T0168376

# Praise for *Eleven Miles to Oshkosh*

*Winner of a Midwest Independent Book Award

"Nostalgic, thrilling, and very engaging. . . . Guhl's straightforward style and unexpected plot twists, combined with a bit of Wisconsin history and plenty of local flavor, make *Eleven Miles to Oshkosh* a memorable, heartwarming and enjoyable debut."—*Milwaukee Magazine*

"A nostalgia trip worth taking."—*Isthmus*

"Guhl's craftsmanship is remarkable. . . . *Eleven Miles* will captivate readers of all ages."—*Peninsula Pulse*

"A charming portrait of a place and time."—*Reviewing the Evidence*

"Deftly written by an author with a genuine flair for originality and character driven narrative storytelling. . . . An inherently compelling read from beginning to end."—*Midwest Book Review*

"Charming debut novel. . . . A worthwhile ride."—*Kirkus Reviews*

"A gripping novel sure to entertain young readers and give their grandparents a trip down memory lane. Guhl's cleanly suspenseful story delivers hard lessons about greed, violence, racism, and the value of an independent spirit, all in family-friendly language laced with a history of the Fox Valley."—ABBY FRUCHT, author of *Polly's Ghost*

"A fast-paced, heartwarming mystery and coming-of-age tale that will appeal to readers from baby boomers to teens. The likable hero struggles with adolescence even as he searches for his father's killer, and as his small town's neighborliness is tainted with prejudice and corruption."—PATRICIA SKALKA, author of the Dave Cubiak Door County Mystery series

# South
# of Luck

JIM GUHL

THE UNIVERSITY OF WISCONSIN PRESS

Publication of this book has been made possible, in part,
through support from the Brittingham Trust.

The University of Wisconsin Press
728 State Street, Suite 443
Madison, Wisconsin 53706
uwpress.wisc.edu

Gray's Inn House, 127 Clerkenwell Road
London ECIR 5DB, United Kingdom
eurospanbookstore.com

Printed in the United States of America
This book may be available in a digital edition.

Library of Congress Cataloging-in-Publication Data

Names: Guhl, Jim, author.
Title: South of Luck / Jim Guhl.
Description: Madison, Wisconsin : The University of Wisconsin Press, [2021]
Identifiers: LCCN 2021007333 | ISBN 9780299332747 (paperback)
Subjects: LCGFT: Fiction.
Classification: LCC PS3607.U4732 S68 2021 | DDC 813/.6—dc23
LC record available at https://lccn.loc.gov/2021007333

This is a work of fiction. Some events, businesses, streets, landmarks,
and settings are real. Individual homes, farms, and certain other places are
fictitious. Individual characters and their actions are products of the
author's imagination.

For
CARMEN,
*ma chérie*

# South
# of Luck

# Chapter 1

With a plain brown suitcase and nothing else, I stepped onto the train depot platform. Mom had her reasons for sending me—that much I knew. She said it was for my own safety but, hell, I was just a month short of my seventeenth birthday, and figured I could take care of myself. Besides, June, July, and August were the best months of the year in Minneapolis—a time for hanging around with friends. Lyndale Avenue, Lake Street, the movie theaters, the beaches, smoking cigarettes in the alleys—that's how I wanted to spend the summer of 1945. Was I sore about getting shoved off to the hinterlands for three months? You bet I was sore.

I checked the sign on the side of the depot one more time just to make sure I had landed in the right spot. Milltown. Yep, this was it. Who ever heard of Milltown, Wisconsin, anyhow? Only seventy-five miles from Minneapolis, according to the map. As far as I was concerned, it might as well have been halfway up to Hudson Bay.

After a few minutes, I simmered down and looked around. Where was everybody? Where was my ride? Where was this distant relative whom I was supposed to be moving in with—this mysterious great-uncle Hjalmar whom I had never met? I had half a notion to wait for the return train—the southbound one—and head back to my pals from Washburn High and my mom's apartment on East Thirty-Seventh.

I wouldn't do it, of course. Like I already said, Mom had her reasons for sending me here.

I glanced left and right, still looking for Mom's uncle. What kind of a name was Hjalmar anyhow? A Swedish hillbilly kind of name, that's what I figured. Mom said to look for a white-haired geezer in coveralls. I spotted three guys fitting the description, and the nearest one was staring at a war bonds poster on the depot wall next to the main door. LET 'EM HAVE IT! BUY WAR BONDS the poster practically shouted. It showed an American soldier throwing a hand grenade and made me think about my brother, Tom. I spat on my palm, flattened out my hair, and walked over.

"Hello, sir, I'm looking for a man named Hjalmar?" (I pronounced it *Yalmar* like Mom had taught me.)

The man turned to size me up, then stopped short. It was a reaction I had grown used to—like nobody had ever seen a scar on the face of a sixteen-year-old kid before. Of course, mine was a doozy. The jagged gash traveled from the corner of my left eye, right through my nose, all the way to my right ear lobe. It basically split my face full of freckles into two separate continents.

The old coot finally shook himself loose from staring. "Ahh—what's that you say?"

"I'm looking for a man named Hjalmar. He was supposed to meet me here. He's my great-uncle."

"Hjalmar who?" he said. "We've got three that I know of."

"Hjalmar Rehnquist."

"Sure! We got one like that. Everybody just calls him Ham. He drives a Ford truck—a green one. Did he know you was coming?"

"I think so."

"Well, he'll most likely be here then. You just sit tight."

"Can I call him on the telephone?"

"Ham ain't got no telephone. No electricity neither. Polk-Burnett ain't reached him yet. You just stay put. He'll find ya."

The man yanked open the door to the depot and shuffled off, leaving me feeling like a foreigner.

*No electricity? No telephone?* Mom hadn't said anything about those minor deficiencies.

I thought about what I would be doing back home in Minneapolis right now on a sun-shiny Saturday in June. Riding a street car to the beach at Lake Calhoun came to mind first. Slurping down an ice cold, cherry chunk chocolate malted milkshake was a close second.

Then I thought about my brother, Tom, again. *Jeez!* I sure could be an ass sometimes. Here I was feeling sorry for myself because I didn't have a cherry chunk chocolate malted milkshake and what was he doing? Dodging Jap bullets in the Pacific, that's what.

A small part of me was actually envious of him, joining the Marines on his eighteenth birthday. That was one way to escape our messed-up family. Of course, he probably would have signed up anyways because, ever since Pearl Harbor, almost every young fella in America had been itching to get

4

into the fight. That was three years in the rearview mirror and the stinking Japs still hadn't been whipped.

Hitler and the Nazis were pretty well mopped up at least. Just a month ago, May 8, the whole country had celebrated VE Day. VE stood for Victory in Europe, and boy oh boy was it ever a good feeling getting that part behind us. Of course, it cost a ton of American lives, including plenty from near my home.

We all saw the pictures in the *Tribune* and on the movie newsreels. Auschwitz, Dachau, Buchenwald. *Damn!* I saw what the Krauts had done. When I first laid eyes on those concentration camp pictures, I felt sick and mad at the same time. On that day, if somebody had lined up some Nazi soldiers and handed me a machine gun, I'm pretty sure I'd have gunned them all down by myself.

I scanned the inside of the depot. Still nobody. I plopped down on a bench. Five minutes passed. Ten minutes. A half hour. I paced the platform. Off in the distance I saw the row of stores that was Milltown's version of downtown. With nothing better to do, I lit up a Lucky Strike, flicked the match onto the tracks, and hefted my forty-pound suitcase.

Five minutes walking put me in the middle of Main Street in Hayseed Heaven. The shops and businesses were all prim and proper on the outside—clean-swept sidewalks, freshly painted siding, a few benches and awnings for shade. Their names seemed right out of a comic book. Twetten Hardware, Brask's Tavern, Orban's Gift Shop, Bimbo Grocery. The most impressive joint in the collection was the Milltown Hotel—a spiffy, two-story outfit with fancy spindles on the porch rails.

Then I scanned the street itself. Where in heck did all the cars come from? The way they were packed in, angle parked on both sides of the street, you'd have thought there was actually something to do around here. I looked around again and scoffed. Not even a movie house.

Most of the people walking around were about as plain as dry toast. Farmers in dusty coveralls. Ladies in bland, shin-length dresses who all looked like somebody's mom. I heard two old guys on the sidewalk chatting about President Roosevelt's death. That was almost two months ago. *Let's get with the times, people.*

Looking kitty-corner across the street, I read the words on a sign alongside the main highway.

"What the hell." Out of pure boredom, I walked over.

The tractors and other machines were all parked outside on the grass. They came in lots of colors, with interesting names like Farmall, Oliver, and Case. Like any sixteen-year-old, I enjoyed looking under the hoods of cars and trucks—but tractors? That was a whole new thing. I set down my suitcase and walked up to a bright-yellow one with the words "Minneapolis-Moline" on the side of the engine cover. The name alone was enough to warm my homesick heart. I looked around the lot and didn't see anybody. *Wouldn't hurt to just sit up there and get the feel of the thing.*

The metal seat was hot from the sun and so was the steering wheel. As a little kid, I had always liked sitting in the driver's seat of a car and pretending that I was racing. I used to make sounds like engines roaring and tires screeching. I think every little boy did that. All of a sudden, I felt like doing it all over again. The only trouble was, I couldn't. I was almost seventeen.

I put my hand on the knob of the shift lever and wiggled it a little. I looked around again. Still nobody in sight. I pushed the clutch pedal down with my left foot and let it back up again. It went down a whole six inches. I pumped it again.

*Pretty swell.*

I scanned the buttons and gauges on a square metal plate that served as the control panel. One gauge was for AMPERES. Another gauge said TEMP with green and red color bands behind the glass. A third gauge said OIL PRESSURE. It was all even simpler than a car. Then my eyes landed on a lever that could be flipped from the word OFF to the word START.

*What the hell—no key?*

My left leg jammed down the clutch pedal and my right hand flipped the lever with a *click*. Nothing happened. Then I spied a silver push button, applied my thumb, and the engine roared to life.

"Son of a bitch."

I looked around. A few cars drove by on the highway and a kid rode his bike along the sidewalk. Nobody looked at me or even blinked as I sat up on the Minneapolis-Moline tractor with the engine rumbling and throwing smoke into the blue sky. I juiced the throttle lever and the tractor responded with a growl.

What harm could come from driving it a few feet? I shifted into what I figured was first gear and bumped up the engine a little more. Then, slowly, slowly, slowly—I let up on the clutch pedal. Nothing. I upped the throttle slightly and continued to pull back on my left foot. Seemed like she was trying to grab, but the tractor didn't budge. I gave it even more gas and lifted my left foot further.

You've probably guessed by now what happened. The Minneapolis-Moline took off with a lurch. I pulled my foot all the way off the clutch and the tractor jumped forward like a frog. In a tenth of a second, I went from calm to full panic. The skinny front wheels of the tractor hit something and the whole front end lurched left and started climbing over the top of a metal contraption with pointed spikes all over it. I jabbed the silver button, but it did nothing. It hadn't occurred to me to disengage the clutch, so the tractor kept crawling on top of the spiky thing. Finally, I jammed my left foot onto the clutch pedal and flipped the toggle to OFF. The engine stopped.

I jumped off quick to see what I had done. One of the front tires hissed as it slowly deflated, the victim of one of those metal spikes. A steady stream of oil rained down from a punctured pan. The metal rod from the steering wheel was bent like the letter Z.

I immediately felt my stomach taking a left turn. Instead of puking, I sat down on my suitcase and tried to figure out what to do. Like any kid my age, I had done some rotten stuff before. Shoplifting came to mind. My buddies and I had even kicked in a few car headlights late at night just to prove how tough we were. But to run away from wrecking a tractor? Was I that much of a rat? I looked all around me. A few cars drove by. A few walkers a block away but nobody looking in my direction.

"What the hell," I said out loud. Then I picked up my beast of a suitcase and lugged it toward Main Street. Once I got away from the lot, I tried to walk natural, businessman style, until I had passed behind a Co-op station and around a corner that took me out of eyeshot of the implement store.

For a few minutes I just stood in the shadows on a side street to let the closeness of my crime drift away. I lit up another Lucky and tossed the match, pretending to be cool. My concern about getting caught was interrupted by hunger. With some dough in my pocket from Mom, I stepped back onto Main Street and glanced around for a place to eat. A brown and white sign snagged my attention. The words—LINDOO DRUG—were strung vertically, big and bold above a striped awning over the store windows.

Then my eyes focused on two smaller words at the very bottom of the sign—ICE CREAM. I flicked my cigarette butt, James Cagney style, and walked inside.

When the door swung open, it almost hit a blond-haired boy who had his eyes glued to the glass globe of a gumball machine. I remembered how it felt to stand drooling like that little cobbler, so I dropped a penny in the slot and pulled the lever. We both watched as a blue gumball about the size of a shooter marble popped out.

"That's for you, buddy," I said and walked away.

There were three open stools at the soda fountain counter, so I sat down in the middle one to avoid any unnecessary human contact. I scanned the ice cream and malt selections and found one called "chocolate-cherry," which I ordered, and slid two bits onto the varnished wood. A skinny, scarecrow-looking kid wearing a white paper hat fixed it up in a jiffy, placing the tall glass in front of me with a straw and a spoon.

"Beautiful day, isn't it?" he said.

"Yeah, I guess," I said back. I lifted my eyes to meet his, then dropped them down again.

"Are you just passing through town?" he asked next. By then he had gotten a good look at my scar, no doubt.

"Probably," I said. "Do you know when there's a train back to Minneapolis?"

"Just past five o'clock. Looks like you'll have a long wait."

I shrugged and nodded. Then, wouldn't you know it, a girl sat right down on the stool to my left.

"Hello, Harold," she said to the scarecrow.

"Hello, Rosalyn, nice day, isn't it?"

"Sure is."

Then she turned toward me. "Okay if I sit here?"

I shrugged and glanced up at the girl's smiling face. Not pretty enough to turn heads on Hennepin Avenue, but prettier than I expected to see up here in nowhere-land. She was about my age, maybe a bit older, and had dark-brown hair and wore a bright-yellow dress. I didn't get a good read on her eyes, because I didn't want to stare—blue, gray, green—I wasn't sure. Sparkly was the part I noticed.

"It's a free country," I said. "Sit there if you want to." Neither the paper hat guy nor the girl said anything after that and I immediately regretted the words. *Dammit.* I sure knew how to be a jerk sometimes.

A couple minutes passed and the girl ordered a dish of Grasshopper ice cream with chocolate sprinkles. The scarecrow guy dished it up and wandered off to the other end of the counter. I reached down inside myself and came up with a second try. I looked at the girl again, but her smile was gone.

"Sorry," I said. "I guess I'm a little beat from the train ride."

She nodded, slowly. "That's okay." Then she swiveled away from me, and I knew it wasn't.

While I was trying to work up something else to say, wouldn't you know it, another person sat down next to me—on the stool to my right this time. I glanced over at a six-foot guy wearing black pants, a light-blue shirt, and a frown. He reached up with one very large hand and gripped my shoulder like a vice.

"A little bird told me that you took a ride on my Minneapolis-Moline," he said.

I quit breathing and looked around. The eyes of every ice cream eater in the joint were on me, including the girl and the scarecrow in the white paper hat. Even the kid with the gumball in his cheek gazed at me with worry. When I returned my blinking eyeballs to the man, the frown was still there and so was the grip. I said nothing.

"My name's Gustafson. That implement store is my bread and butter, boy. You think you can destroy my property and just walk away?"

"Sorry," I said for the second time in two minutes—and boy oh boy, did I ever mean it.

"I think you and I had better go for a little walk," said the man.

I nodded, an action that caused him to release his grip on my shoulder. I rubbed the spot to help the blood flow back into it. There was nothing more to say at the moment, and neither of us tried. I left my malt on the counter, hoisted my suitcase, and followed him out the door. He pointed in the direction of a one-story brick building alongside the tractor lot. Together we walked, me in front, Gustafson behind like a cop. Even though I kept my eyes glued to the ground, I knew that everybody on Main Street was watching me. I could feel it. Just an hour in Milltown, Wisconsin, and everybody hated me and had me pegged as a crook. All that, and nobody even knew my name.

# Chapter 2

As we walked, I kept my head down and fought back tears. Meanwhile, Gustafson didn't throw me no sympathy. Why should he have? My insides whined. *God, I just want to go home!*

Mr. Bigshot walked me through the front door, into a small, windowless office, and pointed to a chair across from a large desk as the door clunked shut. His padded leather chair creaked as he sat. My chair was wooden.

"Let's start with your name."

"Milo Egerson," I mumbled.

As meek as I felt, Mr. Gustafson made it worse. First, he skewered me for not getting permission to start up a machine. Then he ripped me up and down for running away from my responsibility to report the damage. By the time he got around to lecturing me about incompetence, my butt was dragging lower than the bottom of a rock in a mud hole. It took a while, but he eventually used up his ammo. He didn't offer me no hanky so I wiped my nose on my bare arm.

Gustafson rubbed his chin as his eyes tracked my scar. "I haven't seen you in Milltown before."

"I'm here for the summer from Minneapolis," I said.

"Where will you be living?"

"Some guy named Hjalmar Rehnquist. He lives on a farm around here someplace."

"Ham Rehnquist? How do you know Ham Rehnquist?"

"He's my mom's uncle."

"That man could crack an engine block just by looking at it."

I shrugged. "I ain't even met him yet."

"You haven't?"

"Nope. He never showed up at the train depot."

"Oh well. He forgets things sometimes. Right now I have to figure out what to do about *you*."

I said nothing as Mr. Gustafson tapped his pencil slowly against a ceramic cup. I glanced up just in time to see his frown drift even deeper.

"What I should do is call the cops," he said.

I went back to staring at my folded hands.

"I should call the cops and let them deal with you. That's what I *should* do."

I didn't even twitch.

"Of course, then you would probably run home to Minneapolis and I'd never get paid for the damage. You got any money?"

"Twenty-six dollars."

"Hmmph!"

For a minute or two, neither of us talked. The only sound was the creaking of that leather chair and the tapping of his pencil.

"How old are you?" he finally asked.

"Sixteen."

"Have you got a job lined up for the summer?"

"I was planning to help out my great-uncle on his farm."

"Could you come in a few hours each day to work off your debt?"

"I guess so—if he doesn't mind, that is."

"Have you ever worked on fixing cars or anything like that?"

"A little bit," I said, playing coy.

"Well, a little bit is better than nothing."

Mr. Gustafson slapped his palm on the desk. "You get your ass in here by seven o'clock Monday morning—you hear me, boy?"

"Yes, sir."

"By then I'll have the damage tallied up and we can decide how you're going to work it off."

"Yes, sir."

"Grab your suitcase, I'll drive you over to Ham Rehnquist's."

After two minutes in Mr. Gustafson's '41 Buick Roadmaster coupe, I got the feeling that Milltown might not be so backward after all. Even before I got inside, I was studying my own reflection in the glossy maroon paint job on that sleek-looking car. It had a body shape that reminded me of the muscles on a running greyhound. Made a guy think—SPEED!

On the outside, I was minding my p's and q's and staying quietly ashamed, but on the inside my thoughts were—*Gosh! This car is nifty as hell!* My hair flew every which way as we cruised out of town on Highway 35.

Mr. Gustafson slowed down to take a right turn onto bumpy gravel. A few minutes later, he took another right at a cattail slough, and we found ourselves bumping along in a pair of muddy wheel ruts with grass and weeds scraping at the undercarriage.

Ham Rehnquist's farmstead was in rough shape, beginning with a house that probably hadn't seen a coat of paint since President Coolidge. The roof sagged and green moss grew on the eaves. The screen door hung at an odd angle from a single hinge. Around the house, there was no lawn—just tall grass and weeds. A couple of junky farm machines sat out front.

"I like Ham," said Mr. Gustafson. "But I sure wish he would clean up this mess."

A bunch of chickens scurried across the wheel ruts and sneaked into the weeds on the other side. A pair of mud-caked pigs snorted and gazed at us from their pen beside the barn.

For a couple seconds, I had a notion to just ask Mr. Gustafson for a ride back to Milltown. I had seen *House of Frankenstein* at the Boulevard Theater. Little did I know I would be moving into the place.

The crooked screen door moved, and a scary face pressed up against the mesh.

"Who's there!" the face shouted. The light going through the screen door reflected off of something shiny, and all my mind could think was— GUN!

"Take it easy, Ham. It's Nils Gustafson. I've got a young man here, says he's your nephew or some such."

One hand grabbed onto the broken screen door and half-lifted, half-slid it out of the way. The old man looked like Santa Claus in bib overalls, and instead of a gun, he held a tin coffee cup as he walked toward us with a wobbly and bowlegged gate. My heart beat back down.

The guy's mouth was completely covered by bushy white whiskers, and what I could see of his face was a nose and two eyes. That nose was an amazing thing, too. Lumpy and crooked, it took a turn to the right—likely busted and never fixed. His eyes were friendly though—they sprayed wrinkles out to his cheeks and twinkled. Best of all his unusual attributes, he completely ignored my scar.

The old man reached out to me with what I thought was his right hand, but it turned out to be a lobster claw with two fingers missing in the middle. Like a jackass, I flinched and pulled back. In a second I caught myself and gave it a hearty grip that felt like I was reaching all the way up to his elbow.

"Hi, I'm Milo."

"Call me Ham."

I nodded.

By this point, Gustafson had already placed my suitcase in one of the wheel ruts and had started backing away. "Seven o'clock, Monday!" he yelled out the window of his Buick. "If you don't come to see me, I guarantee that I'll find you. Understand?"

I waved and nodded before returning my attention to my mother's uncle.

"What was that all about?" asked Ham, his eyebrows popping.

"I've got a job working in the tractor store—sort of."

"Pretty ambitious."

I nodded. If only he knew.

"Grab your suitcase and come inside."

What choice did I have? House of Frankenstein, here I come.

We walked into the kitchen and I was surprised to find that it was halfway clean. A ceramic-topped table occupied the middle of the room, shiny and bright. There were a few built-in cupboards, but most of the dishes, pots, and pans were apparently hidden behind the doors of an old wooden hutch. At the back wall, a green pump handle and cast-iron spigot stood above a galvanized steel tub for what passed as a kitchen sink.

The most impressive monument in the room was a wood-burning range—a genuine monster that looked like it probably weighed as much as the whole house. The thing was half black and half polished silver with so many doors, cubbyholes, and hinges that I could only guess what half of them were for. Every door had a silver plaque bolted to it, and on each plaque was either the word "Monarch" or a capital letter *M*. The letters had a nifty swirl to them, and they stood out in three dimensions. The stovetop had cast-iron lids instead of electric coils. I watched as Ham lifted one up with a special handle, revealing a porthole of bright-orange light.

Why he had a fire going in there on a warm afternoon, I didn't know, but it explained the beads of sweat forming on my face and neck. I looked to the windows for relief, but they were already open.

Noticing my attention to the stove, the old man smiled. "They ain't makin' 'em like that anymore."

"Everybody in Minneapolis uses electric," I said.

"This look like Minneapolis to you?"

"No, sir."

He smiled, then winked. "This here stove was made in Wisconsin."

*Big whoop,* I almost said.

I didn't give a damn where the stove was made. My eyes were glued to what the old man was dumping into a green ceramic bowl. Three scoops of coffee grounds and then a whole egg, shell and all. He busted the egg and started mashing it all together with a fork.

*Am I going to have to eat that mess?*

The old man must have seen me gawking, because he answered my unspoken question with one of his own. "You drink coffee dontcha?"

I nodded. Maybe twice a week, I drank a cup of coffee with my mom. That still didn't explain the egg.

"As I was saying," said Ham, "this Monarch Malleable range come from Beaver Dam, Wisconsin. Hell of an innovation in its day. Made thousands of them—spread 'em out across the woods and prairies."

"That's swell," I said, trying hard to be polite. "So, why are you mixing up the coffee grounds with an egg?"

He put down the fork and spun on me. "You're a Swede, ain't ya?"

"Yeah, I guess."

"And you ain't drank Swedish egg coffee?" He squinted his eyes at me and said something that sounded like *"Doo ar allt bloogd doo!"*

I kept my yap shut and watched as the geezer scooped the mush from the bowl into a pot of boiling water on the stovetop. It was getting uglier by the minute, so I shifted my attention to the rest of Ham's kitchen.

The walls and ceiling all appeared slightly darkened by years of wood smoke. The bottom half of the walls were vertical planks, painted the color of week-old butter. The top half was wallpapered—strawberries on a light-blue background—something a lady would have picked out. On either side of an open window hung matching kerosene lamps, the kind with glass chimneys. A box of Diamond matchsticks sat on the sill. Above the sink was mounted a fancy blue-and-white plate showing flowers in the center and around the rim—another lady thing.

The last object on the walls was over by the hutch—a photograph in an old-fashioned metal frame. I walked over for a closer look at the lady and a man, probably in their twenties, standing in front of a team of horses and old-fashioned wagon. I looked closer at the picture because at first it looked like my mother. It wasn't, though. She was almost as pretty as my mom, but not quite. Not surprising, really. There wasn't anybody prettier than my mom.

"Who's this in the picture?" I asked.

"That's me and my wife, Isabella. I was married once."

"I didn't know."

"Prettiest girl in three counties. Sweet, smart, and hardworking too. She was from St. Croix Falls. Married her in 1903 on the same day the Wright Brothers went airborne. Then I bought this farm two years later, and for a while we was as happy as mice beneath a haystack."

Ham turned toward the stove to see if the mush had boiled long enough yet.

"What happened to her?" I asked.

As I looked at the old man's back, I saw his shoulders rise and slowly fall. "She died in childbirth. The baby died too."

I swallowed. "I'm sorry," I said to his back.

He nodded and we both stayed quiet for a minute while I kicked myself for asking.

"Both are buried in a grove of pines on the knoll in my big field out back," Ham continued. "Sheriff said I couldn't do it that way but I done it anyways."

I rubbed my hands together under the table. Weren't we supposed to be talking about the weather or something?

Uncle Hjalmar placed a glass tumbler in front of me. "You like it black?"

Desperate to get away from the dead wife and child, I didn't hesitate. "Sure."

I watched as he lifted the pot, and using a fork for a strainer, poured the hot coffee into a kettle, leaving a dark-brown lump behind. From there he poured the coffee from the kettle into my glass tumbler and then his own tin cup.

*What if I throw up? Will he send me back to Minneapolis?* Hey, it was something to hope for, but then I remembered Mr. Gustafson's promise to track me down.

We both slurped the brew at the same time. My taste buds buzzed pleasantly, so I sipped again. I looked wide-eyed at my great-uncle. "Hey, this is good!"

"Of course it's good, city boy. It's the best way to make coffee." He pushed a small plate in my direction with what looked like thick cookies laced with chocolate and sprinkled with powdered sugar. "Try one of these."

I did and my taste buds buzzed again. "Wow! What are they?"

"*Chokladbiskvi.*"

"What does that mean?"

"Chocolate biscuits."

"Did you make them?"

He looked around the room in a sarcastic sort of way. "It's just me living here—or was." He poured me some more coffee and pushed the plate closer. "Have another," he said.

After polishing off two cups of egg coffee and three biscuits, Ham led me outside, where it wasn't so hot. For almost a full hour he showed me around his property. We walked through the barn, where I was introduced to enough animal crap to fill my bedroom back home. I tiptoed around the piles as the old man rolled his eyes.

Somewhere on the shit tour, I met a pair of Belgian draft horses named Bullet and Smoke. They were both brown, sleek, and huge. Smoke had a black mane and Bullet's was oatmeal colored. I scratched them both on the white streaks just above their noses and they seemed to like that.

Then I got introduced to eight brown-and-white cows that the old man called Guernseys. All eight of them were lying down in a pasture, just working their jaws like a bunch of gum-chewing teenagers. A calico cat followed us, and I learned that her name was Peacock. The two pigs were nameless, like the cows.

"How do you keep up with all this?" I asked.

"Not very well, I'm afraid. As you can see, the house and yard have gone straight to hell."

I nodded. "Maybe you can show me what to do, and I can help you."

"Them was the same thoughts your mother had in her letter when she asked about your coming here."

"What else did my mom say?"

"Oh, she went on and on about how a summer in the country would be good for you, and how it would be nice for the two of us to get acquainted. Then she talked about the benefits of fresh air and learning about animals and plants and farm life."

I nodded.

Ham tilted his head closer to mine. "You and I both know that those ain't the real reasons."

There it was. I didn't want to answer, so I shrugged. We both knew it had nothing to do with fresh air and farm life.

Ham's eyes remained locked on me. "The real reason you're here has got something to do with that scar on your face, I reckon."

It wasn't a question, so I didn't answer.

"Am I right?" he asked.

I stayed silent—kicked a stone in the direction of the pigs.

"You don't have to tell me if you don't want to," he said.

I flicked a beetle off a fencepost.

"We can talk about it now or later," he said.

"There's just a guy I need to stay away from."

"What do you mean, 'just a guy'?"

"A guy who wouldn't mind hurting me, okay?"

"Hurting you?"

I turned my back to the old man and that shut him up.

My Uncle Ham didn't deserve that. Well, maybe I didn't deserve certain things neither.

# Chapter 3

Back in the kitchen, a breeze flowed through the open windows, and at least it wasn't so danged hot anymore. Ham worked the handle on the green pump at the kitchen basin, producing two large glasses of water right out of the ground. It was cold, sweet, and down my throat in about three seconds. With a few more pumps of the handle, I filled it again and sat down.

"What's next?" I asked.

"Evening chores," said Ham.

"Just tell me what I need to do."

Ham lifted his claw hand and studied it. "This thing gives me more and more trouble every year," he said. "I'm gonna need you to take over with the cows."

During the next three hours, I learned that tending to eight Guernsey dairy cows was no stroll down Nicollet Avenue. The first step was getting them to come in from the pasture.

"Just say 'Come boss' as loud as you can," said Ham.

I shrugged, cupped my hands around my mouth, and cut loose. "Come boss!"

Out of eight brown-and-white Guernsey cows, two looked in my direction, and not a single one stood up.

"Try it again, from your gut this time."

I took a deep breath and let her rip. "Come boss! Come boss! Come boss!"

They didn't stampede. I'll say that much. But they did stand up, and then, sure as hell, they all marched in single file like a troop of scouts straight into the barn and, to my amazement, right into their assigned stalls, putting their heads into each stanchion.

"Good work," said Ham, and I felt a spark of pride. We clanked the stanchions shut around their necks.

"Now give them something to eat."

"But haven't they been munching on grass all day long?"

"Sure, but they need more than that, corn silage mainly."

I looked around. "Where do you keep that?"

"Did you see the silo next to the barn?"

"Yeah."

"It ain't there for decoration."

Climbing up that doggone thing felt like going up one of the grain elevators at the Pillsbury flour mills. I climbed through a square opening into the dim light inside the silo and found a pitchfork waiting for me. The job wasn't complicated. For five minutes I pitched chopped-up corn stalks down the chute and then climbed back down to the ground, where I wheelbarrowed load after load to the cows. Three shovels full for each one right below their head. *Jiminy*—this job was half grunt worker and half restaurant waiter. Then, as if that weren't enough, each cow needed a Folgers coffee can of supplement that came from a big sack in the feed room.

I was huffing by then and filthy too. I brushed the dust off my pants and leaned against a big wooden timber for a minute or two just to watch the cows eat.

"They sure do look happy," I said.

"You made them happy," Ham answered.

It felt good, just watching them, those beautiful brown-and-white animals nodding their heads and chomping sideways with their huge jaws.

I looked at the old man. "What next?"

"Water. A full pail for each animal."

That meant four trips to the pump house and back. I think my arms stretched a couple inches.

At long last, we got to the milking. At first I was worried about getting down there and touching anything. Ham showed me how to do it: where to place the stool, how to lean my head into the cow's flank, how to wash the tits with soapy water.

The serious part came next. "How do I get the milk out?" I asked.

Ham scooted up next to me and gripped the front-passenger-side tit with his non-claw hand.

"Just squeeze hard and pull down." The stream came out fast and loud as it rang the bottom of the metal pail. He moved aside. "Now you try."

I was tentative at first, wrapping my fingers around what looked like a pudding-filled finger from a rubber glove.

"Go ahead, squeeze hard and pull down," said Ham.

I did what my great uncle told me and got the metal pail to ring just like he had.

"Hot damn," I said. "How's that?"

The old man nodded and winked. "I'll milk four and you milk four," he said. An hour later we both finished at the same time, even though he was missing half of one hand.

~

Suppertime finally came just as the sun was disappearing below the distant woods. By the fading light through the kitchen window and the dim glow of two kerosene lamps, I peeled potatoes and chopped them up while Hjalmar stoked up the fire in the stove again. He emptied a mason jar of beef chunks into a frying pan and stirred it up with another jar of canned tomatoes. With potatoes boiling and beef sizzling, the kitchen got hot and steamy all over again.

There wasn't much talking as we ate. Together, we gulped down every scrap of meat and every shred of potatoes in those two pans. Hjalmar got out two pieces of Wonder Bread and handed me one. He wiped his plate clean with it and ate the soggy bread. I did the same.

Together, we washed and wiped the dishes. "I'm turning in," Ham said. "Your bedroom is on the left at the top of the stairs. You've had a hell of a first day."

I nodded. Gawd, was that ever true. And the old man didn't even know about the Minneapolis-Moline tractor.

Ham handed me a chunk of cheese and four mouse traps.

I looked up, bewildered.

"Put one of these traps in each corner of your bedroom. I'll wake you for milking at 5 a.m."

"Did you say 5 a.m.?"

"That's right."

I gulped and returned my attention to the mousetraps.

On my walk down the path to the outhouse, I took a pause to admire the sky. Maybe I had seen a zillion stars all at once before, but it wasn't on Thirty-Seventh Street in Minneapolis.

# Chapter 4

There was no mistaking the sound of those heavy boots coming up the wooden stairs. *Kallump—kallump—kallump.* The same sound I've heard a hundred times before. Drunken evil. Headed my way. I tried to kick off the blanket to slam shut the bedroom door, but my body wouldn't move. *Kallump—kallump—kallump.* I didn't even need to see him to know that there was a long-blade knife in the grip of his right hand. It only figured that he'd want to finish the job the way he started it. Why couldn't I move? Why couldn't I run? *Kallump—kallump—kallump.* A dim backlit glow revealed the man standing at my bedroom door.

"Wake up, boy."

"Huh?"

"Those cows can't wait."

My eyes sprang open to a face full of white whiskers in the light of a kerosene lamp.

"What time is it?" I whispered the words as the fading image of a killer evaporated from behind my eyeballs.

"Ten past five. Get dressed."

I gulped a breath of air, then swung my legs off the bed and sleepwalked into yesterday's clothes. *Have I been drafted into Stalin's army?*

I gulped down a bowl of Wheaties and hauled my ass to the barn. It was all just like the evening before. Silo-climbing, pitchforking, wheelbarrowing, tit-squeezing, milk-can-filling and hauling them over by the milk house door. He showed me how to steal the eggs from underneath chickens in the coop, and how to find the hidden ones from those hens that wouldn't comply. The big draft horses and pigs needed feeding and Ham showed me how. It wasn't complicated, but *sheesh*—I was still gassed from yesterday.

I got into the habit of touching the animals like Ham did. While making the rounds, I patted their necks or scratched the tops of their heads. Sometimes they would glance at me. Other times they would inch over a little bit or lift their back just a tad like a cat might. It felt good to have those animals warm up to me like that. In fact, it was the only thing about chores that I actually liked.

When the work was done, we released the cows and horses to the pasture again, and I had a notion to crawl back into bed. Ham looked at me like he had read my mind. "Time to go to the creamery," he said.

"On a Sunday?"

Ham nodded.

It irked me of course. All that work on a Sunday morning and I still couldn't call it done? Weren't Sunday mornings supposed to be for reading the funnies in the *Minneapolis Tribune* and listening to Cedric Adams on WCCO?

Ham lifted his eyeballs like he had picked up on my signal again. "Got to," he said. "Without no electricity, the milk might go bad otherwise."

The ten-gallon cans of milk from the day before stood, half-submerged, in a stone and mortar basin full of well water. Those, combined with four more warm cans from that morning, stared at me waiting to be hefted into Ham's pickup. Were my skinny arms up to the task? Ten minutes and about a hundred grunts later, those cans all stood upright in the truck bed, looking like bombs on a mission to Tokyo.

*How had the old man done all of this by himself?* I wondered.

Hjalmar's green Ford pickup must have been built before I was born. The tires were skinny with spoked wheels, and the thing had a cab that was as square as the box behind it. The only curved parts were the fenders, and they swept up and over the wheels like ocean waves. The thing was ready for the scrap heap by my reckoning.

I was getting ready to climb in the passenger side when Ham handed me a Z-shaped metal rod with a handle on one end.

"Give it a crank," he said. "I'll work the choke and throttle."

I'd seen crank starters before but never actually worked one. Down low, just beneath the radiator, there was a spot where it connected. As you can probably imagine, it was no easy task turning four big pistons all at once. Well, I did it, and the engine didn't backfire or break my arm off or anything. In fact, the truck started right up—second try.

"That was easy," I said as I got in the passenger side.

"Easy in the summertime. Winter is a different ball game."

The old jalopy ticked and sputtered, but it went. We bumped along through potholes and washboard stretches that rattled my teeth in the cool sunshine of mid-morning. Before long we passed in front of Mr. Gustafson's implement store again, and I gazed at the wreckage of the Minneapolis-Moline from yesterday.

With a left turn, we rolled right down Main Street and I got my second look at all the stores, bars, and shops that the whistle-stop called Milltown offered. We puttered past the hotel, all white with fancy spindles on the porch rails. We rumbled past Twetten Hardware, Lindoo Drug, Larson's Barbershop, and Brask's Tavern.

A few families in town were walking to church. I spotted one pretty girl, trailing behind her parents, and danged if it wasn't that same one who sat by me at Lindoo Drug eating grasshopper ice cream. My instincts tried to put on a tough-guy face again, but then my brain spoke up and reminded me that having a friend in town might not be such a bad idea.

"Good morning!" I shouted out the open window.

She looked up in surprise and recognition. The girl snapped her eyes back to her mother and father and even sped up her pace to catch them. At first it irked me getting the cold shoulder like that, but then I thought about it from her point of view. Scar-faced mug, marched off for being a crook. Who could blame her?

We kept driving through town, giving me a chance to rubberneck the other shops and businesses. I counted seven gas and service stations altogether.

*How do they all keep busy?* I wondered.

Minutes later, we pulled into a big lot next to a building with steam puffing out of a metal stack. Several other farmers with trucks were lined up, and a couple of old timers even came with horse-drawn wagons. Apparently, everybody was doing the same thing—unloading milk before it went bad. Some of them were wearing Sunday clothes. Others stood there, all dusty and crusty, like me and Ham. I spotted one young fella who I figured to be my age or maybe a year older. He was part of the shit-kicker bunch, except his clothes were tattered worse than a shot-up Civil War flag and caked thick from the knees on down with greenish-brown crap.

"Hello," I said, still trying to shake off my bad behavior from yesterday.

He looked at me, apparently surprised somebody would even talk to him. Like almost everybody else, his eyes tracked my scar.

His stuttering voice was thin and quiet. "H-h-hello," he said back.

He turned away from me then, and I noticed a hairless patch on the back of his head that must have come from an injury even worse than mine. The scar was deep and shiny and pink, not properly tanned like his arms. What was that kid's story? He squeezed through the group of men and escaped me like the girl had.

While waiting, I snooped around the creamery windows. Inside, I spotted gigantic metal tanks with lots of pipes and dials connected to them. Next to the tanks were a pair of large steel vats, and I had a notion that they had something to do with making cheese.

It took twenty minutes, but our turn finally came to unload our milk. When the cans were empty, the two of us rinsed them inside and out with a hose. Then a man with blue pants and a white shirt wrote out a slip and handed it to Ham. He looked at it and frowned, shoved it into his pocket, and gave me the "let's go" gesture with his claw hand. Back in the truck, he signaled for me to turn the crank again. It started and we were on our way.

"Let's drive around a little bit," said Ham, "get you familiar with the country. My farm is north of Milltown and south of Luck—about halfway in between."

"There's a town called Luck?"

"Yep. We'll swing through there eventually."

As we chugged along the back roads, I noticed that the countryside in northwestern Wisconsin was much like Minnesota—lots of farms with red barns, white houses, sheds, and almost always a silo. The land rolled gently with patches of woods mixed in with corn fields and pastures.

"That's a pea field over there," Ham said, "and them are rutabagas on the other side."

"What's a rutabaga?" I asked.

Ham looked at me like I should know better. "They're like oversized turnips. Down in Centuria, there's a dehydration factory where they dry and pack rutabaga to ship overseas for our soldiers."

We kept rattling along on country roads while Ham pointed out fields of potatoes, oats, barley, and beans. At one point, we got stuck behind a bright-blue painted wagon pulled by a two-up hitch of mules.

"That's Oskar Johnson. Some folks shouldn't be on the roads, and he's one of them." Ham tapped the horn, but the wagon just kept on swaying from side to side, hogging the whole road so that we couldn't pass. "Out of the way, Oskar!" Ham yelled. More horn honking. "He's mostly deaf. That's half of the problem. The other half is that he barely speaks English."

Ham leaned on the horn and let loose with a solid blast, foghorn style, that finally got Oskar and his mules to pull over to the right. As we chugged alongside, I looked over at the toothless smile of a man who had to be ninety years old. He waved and I waved back.

We continued south and came upon a lake.

"This is Half Moon Lake," said Ham. "If you ever feel like going swimming, this is a good place."

I nodded and looked over the beach. Two rafts floated at anchor off shore. One of them even had a diving board. The drive continued, and for the next hour, we visited lake after lake with names like Balsam, Bone, and Big Round. A little further down the road, we came upon a stream that flowed under the road in a culvert, and Ham pulled the truck over and stopped.

"Have you ever caught a trout?" he asked.

"I don't think so."

"This is McKenzie Creek. Best place I know of for trout fishing. Maybe one of these days you can come back here and catch our supper."

I pondered the puny little stream. Back home we did our fishing on a real river—the Mississippi—where it was wider than the length of a football field. *McKenzie Creek?* I didn't say anything to the old man, but to me, it seemed about as likely a place to catch a meal as the street gutters in front of our apartment on Thirty-Seventh Street.

Ham kept driving on the back roads—some paved and some gravel. Just like around Milltown, there were farms scattered across the countryside, but as we kept going north, more and more forest took over. My right elbow was hanging out the window and my hair was whipping around in the wind as the old man had our speed cranked up to forty-five.

"Where to next?" I asked.

"Dinner."

"Good, I'm starved."

The city of Frederic was bigger than Milltown but, in many ways, the same. State Highway 35 ran through it, for one thing. They also had the usual businesses—a hardware store, drug store, gas and service stations, bars, and places to eat. They had a hospital too, just east of the main intersection, and a movie theater with a nifty sign and movie posters in the windows. *The Body Snatcher* was showing presently, with Boris Karloff and Bela Lugosi. The poster was weird and menacing, showing the green face of the bad guy with his hands and fingers stretched out like he was ready to grab at someone. I remembered my nightmare with the killer glowering at me and brandishing a knife. That killer had a name, too, Mr. Wayne Borsthagen. With a vigorous head shake, I tried to clear the creep from my brain.

We parked the car at an angle in front of a restaurant, went inside, and sat at the well-lit dining counter. A fire hydrant–shaped waitress came over and handed us each a menu. "Special today is the meatloaf dinner," she said. "It's eighty-five cents and includes green beans, mashed potatoes, and a drink."

"That'll do," said Hjalmar. "Coffee, black."

*Doggone-it. Why did the codger have to order so quick?*

All I knew for sure was what I *didn't* want—meatloaf with green beans and mashed potatoes. The waitress hovered at my shoulder. What I really wanted was a Juicy Lucy, the cheese-filled burgers they served at the 5–8 Club at Fifty-Eighth and Cedar back home in civilization.

"A cheeseburger and french fries," I said. "And a cherry chunk chocolate malted milkshake."

"Cherry chunk what? We've got vanilla and chocolate," she said. "Take your pick."

"Chocolate."

The lady scratched it all down on her pad of paper with a yellow pencil that was worn down to the nub. Then she clipped the piece of paper above the window to the kitchen and shouted, "Order!" before waddling off to refill cups of coffee for the masses.

Out of habit, I tapped a cigarette out of my pack of Luckies and searched my pocket for a match.

"Do you mind waiting until we're outside?" asked Ham.

I gave him an annoyed look and rolled my eyes. Then I tried to look cool, like I didn't even care, as I slid the cigarette back in the pack again.

Still sore about Ham's comment, I looked around the diner to avoid eye contact. The place was mostly filled with old men, and they were all dressed the same. Denim overalls with suspenders, checkered shirts, sleeves rolled up.

*Hayseeds*, I said to myself.

I spotted two high school–age girls in knee-length skirts walk by the picture window. One shaded her eyes and looked through the glass, but all she saw were farmers, me being one of them. The girls kept on walking. As we finished our food and I slurped the dregs from my milkshake glass, the waitress dropped the check at our table. Mom would have wanted me to offer to pay. She had given me twenty bucks, and I had another six of my own. I just sat there and said nothing. I put my right hand on the table like I was thinking about grabbing the bill, but I wasn't really.

"That's for me to get, Milo."

"Are you sure?" I asked. "Mom wants me to pull my own weight."

"Neither one of us is Henry Ford," said Ham. "But as long as you're helping me work the farm this summer, I'll pay for the food."

At the counter, the lady rang up $1.78 on the cash register. I watched Hjalmar's eyes get larger. Slowly he pulled out his wallet and reached for the only bill he had in there—a fiver. She handed back three dollar bills, two dimes, and two pennies. I watched the old man's lips move as he tried to square up the math.

Very carefully, he pinched the two dimes and slid them on the lunch counter for a tip. He saw me watching, lifted his eyes, and winked. "I don't want them all to try to marry me, ya know."

I laughed out loud—for the first time since leaving Minneapolis.

# Chapter 5

I figured we were going back to Ham's place, but we weren't.

"So long as we're this far north, I think we'll visit a friend I haven't seen in a long time. He's an Indian. Lives just west of here with his granddaughter."

I didn't say anything. The only Indians I had ever seen were drunk or vagrant in front of the bars on Franklin or Washington Avenues. For my whole life, I had avoided them. Now I was heading over to knock on their front door. *Great!*

Ham pondered a left turn, then changed his mind and went right. He jutted his chin and screwed up his face, trying to decide which gravel road the Indian fella lived on. With each turn of the steering wheel, we seemed to be moving into more and more remote country. Scruffy-looking oak trees and spindly jack pines. The roadside was turning sandy too, and I figured it explained why we weren't seeing as many farms. Some birds jumped off the ground and scattered.

"Them are prairie chickens," Ham said. "There used to be thousands of them. Now they're getting rare."

"Does it matter?"

Ham applied the brakes and stopped the truck, then he blasted me with a long, hard stare. "Does it matter that the prairie chickens are going away? Of course it matters. What do you think, that this land is just a big jar of honey for us to suck on until it's gone? This land was here long before you and I came along, Milo. It's our privilege to live on it, but we've got a duty to take care of it too. Do you understand what I'm saying?"

"Yes." *Jeez—how did I get twisted around his axle?*

Ham stared at the side of my head for a while longer. Then he put the truck in gear again and we kept going down the road.

*Whew.*

Another left turn was followed by another right and another left. Suddenly, Ham hit the brakes and skidded to a stop in the gravel, throwing up a cloud of dust.

"Are we lost?" I asked.

"We're there."

Through the brush and tall grass, my eyes found the house. A lot like Hjalmar's place, maybe worse.

*Great. Another shithole.*

The house was a low-to-the-ground one-story outfit with a saggy roof and rickety wooden steps. Of the two windows facing the road, one was open and the other had boards nailed across it.

"What's the guy's name?" I asked.

"Grayburn Jackson."

"That's a dumb name for an Indian. Sounds like the ghost of some Confederate general or something."

That smart-alecky comment earned me a scornful look that nearly burned another hole through my head. Ham held his gaze until I looked away.

"He's a Chippewa Indian. One who deserves your respect," he said.

"A Chippewa?"

"A Chippewa elder. You might do yourself a favor by not shooting your mouth off. Don't show your ignorance by asking about teepees and buffalo hunting either. The Chippewa aren't like the tribes you've probably seen in the movies."

"They're not?"

Ham shook his head. "These are forest and lake people. A young slicker like you probably never heard of it, but the northwest Wisconsin Chippewa were known for a long time as the Lost Tribe."

"The Lost Tribe? Why?" I sat up taller, actually interested. I was also still kicking myself for that stupid Confederate general crack. *Gawd!* I could really be an idiot sometimes.

Hjalmar took a breath and relaxed the muscles around his eyes. "I'm not sure when the fighting started between the Sioux and the Chippewa. Back a couple hundred years, I reckon. Anyhow, they had been squabbling over territory around here for a long time. That, combined with more and more European settlers coming every single year, made for a pretty doubtful future for all of them. Some things happened in the 1850s, and the first was an attack by Sioux warriors against a large group of Chippewa just southwest of here, where the Apple River flows into the St. Croix. The Chippewa were collecting sap from maple trees for the sugar. That's when the Sioux attacked and killed a large number."

"Was that how they became the Lost Tribe?"

"That was a part of it. Then at LaPointe it got worse. The government set up a treaty meeting on an island in Lake Superior, a sacred place for the Indians. Most of the Chippewa bands from around Wisconsin and Minnesota showed up. The St. Croix Chippewa band didn't because, as I understand it, they were still torn up from the Sioux attack. At the gathering in LaPointe, the US government set aside reservation land for each group that attended. It was a raw deal, but at least they got something. The St. Croix Chippewa got nothing and were left for lost. The result was a sort of scattering of them in small groups throughout northwestern Wisconsin to manage as best they could with basically no land of their own."

"The Lost Tribe," I said, pondering that storybook notion.

"That's right," said Ham. "Set adrift, you might say."

"And then the pioneers moved in and staked out claims on the land all around them, I suppose."

"That's right."

"And then I suppose the loggers came in and cut down most of the forest."

"Now you're getting the picture."

"Did they ever get their own land to live on?"

"About ten years ago they did, except by then the Chippewa from these parts were pretty well scattered. Some are down around Balsam Lake. Others up in this region here. All the other land had been gobbled up by settlers like our ancestors and bumbling farmers like me."

*The Lost Tribe?* I pondered it all. *How come we never learned about this stuff in school?*

Ham opened the truck door. "Come on, let's go talk to Grayburn Jackson."

I followed him and thought: *This is the last place I want to be.*

Grayburn Jackson must have had his eye on us the whole time, because he was standing outside the front door before we got halfway there through the tall grass. Right away, I hoped that he wasn't a mind reader.

As I looked the guy over, I decided that he was probably tall once. His body was bent in so many places that it might have shrunk half a foot over the years. He had one hand on a metal railing and the other at his hip. His face was brown and leathery, with so many wrinkles and deep creases that it made a fella think—*roadmap.* Every hair on his head was silvery white, and the whole lot of it lay in disarray down to his shoulders and even longer. I seriously wondered if that old Indian might be coming up on a hundred years old.

"Grayburn! Long time no see," said Ham as he reached out his claw hand.

The Indian responded with his own right hand. "Why don't you come see me anymore, Feather?"

"Just trying too hard to be a farmer, I reckon."

"Yes. That's always your excuse."

Ham turned toward me and touched my shoulder. "Grayburn, I want you to meet my grand-nephew, Milo. He's come up from Minneapolis for the summer to help me milk cows and such."

Grayburn looked me square in the face but didn't change expression. Most people when they saw me tracked their eyes with the path of my scar. The old Indian didn't do that. He looked all over my face like he was mystified to see so many freckles.

"You must be highly respected in Minneapolis," he said.

"Huh?"

"You've got an interesting face. Part warrior and part chief."

I stood a little taller and straighter. "Thank you," I replied.

He nodded and then pointed to a couple of cushioned chairs where we could sit down. Ham slid into the red one. I hesitated and wondered about the flea population in the green one. Tentatively, I settled my ass on the front edge and leaned forward.

The two old men embarked on a long, wandering conversation about people they both knew in the area and what had changed since the last time they talked. They spent at least twenty minutes on the subject of who had died and who was close to dying. The list was long. They discussed the names of men who had been killed in the war, others who were still fighting, and still other young men who never went.

While all of this was going on, I scanned the walls and floor for interesting objects. A pair of old snow shoes was propped up in a corner, and there was a stack of long, flat boards, each rounded on one end, that I couldn't figure out. Rolled up and tucked alongside the chair I was sitting on was something that looked like a blanket. I picked it up and it was soft and fuzzy like animal fur. After a closer look, I realized that it actually *was* animal fur that had been cut in strips that were sewn together at the ends so they could be woven, basket style, into the craziest, niftiest blanket that I had ever seen.

"That was made by my granddaughter, Raina," said Grayburn. "She snares rabbits in the winter and makes blankets and mittens—things like that. She also makes rabbit stew. Maybe you should come back and try it sometime."

"Maybe," I said, still following the weave of all those strands of mostly white fur. I wrapped the blanket around my bare arm and could feel the warmth.

A screen door clicked open, then twanged and slapped shut from the direction of Grayburn's kitchen. "Raina, come here. We have visitors."

The girl stepped into view timidly, like a deer. All I saw was one shoulder and half of her head, including one dark, mysterious eye. She looked at Ham and must have recognized him, because she stepped all the way into the room and offered him a nod and a smile. She then turned toward me again and the smile washed off her face.

"This is Feather's nephew, Milo," said Grayburn. "He likes your rabbit blanket."

I shrugged, acting like I didn't care one way or another.

If anything, her eyes became darker. I'm not sure how, but she knew what was inside of me. That girl knew about my dirty, rotten feelings about Indians. She knew about white boys and how they talked. A small part of her still looked afraid, like a deer, but a bigger part of her now looked something like a mountain lion.

I stammered and looked at my own feet. Then I tried again.

"It's just that, I never saw a blanket like this before."

"My grandmother taught me how to make it. She taught me how to snare rabbits too."

"Why don't you just shoot them?"

"Some animals are best trapped."

It sounded like backward thinking to me. Why not just blast them with a shotgun the way everybody else went after rabbits? I squeezed the rabbit blanket in my right hand.

Her eyes remained dark. "Yes, it is warm," she said, answering my question before I could ask it.

*What the . . . ?*

Grayburn looked up at the girl, then at me and Ham. "You want some tea? Raina will make it."

Ham waved her off and she looked disappointed.

Grayburn turned to me. "How about you, Milo?"

"Tea sounds good," I said. "If it's not too much trouble."

"English tea or Chippewa," she asked, unsmiling.

Now, there was a curveball I didn't see coming.

"Chippewa," I said.

Ham gave me a look. "Better slow down, boy."

"Huh?"

"From Swedish egg coffee to Chippewa tea in two days. What's next? White lightning right out of the jug?" Grayburn laughed. Raina didn't.

A few minutes later, Raina came back with a juice glass of hot tea, orange in color.

"Thanks," I said.

She turned her back and I watched her return to the kitchen.

*Tough girl. Tough and pretty.* My thoughts surprised me.

I took one sip of the tea and swallowed it down. I didn't say anything, but my mind thought—*Yuck!* I tried very hard not to make a face but couldn't help it. "What's in this?" I asked.

"It's from a swamp plant," said Grayburn. "Too bitter? Raina, bring some maple sugar."

The girl came back with a jar of brown lumpy stuff. She handed the jar and spoon to me without eye contact. Again, I watched her turn and disappear into the kitchen. Grayburn and Ham both had their eyes on me like they were waiting for act two in a play. I took a scoop of the maple sugar and mixed it in, then took another sip. It was better this time, and I gave them both the nod.

While I was sipping the stuff, determined to get it all down, the conversation waned between Ham and Grayburn Jackson. I had been waiting for an opening, so I took my shot.

"Mr. Jackson, why do you call my great-uncle Feather?"

"Because he likes birds."

"Not really," said Ham.

"Yes, he does," said Grayburn. "I have watched him in the forest."

"That's just nonsense."

"Well, you liked those prairie chickens," I said.

"He likes all birds," said Grayburn. "That reminds me, Feather. I have a gift for you."

Ham was flustered. "No gifts, Grayburn. We just stopped in to say hello."

The old Indian disappeared into the kitchen, and I heard the screen door open and close. A minute later he was back, walking slowly into the living room with a crow sitting on his left shoulder.

"Well, will you look at that," said Ham.

I had no words.

Grayburn walked over and slowly transferred the large black bird to his hand and then to Ham's shoulder. To my amazement, my great-uncle didn't object. The twinkle in his eye was brighter than ever. He was trying to keep down a smile but losing the fight.

Raina had emerged from the kitchen to watch. "He really does like birds," she whispered.

Grayburn nodded. "I told you so."

Ham gently reached up and stroked the crow's feathers. The bird then hopped to Ham's knee and they looked at each other like long-lost friends.

"Is it a boy or a girl?" asked Ham, looking at Grayburn Jackson.

"Girl."

"What's her name?"

"Black Cat."

"That don't make no sense."

"You've got a three-color cat. What's her name?"

"Peacock."

"See. It all evens out."

*Cawww!*

"She wants to go with you, Feather."

"I can't take her," Ham continued, shaking his head.

"You have to. She's tired of being with me, and she obviously likes you now."

*Cawww!*

"Besides, if you don't accept my gift, I might be insulted and you don't want that."

"Baaagghh."

*Cawww!*

"That does it," said Grayburn. "You heard her."

~

The rest of the afternoon's drive amounted to a sightseeing tour that really opened my eyes about the beauty and industry of the whole region. Through the windshield of the Ford truck, we saw a huge dam and power plant on the big St. Croix River. The old man told me that the river was almost as big as the Mississippi and that it was a shame to plug a natural waterfall like that. I wondered about that, because the whole world needed electricity. But, having already been burned by my prairie chicken comment, I kept my mouth shut this time.

We drove south along the river through a state park where sheer bluffs rose up on both sides. From there we headed east through some hills that were big enough to ski on. East of there we found a little, dinky town with the funny name of Ubet. The town had a general store and not much else. After a few more right and left turns, Ham slowed to a stop on the side of the road and stared hard at a collection of buildings amid a grove of trees and surrounded by fields.

"What's this?" I asked.

Ham didn't answer at first. His eyes were locked, studying the mystery farm.

"What is it, Ham?"

At last, he shook himself loose from staring and his sad eyes met mine. "That's where I don't want to end up."

"Huh?"

"It's the Polk County Poor Farm," said Ham.

I looked at the buildings and back at Ham's eyes. *Jeez!* He was scared of the place all right, almost as much as I was of a certain person who showed up in my nightmares wielding a long-blade knife. I kept my yap clamped shut as the old man took his time hurling lightning bolts from his elderly eyeballs at those buildings. At last he found the gearshift lever with his shaking claw hand, and we puttered again down the road.

~

We arrived home just in time for milking and the rest of the chores. Ham brought Black Cat right inside the barn, where she stood on the wooden rail of one of the empty calf pens the whole time. After chores, we cooked up a supper of canned beef, tomatoes, boiled carrots, and two pieces of Wonder Bread each. Ham went to bed as soon as supper was done, leaving me alone. The house was still too hot, and getting hotter from the Monarch range. I stepped outside. It wasn't even close to being dark yet.

I went back inside and up the old wooden steps, opened my suitcase, and dug down through a couple layers of clothes. The homemade radio was about the size of a toaster in its dark-stained wooden case. I was proud of it, having built the thing in shop class with the help of my teacher, Mr. Sheldrop. It wasn't some stupid crystal set either. It was real. A working radio with vacuum tubes and sockets, resisters, condensers and two knobs, one for volume and the other for tuning. For the antenna, Mr. Sheldrop helped me make a coil of wire that we concealed right into the lid of the box. And for power? Well, luckily for me I had made it battery powered, with two wires coming out the back. The battery was a six-volt about the size of a lunchbox, and it was so danged heavy that it came with a carrying handle on top.

I hauled the radio and battery down the stairs, out the kitchen door, and up the lane that made the border between the cow pasture and a vast field of weeds. I walked diagonally through the weed field until I had reached a grove of pine trees that marked the highest spot. Inside the grove, I found a closely mowed patch of grass marked with two large stones, the gravesites of Hjalmar's wife, Isabella, and their stillborn daughter.

I stepped back from that sacred ground and found a different place on the edge of the pines to set things up. The red alligator clip went to the positive terminal and the black one to the negative. After waiting a minute for the tubes to get warmed up, I dialed up the volume and started tuning for a station.

From my bedroom on Thirty-Seventh Street, my radio could pick up a dozen stations, easy. From out here on Hjalmar Rehnquist's knoll, I could only pick up two. KSTP from St. Paul came in good, but not great. WCCO out of Minneapolis came booming through as strong as if I were sitting at the top of the Foshay Tower. I recognized Cedric Adams's voice right away, as he started off the evening news with a commercial message about "Crisco—the pure all-vegetable shortening."

Cedric had the kind of voice that settled me down in the evening and gave me a vague feeling that everything was going to be okay. I think his big, friendly laugh might have had something to do with it. And I wasn't the only one who felt that way, neither. I knew plenty of people who found comfort at the end of the day listening to Cedric Adams reading the news. On this particular evening, he was talking about a raid by US flyers on a Japanese plane base that they had been using to train Kamikaze pilots.

*Good!* I thought to myself. *Let's get Tom back home—pronto!*

~

I set four mousetraps again, one for each corner of my bedroom. Through the open window, a cool breeze trickled through. I heard the flapping of wings and saw the old man's crow take a perch in the maple tree next to the house.

Lying there on top of my bedsheet, it was still too hot to sleep. My thoughts wandered from Tom to my mother. From there they took a nasty turn. Sometime this summer I knew that Mr. Wayne Borsthagen would find and try to kill me with his long-blade knife, the only questions were where and when.

# Chapter 6

At first light Monday morning, I was shook out of my sleep again by the sight of that claw hand, broken nose, and face full of white whiskers. Neither of us talked. I pulled on my pants and noticed that they were getting pretty rank and even rigid from all the dirt, dust, and animal by-products that seemed unavoidable around here. I was going to have to wash them soon and wasn't looking forward to doing it all by hand.

There were two dead mice in the bedroom corners. That was two less than the day before, so I chalked it up to progress. I would deal with their carcasses later, if Peacock didn't find them first.

I walked out the door to the sound of dew dripping off the eaves onto an upside-down wash basin that played them like a drum. A banana moon still hung up in the deep-blue sky like it was pasted there for a high school play.

Ham sat on a wooden chair amid the weeds, Black Cat clinging to his forearm and gobbling down blueberries from an open hand. *Talk about your pampered pets.* I couldn't see the old man's mouth, but his eyes were grinning. Grayburn Jackson had him pegged all right—Hjalmar Rehnquist really *did* like birds.

"I'll pitch down some silage and start milking," I said. "Gotta get to my job at seven."

"Take the bicycle," he said.

"What bicycle?"

"In the shed, by the barn."

While he was talking to me, Ham never took his eyes off that crow. And his eyes never quit smiling about it either.

*Goofy old crow! Even goofier old man!*

I turned my back, marched to the silo, and struck a match against the side to light up a cigarette. Taking a long, slow draw, I puffed a ring of smoke that floated perfectly for two seconds before falling to pieces. I put the cig tight in the corner of my mouth like a sailor, climbed the silo ladder, and crawled inside through the small, square opening.

I don't mean to brag, but I was a quick learner when it came to this dairy farming stuff. It was hard work, that was for sure, but it wasn't any complex algebra. I pitched silage, scooped shit, tossed hay, and pulled tits for just over an hour. The cows were getting used to me, and I was getting used to them too. Gosh—it was a swell feeling to see how they already trusted me.

By the time we had all eight milked and fed and the milk cans standing in cool well water, it was time for me to get to town. I slathered some raspberry jam in between two pieces of bread. There was no time for coffee. I pumped myself a glass of water and swallowed it in two gulps, then headed outside to find the bicycle.

The shed turned out to be a rotting heap. No paint left on the planks, wild grapevines growing all over three sides. I managed to shove the sliding door open and found the bicycle. Not surprisingly, it was a relic. The thing had a cracked, leather seat about as hard as a slab of granite and a piece of pipe with no grips for a handlebar. Attached to that was a wire basket, and beyond that it was all rust—especially the chain. I perused the dusty workbench in the shop and found an oil can. Once I got the chain good and saturated, I lifted the rear wheel and gave it a few turns of the crank. The tires were flat, of course. I looked around and found a hand pump hanging on the wall. Amazingly, both tires held air.

Twenty minutes of hard cranking on that rusty chain got me to Milltown, where I leaned the bike alongside the brick building at Mr. Gustafson's implement store. It was just two minutes past the seventh gong of the church bell when I strutted in the door—right on time, by my reckoning. I looked around but didn't see anyone. There was a light on in Gustafson's office.

"Get your ass in here!" he yelled.

I swallowed hard and stepped into his office. "Good morning, sir."

"To hell with good morning! What I want are employees who get here on time!"

"Sorry." *Damn!*

"When I said seven o'clock, I meant seven, sharp. Understand?"

"Yes." *What a prick! I'd like to see him on that bicycle.*

"Okay, kid . . . What's your name again?"

"Milo."

"Milo, here's the story. I tallied up the damage on the repairs to the Minneapolis-Moline and the harrow. It comes to seventy-two dollars."

I could feel the skin around my eyeballs stretching. It was worse than I thought. That was two hundred tickets to the Boulevard Theater. That was three hundred packs of Lucky Strikes. That was practically a down payment on a brand-new car, for crying out loud.

Gustafson continued. "You'll be paid forty-five cents an hour, all of which will go toward the repair of the equipment that you damaged. You'll work four hours a day, from seven to eleven. That will still give you time to help your uncle in the afternoons. That's every weekday morning, from Monday through Friday, 7 a.m. sharp, understand?"

"Yes."

"If you do good work, I'll give you a little bump in wages mid-summer. If you give me any trouble, I'll drop you to the minimum of 40 cents. You understand?"

"Yes."

"You'll be working for my maintenance and set-up man, Mr. Krankel. You'll do whatever he tells you to do. Whatever it is—sweeping, painting, deliveries—you do it. Understand?"

"Yes."

"Come with me. I'll introduce you."

We walked out of Mr. Gustafson's office and through a door that led to the shop. One man with dark goggles and a torch was welding something that looked like a big axle. Another mug, at a workbench, held a rotary grinder to a large chunk of iron. The sparks were really flying. We watched for a little while and I thought it was all as nifty as hell—especially the guy with the welding torch and goggles. Man oh man . . . would I ever like to learn that!

Our little tour continued through another door into a room that was full of all sorts of supplies and spare parts on heavy duty metal shelves. In the corner of that room, we came to a cluttered desk where a man scoured the pages of a fishing catalog.

"Carl!"

The man snapped his head around, bug-eyed, while frantically shoving the catalog into the top drawer of his desk and banging it shut.

"Yes, Mr. Gustafson."

"I want you to meet Milo . . . umm . . . What's your last name, kid?"

"Egerson."

"I want you to meet Milo Egerson. He's the new kid who will be working for you this summer."

Carl Krankel stared at my scar. While he was doing that, I studied him right back. His head resembled a light bulb—the forehead wrinkled like screw threads beneath a shiny baldness. His nose was hooked like an eagle's beak, and he was about two days overdue for a shave. Krankel wiped his right hand on his pants and reached out to shake. I grabbed it and found myself on the losing end of a hand-crushing contest.

"Show him the ropes," said Mr. Gustafson to Mr. Krankel. "Put him to work on whatever you got."

My speculations wandered in the direction of welding, grinding, machining, and assembly. I would certainly be turning wrenches and drilling holes along the way. I could almost imagine the complexity and challenge of taking apart a large farm machine and then putting it all together again. To be honest, I couldn't wait.

I felt a whack on the shoulder from Mr. Gustafson's encouraging hand. "Good luck, kid." Then he walked back out the door and it was just me and Carl Krankel.

I looked him over again, and didn't like the way his mouth hung half open like a zombie. He clamped it shut and his bloodshot eyes locked onto mine.

"Where did you get that scar?" he asked.

"None of your beeswax," I blurted out before thinking.

"Tough guy, eh?"

Guess what I did for four hours on my first day on the job at Gustafson's Tractor and Implement? Scrubbed toilets and mopped floors. That's what. Was I sore about it? You're damned right I was sore about it.

By the time the church bell gonged eleven times in a row, I was ready to shove that scrub brush up a certain part of Krankel's anatomy and leave it there. I had a notion to chuck the mop and bucket on the roof while I was at it. Then my plan was walk out the door with a middle finger salute to Gustafson. All of these ideas played like a movie through my brain. In the end I just filled out my time card with four hours of work at $0.45 an hour and did the math. $1.80 down, $70.20 yet to go.

With most of the day still ahead of me, I straddled the rickety bike and pedaled up and down almost every street in Milltown. In part, it was a way of blowing off steam. I was still burning on the inside after getting bossed around all morning by that dimwit Carl Krankel. Mostly, I rode past places I had already seen. Twetten Hardware, Lindoo Drug, Brask's Tavern, and another bar called Rosies. At the Co-op station, I cut the corner and, just for yuks, dinged the bell cord. Wouldn't you know it, a guy jumped out and started yelling.

"Hey, why don't you move back to Minneapolis?"

*Huh?*

I snapped my head around to take a look at the prick. Just some high school goon—stocky build with a round head, acting tough. I'd seen a hundred of 'em just the same back at Washburn High.

Another zig and another zag. There it was, Milltown Public School. It was a dandy building too—red brick, two stories, big gymnasium right next door. *Criminy!* For a two-bit town, they had a school right up there with some in the cities. Even the ball fields were in tip-top shape.

As I worked my way back, I passed two churches and the Milltown Hotel again. Then my eyeballs landed on a small shop that had eluded me before. STENLUND RADIO were the words in red and white over the front door. *Shit yeah!* I hammered the brakes, flipped the kickstand, and grabbed the door handle. Wouldn't you know it? The place was locked up.

I pressed my face against the glass between cupped hands and eyeballed at least three dozen modern radios for sale on the shelves. Philco, Emerson, Crosley, Zenith, and RCA. I could see them all. I even spotted an Arvin 524, the kind with those minitubes I'd read about in Popular Science. Behind the counter, I could see that they had components for sale too. Everything a guy needed for repairing home-builts, like mine. It was a top-flight shop, and since I was sort of a nut about radios, I was certain about coming back.

That little bike tour took about twenty minutes. *Big whoop!* Well, at least Stenlund Radio was a score. It was time to head back to the farm, but just then an ice truck crossed the intersection. I followed it to a house on Bank Street and stopped. The ice man came out dragging a block with a pair of giant tongs.

"Could you spare a chip, mister?" I asked.

He lopped off a corner with his scraper tool and chucked it over.

"Thanks!"

"No problem," he said. Then he slung the ice block over his shoulder and walked toward the side door.

I chewed down the ice chip until I could fit the whole thing in my mouth. Then I jumped back on my bike and aimed myself back across town so I could ride back to the crummiest little farm on planet Earth. I almost made it to the town limits on State Highway 35 when an oddity stopped me.

A field of brownish-green tents. Rows and rows of them, and big too. I counted at least thirty in three rows and a huge one in the center. There were also a couple of long, narrow buildings close to the road, and around the whole works was a fence. Nothing sturdy—just a wood slat snow fence, about chest high. My eyes returned to those perfectly aligned rows of tents. What were they for? *Boy Scouts? A church group? A traveling circus?* And do you know the strangest part of all? Nobody was even around.

"Weird." I jumped on the pedals and pointed myself north on 35. Maybe the old man could give me some answers.

Ham wasn't even home and neither was Black Cat. I gulped down two glasses of milk and made another jam sandwich, then got to work on the mess inside the barn. The afternoon dragged by slow. After four hours of toilets, mop handles, and slop buckets, I was ready for anything other than more shit. One wheelbarrow load at a time, I hauled manure out the door to the barnyard where the old man had started a pile. I kept one eye on my Hamilton wristwatch.

At ten minutes to three, I chucked the shovel in a corner and made my move back to the house, worn ragged and pissed off. Why was I doing all the work while Ham was off on a joy ride with his stupid crow?

I grabbed my radio, the battery, and my pack of Luckies. Then I slogged again out to the pines that marked the high point in the big field. The dial was already set to WCCO, and all I had to do was hook up the battery wires and wait for it to warm up. When the sound came through, a commercial for Wrigley's Chewing Gum was playing. They did a little jingle and ended with their slogan—*The flavor lasts!* I pulled the radio closer to my face and listened hard. Then the voice came through that I'd been missing since I jumped on the train to Milltown, Wisconsin, in the first place. The voice belonged to my mom.

"Hello everyone, and welcome to another edition of *Beauty Banter*. My name is Hedda Egerson, and today we're going to learn about the best way to enhance your appearance with makeup."

I rolled onto my back and used my hands for a pillow, just gazing straight up into the cotton-ball clouds. I could see Mom's face in detailed color. Her bright, cheery eyes and that smile. It was a miracle she was still so pretty after all she'd been through. I took a breath and closed my eyes.

"The most important thing to remember, ladies, is to start out with a freshly scrubbed face. Never apply new makeup over old. Never, never, never."

The fifteen minutes flew by. Then, as her closing comments came near, I pulled a scrap of paper from my pocket and a pencil. I got ready in a kneeling position and aimed my left ear toward the speaker in the radio.

"Thank you for listening, ladies. And remember, keep your best face forward."

As the radio went to a baking soda commercial, I jotted down the words "best face forward." Then I pulled the decoder card from under the wooden radio lid. The card, when held vertically, showed a thermometer, drawn with colored pencils along the right side. The bottom third of the thermometer was colored green. The middle third was colored yellow and the top third red. On the left side of the card, Mom had written down a bunch of different phrases that lined up with different levels on the thermometer. I scanned the words and thankfully found what I was looking for near the bottom.

Best face forward = Low green

Low green was the coolest, safest place to be on the paper thermometer. It meant that, for now at least, I didn't need to be looking over my shoulder for a man coming at me with a long-blade knife. At least for now I was safe from the creep, as I hid in the middle of nowhere like a cricket under a rock. But do you know what warmed my insides even more than that message? Getting to hear Mom's actual voice on the radio. Gosh, I missed her. Gosh, I wished I were back home.

Ham and that stupid crow showed up just past four, so at least I had help with the evening chores. The routine was the same. Then supper, and the menu hadn't changed either—more beef chunks out of a mason jar along with cooked tomatoes, boiled potatoes, and Wonder Bread. I must have grumbled because it earned me a response from my great-uncle.

"You want something different, go out and kill a chicken. Either that or catch some fish."

# Chapter 7

Tuesday, Wednesday, Thursday—the whole week was a blur starting at 5 a.m. Shovel shit, pitch silage, and milk cows. Then ride the bike over to Gustafson Tractor and Implement. Scrub, mop, and shine for Mr. Krankel, then back to the farm.

Don't get me wrong. I had nothing against work. I'd done my share of paper routes, lawn mowing jobs, and show shoveling. It's just that this was about a hundred times harder and, like I said earlier, it was practically nonstop. And to top it all off—to put the cherry on top of my vanilla shit sundae—I wasn't even getting paid because all my wages went to fixing a Minneapolis-Moline tractor. A part of me was actually getting peeved at Uncle Ham, too. I knew he was an old man and everything, but did he really have to dink around with his new pet crow for hours on end?

On Friday morning, when I showed up at work, Krankel was waiting for me at his desk. There was a sparkle in his eye I had not seen before—a bad sign.

"Got a seed planter, just arrived as a trade-in," he said. "I need you to get the rust off it. Then repaint it."

He walked me out to the equipment yard and pointed to an odd contraption with all sorts of hoops, wings, cans, and wheels, every square inch of which was caked with rust, dust, and dirt. Every moving part was froze up solid. Krankel handed me a wire brush. Then he grinned like the devil and walked away—whistling.

*Bastard!*

Right away I scrubbed hard and kept at it. It was personal this time—me against Krankel. Me against Gustafson too. Why stop there—I added Ham to the *Me Against* list. Then there was the big one—me against Mr. Wayne Borsthagen.

Through gritted teeth I repeated every curse and swear word that I held in my arsenal and ran through them a hundred times. All morning long, I stayed at it, head down, not even stopping for water as I shoved and pulled at that wire brush. The sun climbed, the minutes ticked by, and dust caked my hands and arms. When I wiped the sweat from my face with my white handkerchief, it came away reddish brown. I was a spectacle for passing cars. A lady walked by with her little boy and I imagined her using me as an example of why the kid should go to college.

At last, the church bell gonged eleven times. I rose to my feet, took several breaths, and began my walk back to where Krankel was sitting at his desk reading that fishing catalog again. I placed the brush down. It was ruined now, the bristles completely flattened.

He lifted his eyes briefly. "You can finish up on Monday," he said, then returned his gaze to where his finger marked a black-and-white page of musky fishing lures.

I walked away, but not to my bike. Instead I headed toward Mr. Gustafson's office and knocked on the open door.

He looked up from under his green visor, then did a double take at the sight of me. "What happened to you?"

"Scraping rust."

"The trade-in planter?"

"Yes."

Mr. Gustafson took off his green visor and nodded.

"This job stinks."

"What you did on Saturday stinks! Don't forget it!"

I let my head sag.

"I hope you're not getting ideas of quitting, Milo. You've got a big debt to pay."

"I know."

"Just keep doing what Carl Krankel tells you. Just work hard. It's only a couple of months."

I looked up again. "He's got me scrubbing toilets, mopping floors, scraping rust."

"You got yourself into this, boy. Don't come crying to me."

I didn't know what to say, so I simply stood, nodded, and walked away. I found the rickety bicycle where I had parked it. One tire was flat. I walked it down Main Street. I passed in front of the Co-op station with the idea of getting the bike tube repaired. That stocky-built guy with the round head came out wiping his hands on a rag.

"You gonna ding our bell again?" he asked.

"Maybe."

Melonhead dropped the rag and walked right up to me with a snarl. "Why don't you go back to Minneapolis like I told you?"

"Why don't you screw yourself?"

The punch to my gut came quick and hard. It took the wind right out of me so I could hardly breathe. Still holding the bike, I doubled over and gasped.

The goon picked up his shop rag and stared at me for a while. "Get out of here," he finally said, then walked back inside.

I stood there for a couple minutes trying to get some air back into my lungs when a '38 Chevy coupe pulled up to the pumps, dinging the bell cord twice on the way in. Melonhead came out and got busy pumping ethyl, checking oil, and wiping the man's windshield. When he got his hands on the gas nozzle again, I decided to do it. I walked over to the bell cord and jumped on it with both feet.

*Ding!*

The dimwit nearly jumped out of his blue pants and glared at me over the roof of the Chevy. I glared back, betting that he wouldn't leave his station. He was practically twitching, wanting to pound me again, but stayed put instead.

I spat on the blacktop, then walked slowly to Lindoo Drug, trying not to show how much my stomach was still hurting. I parked the rickety bike and strolled inside to the ice cream counter. Beneath the pain, my stomach groaned with hunger. Maybe a treat would make me feel better. I ordered a chocolate-cherry malt from the scarecrow who I'd met on my first day in town. He nodded, wide-eyed and apparently a bit shocked by my appearance, then got busy with scooping the ice cream. I glanced around and spotted a lady with her two kids at one end of the counter and two businessmen talking at the other end. One booth held a group of four kids who I figured to be a couple years younger than me. All four stared at me at the same time, then turned away and giggled.

Scarecrow slid the malt in front of me. "Twenty-five cents," he said quietly.

I slid him a quarter. He grabbed it and quickly walked to the end of the counter by the lady with the two kids.

I sucked down half of the malt in about ten seconds, then took a pause to unfreeze my throat. The bell jingled, announcing somebody at the door, and I turned to look. It was that pretty girl who I'd met on Saturday at the ice cream counter. I remembered the scarecrow calling her Rosalyn. She recognized me and looked at the floor. Still looking down, her feet took her to the end of the counter where scarecrow stood waiting. She had a whispered conversation with him then walked head down and fast through the door and down the sidewalk.

I finished the malt with a long noisy slurp through a straw, then pushed the glass away and shot a quick thumbs-up to the scarecrow. On the way out the door, another little kid stood there, staring at the gumball machine— a little girl this time, wearing what looked like a hand-me-down dress and a pair of scuffed-up shoes. I reached in my pocket and found two pennies. Then I handed them both to the little girl as her eyes popped.

Back outside, I approached the Mobil station and asked the man if he could help me patch a bicycle tube.

"Too busy right now," he said. "Got two brake jobs, a bad starter motor, and an oil change. Can you leave it and come back at five?"

"I'll be milking cows at five."

The man nodded and pointed to his tool box. "Feel free to help yourself. There's a patch kit and glue in the second drawer. Wrenches are right on top."

"Thanks," I said.

"No sweat, kid. Name's Bill Schick." He reached out a greasy hand and I shook it.

"My name's Milo Egerson."

Getting the wheel off was the hard part. After that I easily removed the tire and tube, found the leak with soapy water and pressed on the patch with rubber adhesive. I used a hand pump to fill the tire with air until it was hard. Then I offered to pay Mr. Schick but he waved me off. At least I'd met one nice guy today.

I rode the bike north on Highway 35 and saw that mysterious encampment of tents again as I passed by. A few hundred yards beyond the tents, I spotted a tin building with a steam pipe sticking up through the roof. From the sign, I figured out that it was Stokely's canning factory. About a half mile past the canning factory, the other tire sprung a leak, and with a fizzing noise going round and round underneath me, I coasted to a stop.

I was too tired and sore to swear. Too tired to even spit. Left—right— left—right . . . I walked a long ways and took a right turn on gravel. At the cattails I took another right onto the wheel ruts leading to Ham Rehnquist's farm.

The old man spotted me but said nothing. The dust, dirt, flat tire, my dragging feet, and bent body told enough of the story. While I sat at the kitchen table, he cracked three eggs in a frying pan and another into a bowl with some coffee grounds. Five minutes later I was shoveling scrambled eggs on toast and sipping Swedish egg coffee between bites.

The meal and especially the coffee brought me back to the world of the living, but by that point I was quietly scheming again to buy a ticket on the train back to Minneapolis the next day. The killer would probably find me anyway, so why stay? Besides, I was tired of living in a place where nobody except the Mobil gas station man and the little kids at the gumball machine liked me.

I finished my eggs and polished the plate with half a piece of Wonder Bread. I leaned back. Just then Black Cat jumped down off Hjalmar's shoulder and made a move for the last of the bread still in my right hand.

"Get away," I yelled and took a swat at her.

She jumped back. *Caawww! Caaww!*

Not even the crow liked me.

# Chapter 8

Recharged with eggs and coffee, I stood, flexed my arms, and cracked my knuckles. Ham was washing a frying pan with Black Cat perched on his shoulder watching me. As a peace offering, I tossed a corner of bread to the floor. All I got was more anger—*Caawww!*

"Great," I said. "I can't even *buy* a friend."

Ham looked at me, drying the frying pan with a tattered dish cloth. "Don't give up, boy, ya only been here a week."

"I've been trying."

"Folks will come around."

I watched a large fly buzz and bump against the window pane. It finally gave up and circled the room before landing on a spiral-coiled strip of yellow fly paper above the kitchen table, joining a hundred dead companions.

"Who lives in those tents on the edge of Milltown?" I asked.

Ham turned to look at me and smiled. "You found our best kept secret."

"What?"

"Germans."

"What?"

"German prisoners of war. Over three hundred of them."

"What?!"

Ham shrugged. "The army had to put 'em somewhere."

"But Ham! The fence is so flimsy, they could jump right over."

The old man looked at me like I was ignorant. "Where they gonna run to, Milo?"

"I don't know? South? East? West? They could hop on a freight train and make a getaway."

"They're mostly just boys. I've met some of them. North Africa corps mainly. All they want to do is wait out the war. They work in canning factories and do work for farmers."

"That's crazy! They're the enemy."

"They ain't much different from you, actually."

"If I had my way, I'd push them all into the ocean."

"And you're wondering why it's hard for you to make friends?"

Ham hung the wet dish towel on a hook and shuffled toward the door. That arrogant crow watched me the whole time from his shoulder.

"I'm fixing to feed the chickens and pigs," said Ham. "Then I'm gonna check on a cow that's about ready to calve. If you want to make yourself useful, you could get us some groceries in Luck. The list is on the table. Sugar ration coupon is there too. Tell them it goes on my account."

"The bike's got a flat tire."

"Glue and patches are in the drawer behind you. Tools are in the shed." The old man took a half step through the screen door, then stopped and looked at me again. "You know how to patch an inner tube, don't you?"

"Yes."

He nodded and walked out onto the weedy path toward the barn.

I fixed the flat tire in a jiffy and came back for the list.

Wonder Bread
5 lb. Sugar
10 lb. Flour
Pickled Herring
Crackers
Beer

Under the word *Beer*, he had scrawled a note: *To whom it may concern. I hereby authorize Milo Egerson to purchase one quart bottle of beer on my account. Hjalmar Rehnquist.*

Luck was even closer than Milltown, a fifteen-minute bike ride by way of Highway 35. Just like in Milltown, I took a few minutes to check out the dinky little town. As usual, the railroad tracks and depot were set back from Main Street. Just two people stood on the wooden platform next to the tracks.

Main Street was a busy place with cars angle parked on both sides and a bunch of stores selling everything a backwoods hillbilly might need. There was a grocery store of course, a couple churches, and several bars. Among service stations, the Texaco appeared to be the newest. The West Hotel kept its face pretty shiny too. Most of the houses in Luck seemed like they were east of downtown. I took a spin in that direction and found out the reason. There was a lake over there. I asked a kid and he said it was called Big Butternut. After eyeballing the water, I pegged it to be about as big as Lake Harriet in Minneapolis—not bad for Wisconsin, I figured.

Back on Main I spotted an official-looking building with a fancy sign with gold letters on a black background.

D.B.S.

LODGE NO. 186

A gray-haired woman with a cane saw me looking. "It's the Danish Brotherhood," she said.

"Danish? As in Denmark?"

"That's right. Luck was mostly settled by Danes, and folks are plenty proud of it. Up until a couple years ago, the men in that club still held their meetings in the Danish language. Now, of course, all the youngsters and their fancy ways don't hardly care about heritage no more. Don't get me started." The lady looked me over, tracking my scar. "Are you Danish, young man?"

"Swedish."

"Pfft! You and everybody else. Well, at least you're not German."

I thanked the lady for the information and turned the bicycle crank to get back in the direction of the grocery store. The man there helped me find all the goods that Ham had asked for—all except the beer, that is. He asked me if I had a ration coupon for the sugar. I handed it over, and the man studied it for a few seconds under a bright light. Then I told him at the cash register that I was the great nephew of Hjalmar Rehnquist and asked if he could he please put it on his charge account.

"I guess that's why he sent *you*." The man was gazing hard at me over the top of his spectacles.

"What do you mean?"

"We've got a fifty-dollar limit on credit. He's already begged his way up to sixty-three. I reckon the stores in Milltown are wise to him." The man's face tightened up as he shook his head and rang up the total of $1.72. From under the counter, he pulled out a general ledger and looked up Ham's name.

"Wait a minute," I said as I dug in my pocket and pulled out a couple of crumpled dollar bills and dropped them on the counter. The man returned

28 cents and an appreciative nod. Then he loaded everything into a cardboard box with Heinz Ketchup printed on the side.

I wedged the box into the bicycle basket and then scanned the street for a likely place to buy the beer. The Northern Tavern held promise. I leaned the bike beneath the front window and walked inside.

It took a little while for my eyes to adjust to the darkness. A pair of dim yellow lights hung down from the ceiling, barely illuminating rows of bottles, three deep, on the ledge behind the bar. A cash register sat to one side. Seven men, seated at the bar, drank amber fluid from short, clear glasses. Four of the men were farmers speaking quietly in their own little group. Two others, at the far end of the bar, I had pegged as fishermen. One wore brown pants and a green short-sleeve shirt, and the other had a hat with trout flies stuck in the band.

The man closest to me appeared to be pretty well sauced. He supported himself (barely) with both forearms on the bar and his head and shoulders bobbing, bobbing, bobbing, as he fell in slow motion toward his glass. At the last second, he caught himself and sat back up to almost straight again. Then the bobbing started all over.

The bartender was a skinny guy with slicked-back hair and a dish towel tucked into his belt. He walked over suspiciously without saying anything, and I placed Ham's note on the bar.

"What's this?" he asked.

"My great-uncle, Hjalmar Rehnquist, asked me to pick up a quart of beer."

The guy glanced at the note. Then he studied my face for a few seconds and shrugged. Very slowly he ambled back down to the other end of the bar. He said a few words to the farmers, then chuckled at something one of the fishermen said. While he was down there, I noticed some packs of cigarettes stacked next to a jar of pickled eggs.

*What the hell.* I reached over and grabbed two packs of Lucky Strikes and dropped them inside my shirt at the collar. *Easy Peasy.*

Finally, I watched the bartender reach underneath and grab a thick brown bottle and move back in my direction. He put it in a brown sack and placed it on the bar.

"Ten cents," he said.

I placed a dime on the bar, grabbed the sack, and turned to the door. The sunlight smacked me right in the face as I stepped outside and wedged the beer bottle in with the other groceries in the basket of Ham's bike that was still leaning against the wall. I touched the lump inside my shirt where the packs of Lucky Strikes rested somewhere near my belly button. I decided to leave them right where they were for the time being.

The bar door opened and closed. I had my hands on the handlebars but couldn't move, because two ratty-looking leather boots and a pair of dirt-stained pants stood in my way.

"Whatcha got there?" asked a deep voice.

I looked up (way up) and saw a young buck who stood about six foot four. He had dark-brown hair that hung in his eyes, sunburned cheeks, a sharply pointed nose, and a square chin. I figured him to be Tom's age, probably about twenty, and wondered why he wasn't fighting in the war.

"Nothing," I answered back.

Quick as a praying mantis, the guy's arm snapped out and grabbed my shirt, pulling me to him and lifting me onto my toes at the same time.

"I saw you take those cigarettes," he said.

"What cigarettes?"

He gripped my shirt tighter and pulled me up higher. I couldn't do much because my toes were barely touching, but my arms were both free so I socked him twice in the gut. That brought me down onto my feet again. He let go of his grip too.

I should have made a run for it then and there. Instead, I balled up both hands again and set them both loose in a fury of lefts and rights. The first swing of my right fist was a clean miss. Then my left glanced off his shoulder as he backpedaled. Another miss. Another glancing blow and then—*Bam!* He hit me square in the side of the face. I tried to shake it off and kept coming. *Bam! Bam!* I took a shot to the nose and another to my left ear. I staggered back. It was a blast to the gut that dropped me for good—right between two parked cars.

I tried to take a breath but couldn't. Heck, I couldn't even gasp. My legs kicked like a half-dead frog, and I flopped from one side to the other.

While I was down on the ground, the tall guy ripped open my shirt at the buttons, grabbed both packs of cigarettes, and walked back inside the bar. I crawled up the curb. Red droplets, one after another, appeared beneath me on the sidewalk. I pinched my nose to stop the bleeding and stood up. Fortunately, the box of food was still in the basket of my bike. The beer was gone, though. The guy had taken that along with the cigarettes.

I pushed the rickety bike down a side street and ended up behind the Luck train depot, where I found a water spigot. On hands and knees, I washed the blood off my face as a string of box cars slowly rumbled and clicked past me on the rails. Over a mud puddle, I studied my reflection. To my already scarred face I had added a fat lip, a swollen right eye, and a cut above the nose.

A clanking rattle caught my attention and I looked up from my puddle. A girl in a plain blue dress on a bicycle.

*Wait a minute. It's that Indian girl.*

She glanced at me and then looked straight ahead again, pedaling harder than before.

"Hey, you!" I shouted.

No response.

"I know you recognized me!"

Still no response. She just kept pedaling. That's when I noticed the pair of wooden baskets that straddled the rear fender of her black bicycle. They were loaded with plants. The green leaves from each one fluttered in the breeze about head high.

"Where you going?!" I shouted.

She turned the corner, and just as she was about to disappear behind a stack of pine timbers, I saw her glance at me over one shoulder. Then she was gone.

*Dumb cluck.*

# Chapter 9

All the way back to the farm, I grumbled and groaned about the raw deal that was my whole life. First there was Dad dying. Then all of Mom's bad luck.

*Not my fault!*

Then there was the scar that ruined my chance of being normal ever again. That special gift that might as well have been a tattoo on my face. A tattoo of a fist with the middle finger sticking up. One that would have had words underneath that spelled LEAVE ME ALONE!

*Not my fault!*

And as far as friends were concerned, what choices did I have? Do you think I *wanted* to be one of the hellions? Do you think I *wanted* to kick in car headlights and smoke cigarettes in the alleys? I wanted to be on the chess team, if you must know. Maybe I wanted to be homecoming king, too. Did anybody ever think about that?

*Not my fault!*

You know what would have been really nice? To have a big brother at my side to help out once in a while. But no! What did Tom go off and do? He ran off and joined the United States Army to kill Japs. Lucky for him. Rotten for me.

*Not my fault!*

At least I had Mom. Yep—at least I had Mom, who loved me and always would. But then with no warning, what does Mom up and do? She rips me right out of my home and shoves me up north to live on some godforsaken farm with some useless great-uncle who can barely even take care of himself, to say nothing of me.

*Not my fault!*

My legs churned like pistons as the bike chain rattled and spun like an egg beater. Was I finished with my self-pity tour? Hell no, I wasn't!

Milltown, Frederic, and Luck—*Big Whoop!* And what kind of stupid name was "Luck" anyhow? Just some stupid name thought up by stupid people because nobody was bright enough to come up with a proper name like Minneapolis.

*Stinking little towns!*

And wouldn't you think folks could be nice to a newcomer? Fat chance. Bunch of assholes was more like it. There was Gustafson getting on my case and making me work for that idiot, Carl Krankel. Toilet cleaning, floor scrubbing, rust scraping. *Crap!* And what did I get paid for my hard work? Nothing.

Heck—even the kids my own age had it in for me. That Rosalyn girl and the scarecrow at the ice cream counter? *Shoot!* They acted like I had the measles. The melon-headed dick who got pissed off because I dinged his gas station bell. And that tall bastard in Luck who knocked me around. What business was it of his that I stole a couple packs of Luckies? *Christ almighty!* Even the Indian chick wouldn't give me the time of day.

*Stupid, ignorant people!*

I suppose the topper was my great-uncle, Hjalmar himself. And what kind of backwoods name was "Hjalmar" anyhow? Sure, he was· nice enough on the surface, but who did he think he was kidding? A place to stay for my own protection? Free farmhand was more like it. And what was in it for me? Just like with that freeloader Gustafson, not one thin dime.

~

It was a lot of work trying to nail myself to a cross, let me tell you. And with nobody listening while I was doing it? With nobody to feel sorry for me? Hell—it burned my insides all the more. I had half a mind to launch a gob of spit all the way up to heaven so I could smack God right in the eyeball. Wasn't He the one who was supposed to make things right?

That was it. I had made up my mind.

I noticed that the truck was gone and so I knew Ham was gone with it. Just as well. With him out of the way, at least I could make a clean getaway. I put the box of groceries on the kitchen table and flew up the stairs. My suitcase was right under the bed where I had left it, still half packed with the few extra clothes I had brought. I swapped out my bloody shirt for a clean one and got busy stowing my homemade radio. Just as I almost had it surrounded by clothes, I heard the kitchen clock chime three times.

*Beauty Banter!*

I pulled the radio and battery back out and hooked up the black and red wires. As usual, it took a minute—then a commercial for Viceroy cigarettes came on. "The brand recommended by dentists," said a Hollywood voice. The next voice belonged to Mom and, just like last time, it warmed my heart. Her topic of the day was about matching your hair style to suit your face. I waited and waited, imagining Mom's expressions as she talked about how a hairdo was like the picture frame around your face. She said that with the right style, a round face would look less round and a square face would look less square. Stuff like that. When it came time for her sign off, I turned up the volume and put my ear closer to the speaker.

"Join me again on Monday, ladies, and remember—your real beauty is on the inside."

I pulled out the decoder thermometer card from under the radio cover and scanned down the list until I found it.

Real beauty is on the inside = Middle green

That cinched it for me. I quickly packed the radio and battery in loose clothes and snapped shut the suitcase. Just before heading out the screen door, I spotted a slip of paper on the table.

Visiting a friend.
Back soon.
Ham

Probably off to see more Indians is what I figured. *Crazy old man.* For a second, I contemplated leaving a note for the knucklehead. Finally I decided—*Screw it!*

# Chapter 10

The slog to the Milltown Depot with my heavy suitcase took just over an hour. I bought my ticket for the 5:18 to Minneapolis and sat down on a bench. It was just past four o'clock so I had time to kill. I walked back to the ticket window.

"A pack of Lucky Strikes."

The guy looked at me and I could see him contemplating everything at once—my beat-up face, my scar, my age—maybe even my recently earned reputation in the village of Luck. In the end, he reached behind and plopped the pack on the counter. "Twenty cents."

I paid it in three nickels and five pennies to get some weight out of my pocket. Back at the bench, I struck a match and drew my lungs full. A little kid from the other side of the room was watching me, so I made a show out of puffing a smoke ring and then blowing a geyser toward the ceiling.

A freight train rumbled by and kept going. Another took the siding track up toward Stokely's. While I was looking that direction, a whole herd of men appeared, all walking my way. Shift change, I figured.

They got closer. Altogether there were at least three dozen. Young guys, not much older than me. The first gaggle of them got close enough that I could see something written on their pants. Two letters, one on the left leg and one on the right. I looked closer. *P W*. What the hell was *P W* supposed to mean? More young guys kept coming. Two of them goofed around, kicking a stone back and forth as they walked. Something was different about the last fellow in the group. He was carrying something. What was it? In a split second I knew.

*A rifle! An army rifle!*

The rest of the puzzle came together quick. *P W* stood for Prisoner of War. The rifle was to guard the prisoners, and they were all walking from the canning factory, back to the tent encampment next to Highway 35.

*Son of a bitch!* It was the goddamn Nazis.

I jumped to my feet and walked closer to the glass. They all looked so young. Young but evil, I figured.

*Rotten scum!*

Except for the letters stenciled on their clothes, they could have passed for ordinary Americans. Where was the goose stepping? Where was the "Heil Hitler" salute?

"Just regular young men," said a familiar voice behind me.

I turned around.

"Like you and your brother, I reckon," Ham's quiet voice trickled through his white beard. His eyes weren't smiling this time. Black Cat stared at me from his shoulder.

"Hi," I said.

"I would have appreciated a good-bye."

"Sorry."

Ham sat down slowly on the bench, looking older than usual. "Had a hunch I'd find you here when I seen your suitcase was gone."

"I'm going back to Minneapolis," I said. "I don't fit in here. It's obvious."

"One week isn't much of a chance."

"Easy for you to say. You're not the one everybody hates."

"They don't hate you. They barely know you."

"Well, they ain't being fair, that's for sure."

Ham's eyes rose up to the ceiling, where a sparrow flitted from beam to beam. He studied the bird intently for a few seconds, then returned his gaze to me.

"*They're* not being fair? What about you?"

"I done my best."

"I'd say you done your best at being selfish."

I jumped to my feet and felt my hands clench at my sides. Then I realized how foolish I looked and sat back down. Not knowing what else to do, I pulled out another cigarette and lit it with a wooden matchstick. At least it gave me something to do with my hands.

"See there?" said Ham.

"What?"

"You just lit a cigarette and never even offered me one."

"You don't smoke."

"No, but it doesn't mean I can't start."

I reached out with a cigarette and the old man took it. I lit another match and he sucked on the cigarette—then coughed.

"Thank you," he said.

Together we sat there smoking. Ham took a puff from his Lucky and coughed again. He tried a third time and almost hacked up his spleen.

"Mighty tasty," he said.

"You're not mature enough," I zinged back.

For a few seconds Ham watched his cigarette burn, then turned and looked me in the eyes. "You really ought to stay."

I shook my head. "Not the way people have treated me. See this?" I said, pointing to my fat lip and smashed up face.

"What did you do to deserve that?" Ham asked.

"Nothing."

"Maybe honesty isn't the Minneapolis way, but it works pretty well up here."

I felt blood rushing into my face. "Yeah? And what do you know about Minneapolis?"

"What I know is that you got what you deserved around here."

That was it for me. I let loose on the old man with a five-minute tirade, starting with my grievances against Mr. Gustafson and Carl Krankel. I blasted both of them for making me do slave labor—scrubbing toilets, swabbing floors, scraping rust off junk machinery, for Christ sake. Then I piled on about how mean the regular people in town all were to me. The girl at the ice cream counter and the scarecrow. The mug who punched me for dinging the bell at the gas station. The creep who thrashed me on Main Street in Luck. I probably should have stopped there but I didn't. I started firing my bullets at the old man himself. I was sore about his hayseed shit jobs and for making me do all those chores for free. I'd had it with eating five-year-old meat out of mason jars. I was ticked off about my bedroom full of mice and doubly ticked at the lazy cat that wouldn't catch them. And last, but not least, I was sick of that goddamn wood stove heating the place up like the fires of hell in the summertime.

Just when I was getting rolling, the old man's crow took a bite out of my ear.

"Ouch!" I glared at Black Cat. "Stupid bird!"

"Black Cat's pretty smart, actually," said Ham.

"Can't stand him!"

"Her . . . And she knew how to shut you up, didn't she?"

"Whatever." I sucked on my cigarette but got nothing. It had burned out during my rant. Now what was I going to do with my hands? I touched my beat-up nose, turned away from the old man, and stared out the window. Where was that train anyhow?

Time passed. I sniffed. More time passed and I sniffed again, embarrassed. A moment later, I wiped a tear from one eye.

"I wish you'd stay," said Ham. "I need your help. You're a quick learner and a hard worker. You're good with your hands and good with the animals."

"I'm going home."

"I'll be lost without you. The farm is too much for me anymore."

"I'm going home." *He can rot in the Poor Farm for all I care.*

"What about your debt to Mr. Gustafson?"

"I'll mail him the money from Minneapolis."

"Seems unlikely from a proven thief."

I shot the old man an angry glare. "I ain't no thief."

"That's not what Henrik Jespersen over in Luck told me."

All of a sudden, my tough-guy act melted away. *God almighty! Look at me!*

I *was* a thief and a liar too. A deep shame surfaced inside of me and rose up beyond my anger. My head fell into my hands and my chin quivered. I began to cry. A minute later, I was full-blown sobbing . . . a Mississippi River at flood stage sort of crying. How *was* I going to pay Mr. Gustafson back? How *was* I going to make things right about the stolen cigarettes? How *was* I going to keep my great-uncle out of the Poor Farm? How *was* I going to ever get any decent friends for once?

A weird thing happened next.

Black Cat made a soft sound and ruffled herself. Then, just like that, she jumped off Ham's shoulder and onto mine. She stayed there too. All the way out to the truck. All the way back to the farm.

It didn't make any sense.

Some things don't.

# Chapter 11

*You'll be just like him.*

My eyes popped wide open at the sound of the voice that refused to leave me alone. My heart hammered inside of me. My lungs pumped air like a bellows. I didn't know where those words kept coming from—maybe God—maybe the devil—maybe my own messed-up mind. All I knew was that they scared the hell out of me.

I scrambled out of bed, fell down, and crawled in desperation to escape pitch darkness. My right hand swept the emptiness and finally whacked into something hard. My fingers found a knob, then the top surface of the dresser. Frantically, I groped until a whole box of Diamond matchsticks spilled all over the floor. I managed to grip the box and pick up one of the matches. Quickly I scratched the stick to the box. Wrong side.

*Come on, Dammit!*

Rotating the box to another surface, I tried again and finally found the side with the striker as a spasm of yellow light filled the small room and burning sulfur stung my nostrils. As the flame settled down, I got to my feet and used the lit match to find the kerosene lantern, also on the dresser. The wick produced a separate, tiny blue flame. I dialed it up higher with the brass knob and it brightened to yellow.

Slowly I paced the floor as my heart beat back down before squatting at the open window. No moon showed itself. No stars either. For that matter, not a single light anywhere. The only sound, the nightlong trill of frogs from the cattail marsh.

*Why didn't I just wait for that train?*

Still exhausted from the previous day, my body and mind both needed sleep. I knew that wasn't going to happen. I lay my head on the window sill and relaxed the muscles in my stomach and back.

*What's to become of me?*

The question was surrounded by a certain dread—a certain hopelessness. The clock in the kitchen chimed three times. In another two hours, the routine of chores would kick in all over again. At least there would be daylight.

Then a sound hit my ears out of the darkness. A low moaning sound. An awful, horrible, something's dying sort of sound. My head rose off the window sill. My ears waited. Was it my imagination? Then it came again— so pained and sickening that I couldn't ignore it. I pulled on my pants and, with the lantern in my hand, scurried down the steps, through the kitchen, and out the single-hinged screen door.

Again I heard it and my feet took me toward the pasture where the cows would be resting. I lifted the wire loop from the fence post, pushed the gate, and secured the loop again after passing through. Again, the moaning sound punched a hole in the night. I held up the lantern and counted seven brown faces looking back.

"It's okay, girls. Where is she?"

As if on cue, the death moan sounded again, from the far side of the pasture. With long strides, I moved diagonally through the field. I saw nothing as I neared the place where the fences met at a corner. Carefully, I listened and heard a rustling from an area of scrubby bushes. I walked right into the thicket and felt thorns tearing at my arms, piercing my pants.

I could hear breathing now and lifted the light higher. There she was, the eighth cow, and I remembered Ham telling me that a new calf was due to be born any day.

"Easy, girl," I said, and sat down beside her head, patting my hand against her neck. Her gigantic barrel of a body heaved with each breath. She groaned again and stiffened.

"It'll be okay, girl. You'll see."

Not knowing what else to do, I got up and walked to her back side, still holding the lantern in front of me. I moved in close and *whoa!* There were two little hooves sticking out. I took a step back.

"Damn. Now what?" The cow moaned again. Was she dying?

I watched for five minutes, hoping for a miracle. The cow tried and tried to push that calf out but wasn't getting any closer. I almost took off at a run to get Ham, but then a distant memory popped into my head. I couldn't remember who talked about it, maybe Mr. Murkowski in biology class, but somewhere along the way I had heard that a person could help a stuck calf by pulling on it. I scratched my head. Hell—the handles were right there—sticking out. I put down the lantern and moved in closer. The cow groaned again, a real painful sound for sure.

That was it. I would try. Each of my hands grabbed one of the protruding legs just above the tiny hooves. I squeezed tight and pulled, but they were so slippery I lost the grip and fell on my butt instead. The cow moaned again and her whole body shifted.

"Sorry, girl."

I rubbed my wet hands on my pants and pulled out a handkerchief from my pocket that I wrapped around both legs. It worked on opening jar lids. Maybe it would work on pulling out calves.

With the handkerchief in place, I gripped again. Then, believe it or not, I even put one boot on the cow's rump for leverage. I took three deep breaths of air and *pulled!* Let me tell you—it was a noisy spot, with her moaning and me grunting at the same time.

First the rest of the front legs came out and then the nose. She was stuck again. I took another deep breath, doubled my grip and tugged. The head popped out, brown and white. After that, everything happened in about two seconds. As I tugged and the cow pushed, the whole calf came out about as quick as a watermelon seed squeezed between two fingers. There it was, a slimy little brown-and-white critter at my feet with eyes open and tongue hanging out—breathing and everything.

"Good job, girl!" I said.

I sat and watched in the flickering lantern light. It took a while, but the mother found the energy to stand, then turned toward her baby, licking it again and again on the face and neck. The calf wobbled, then shook its head and tried to stand. No luck. The mother cow nudged it and kept on licking until the little fellow tried again, successfully this time.

"Shazam!" I said right out loud.

The little guy pushed its nose up against his mother's side, followed that flank in the direction of her udder and—bingo. The little critter had his first meal. In the eastern sky, a pale-violet light glowed, and I blew out the lantern flame. All was good. All was calm. All was bright.

Taking a breath of cool air, I looked up at a single fading star and then back at the mother cow and her suckling calf.

"No," I said to the glow in the eastern sky. "I will *not* be like him."

~

The smell of fried eggs and bacon drifted through the screen door as I approached. The heat of the Monarch Range hit me in the face and even felt good for a change. Uncle Ham glanced and nodded before turning back to the eggs, but just as quickly he turned all the way around and looked at me again. Maybe it was the expression on my face, the thorn scratches on my arms, or the wetness of my knees, but he knew where I had been.

"The calf?" he asked.

I nodded and smiled.

"Was she stuck?"

"Not anymore."

"You pulled it?"

"I pulled it. The cow and the calf are both standing and doing fine."

All was quiet but for the sizzle and pop of bacon. Ham looked at me all squinty-eyed with his mouth hanging open. Even Peacock lifted her head from a dish of warm milk to ponder me.

"You ever pulled a calf before?" asked Ham.

"No, sir."

"How did ya figure it then?"

I shrugged and put a twist in my mouth, enjoying the moment. "I knew the cow needed help and . . . well . . . the handles were both right there."

Ham's mouth went crooked like mine, and for a second we looked like a couple of goofs. Then he busted all the way into a full-blown smile. "Well I'll be damned."

All I did was nod. I was proud, of course, but trying to be cool at the same time. My lips were clamped tight but there was a smile coming up and it was ready to bust through.

Ham dropped the spatula and walked over to me, pressing his good hand on my right shoulder and his claw hand on my left. He looked in my eyes with wonder. "For a Minneapolis boy, you got more gumption than I thought."

My smile busted out all the way.

"Bestämdhet och mod!"

"What's that?" I asked.

"Never mind. I'm just proud of you, that's all."

Ham went back to rescue the bacon and eggs. But his eyes kept flashing in my direction and the sparkle never washed out of them. He asked me to tell him the whole story, and I did. From the moment I first heard the cow moan to the moment the calf stood on wobbly legs and suckled milk from its mother's tit. It was a celebration, nothing less. Yep, a celebration at five o'clock in the morning, and I was the guest of honor. The Swedish coffee flowed nonstop. The mouseproof tin of *Chokladbiskvi* emerged from the cupboard. That, combined with the bacon, eggs, and Wonder Bread, and, by golly, we were both acting like a couple of drunken lumberjacks.

The clock finally sounded its reminder to us with one chime at 5:30 sharp. Ham sneered at it—even snorted. With his claw hand on my shoulder, he shot me a wink and another admiring smile. "I'll get started," he said. "You take your time and finish up breakfast. Come out when you're ready." I watched as Hjalmar Rehnquist headed out the screen door and walked to the barn. There was something about his quickness this morning that warmed me even further.

So, did I take my time finishing up breakfast like the old man said? Did I dawdle and bask in my glory? Hell no! The old man needed me out there. There was my silo to climb, my pitch fork to grip, my pails of water to deliver, and my cows to milk.

I wiped the yolk and bacon grease off my plate with a half slice of Wonder Bread and walked out the rickety screen door. The sun was a golden face, smiling down. The weeds that bordered the trail all sparkled with their diamonds. And there was the silo, about as tall and straight as the Jolly Green Giant.

I think I might have been taller.

# Chapter 12

Thank goodness for weekends. It was the start of two days off from my lousy job. Carl Krankel's donkeywork at Gustafson Tractor and Implement would just have to wait. I went to the kitchen pump and downed three full glasses of water while Ham perused the advertisements in the *Polk County Ledger*. As I stood there, I noticed a stink and wondered where the heck it was coming from. Then, I took a whiff of my left armpit and got the answer.

"Umm . . . Ham?"

"Yah?"

"Do you have anything like a bathtub? And maybe some kind of clothes washing machine?"

"Yah! It's behind the shed. You'll have to carry pails of water from the pump to fill it up. There's a bar of soap out there too."

"Thanks."

The round, steel tub was about four feet across and two feet deep. The washing machine was a slab of corrugated steel. I would wash myself first and the clothes second, figuring that the biggest stink ought to take priority.

The first order of business was to get the spiders and centipedes out of the tub. It wasn't easy, as they were well entrenched. That done, I started toting water from the kitchen well. Six buckets seemed like enough. Heck, I wasn't going to prom. I found the soap, a brown rectangle that smelled like lye, and scrubbed myself in that freezing cold well water. The dirty clothes came after that. Buck naked, I spread every stitch in the sumac branches to dry.

*Now what?* I wondered.

Like a thief, I snuck back into my bedroom, grabbed the blanket off my bed, and wrapped it around me like an Arabian sheikh. From there I grabbed my radio set and headed off to the knoll in Ham's big field. I lay the blanket down in a sunny spot and sprawled out, buck naked, on my back like one of them Nature Boys from California.

I dialed up Cedric Adams on WCCO radio out of Minneapolis and listened to all the news from around the world and back home. After an hour or so, I moseyed back to where my clothes were drying in the sumac branches and got dressed again. When I stepped back in the kitchen, Ham's eyebrows really popped.

"Better get yourself over to the ballroom," he said. "The girls will be lining up."

I made a face. *Girls lining up for me?* I'd have settled for a one-minute conversation with a certain one named Rosalyn. My thoughts drifted to her pretty face at the ice cream counter.

All of a sudden, a flash of black came soaring at me like a jet. Black Cat slowed down with the back-flapping of her wings and found a perch on my shoulder.

"I'm wounded," said Ham. "That bird likes you more than me now."

"Naw. She's just trying to get you jealous."

"No. She likes you all right, boy. All the critters do."

I pinched a grasshopper off a weed and held it out for Black Cat. She snatched and swallowed it, then looked to me for another. "Wish some of that critter-liking would rub off on people."

"Folks will come around."

"Are we going to the creamery today?" I asked.

"Milk should keep until tomorrow morning," said Ham. "Go and do something fun with your day off. Get out of here. Take the truck. I'll stick around and tend the homestead."

"Really? Take the truck?"

"Sure."

I gave a glance to my boots, then back at Ham. "Do you reckon the theater in Frederic is showing a matinee?"

"Two o'clock," he said." You got plenty of time."

"Hot dog!"

"If you want to catch us a few trout for supper, you can do that too. Remember the McKenzie Creek I done showed you?"

"Yes."

"Just take the county road straight east out of Frederic. Fishing pole and tackle are behind the truck seat."

"Okay. Do you want to come along? I think they're still showing *The Body Snatcher*."

Ham held up two open palms. "I'm sure."

We had jam sandwiches, carrot sticks, and boiled potatoes for dinner. It seemed weird not having any meat, but I kept my mouth shut about it. The old man gave me a few instructions about running the truck. Using the crank start without a helper was the trickiest thing. Otherwise, it would be just like driving cars up and down the alleys and side streets in Minneapolis.

"How are you at working a clutch?" asked Ham.

"I'm good," I said.

That earned me a raised eyebrow. How much did Uncle Ham know about the Minneapolis-Moline?

"I have one more condition before you go," he said.

"What's that?"

"I want you to stop at the Northern Tavern in Luck and apologize to the owner for stealing those cigarettes."

"But . . ."

"No buts. You have to apologize, face to face. Understand?"

"Yes, sir." I felt two boulders and a cinder block settle into my gut.

With that, the old man set me loose. I gave a wave out the open truck window just before turning off his wheel ruts and onto the gravel. I took it slow until reaching Highway 35. Then I cranked her all the way to fifty.

I had to slow back down pretty quick, of course, because Luck just wasn't that far away. Took a right turn on Butternut and then the left onto Main. There it was. The Northern Tavern. I parked one block away and across the street, then walked real slow.

Inside it was dark like before with a few men on barstools and a few more standing around. Nobody paid any attention to me. Then the bartender from my previous visit saw me and his eyes locked down hard. There was another man behind the bar and we recognized each other too. He was the guy who roughed me up. By my thinking, getting punched in the face and the gut had been punishment enough, but mine wasn't the thinking that mattered.

I swallowed hard and walked closer to the two men. "I came to apologize for the other day," I said. My voice was barely above a whisper.

"We can't hear you," said the young one.

I leaned over the bar and cleared my throat. "I came back to apologize. I'm sorry about stealing the cigarettes. Real sorry."

The regular bartender didn't say anything but the young oaf walked up to me and leaned in until we were nose to nose. "I heard you're from Minneapolis. Is that right?"

"Yes."

"You're staying the summer with Ham Rehnquist?"

"That's right. He's my great-uncle."

"You'd best not pull another stunt. You understand?"

"Yes."

"If you do and I hear about it, even if it's somewhere else, I'm coming after you again. You understand."

"Yes."

"Okay. Get out of here."

I walked calmly and politely out the door and pushed it shut behind me. Then I flew like a spitfire to Ham's truck. As near as I could tell, I hadn't crapped my pants. With that bit of success, I kept on going in the direction of Frederic.

The drive north took ten minutes. All I had to do was stay on State Highway 35 and then turn left at Oak Street, where the theater was on the left side along with the usual small-town stores. I was early and nobody was lined up yet for tickets, so I decided to park the truck and take a stroll through town. Off to the west was the railroad depot, a two-story job with a half-dozen people outside. A string of box cars rolled by slowly and I didn't want to wait for them, so I spun on my heel and walked east. There was the restaurant where Ham and I had stopped for a meal. I scampered across the highway, walked past the hospital, and kept going. Then, just like in Luck, I came upon the town lake. It was a dinky little thing, no Lake Harriet this time. Pretty though, with trees all around and reflecting the blue sky.

"How are they biting?" I asked an old man with a cane pole and a wooden bobber.

"Pretty fair," he said, "if you like fish with whiskers." He pulled up a stringer of five or six slimy bullheads. I nodded but didn't say anything.

I kept walking along shore and skipped a few stones. Then, after wasting enough time, I zipped back across the highway to the theater, where folks were lined up for a city block.

I started walking toward the end of the line thinking the population of Frederic must be bigger than I thought. But then I started recognizing faces. The scarecrow from the Lindoo ice cream counter was in line with some buddies. He nodded to me and I nodded back. Then I came upon Melonhead from the Co-op station, and he was with some of his pals, too.

Just as I was getting to the end of the line, guess what. There was that pretty girl named Rosalyn. My heart started to thump pretty loud inside my chest as I tried to think up something clever to say. Then I noticed that she was standing in line with a tall, good-looking fellow with comb lines in his hair. On his feet, he wore brand-new two-tone wingtips, and I wondered how he got the ration coupons for them. Next, I looked down at my own leather boots and kicked off a greenish-brown clump.

Rosalyn glanced at me briefly but then turned away and grabbed hold of the movie star's hand. She knew what she wanted, and it wasn't that Minneapolis prick with the slash across his face. I dipped my head and wished I had a wide-brimmed hat.

# Chapter 13

From my hiding place in the very back row, I waited for the lights to dim so nobody could gawk and whisper about me. The newsreels played first, with updates from the war. The first half showed our troops cleaning up the huge mess in Europe. The second half showed our men still fighting, island to island, across the Pacific. They had pictures of guys sweating in steamy jungles. Soldiers firing machine guns up hillsides. Then there were pictures of bombs dropping out of planes and exploding on Tokyo. Through it all, I leaned forward in my chair and watched for a glimpse of Tommy. He hadn't written me or Mom a letter in a long time, but we hadn't received a government telegram neither. He had to be out there somewhere. Right?

*The Body Snatcher*, in case you're wondering, was a doozy. There was an evil doctor who needed more dead bodies for his science experiments. Well guess who played a deranged taxi driver to help him out by digging up graves. You got it—Boris Karloff. The whole theater was buzzing after the movie ended, and everybody was happy to get back outside in the sunlight. I made a dash for Ham's truck since I didn't really want certain people seeing me anymore.

Next stop on my Saturday off was that dinky little stream where Ham wanted me to catch some trout for supper. I drove a few miles east of town on the county road like the old man said, and there it was, McKenzie Creek, that stream so puny I could have almost jumped over it. I wasn't feeling lucky.

From behind the truck seat, I pulled out a bamboo pole, a small box of tackle, a wicker creel, and an empty tin can. I shoved over a rotting log and scrounged seven worms and a grub for the can. I rigged the hook with a worm and flicked the line in the water right there from the road.

I remembered Ham telling me to toss the bait upstream and let it drift back. His other advice had been to keep it close to the edge because the brook trout liked to hide in the undercut banks. I did like he said, and watched as the line went straight. I pulled up on my pole and felt the *tug-tu-tug-tug* of a real fighting fish. The thing flashed and jumped. As I lifted the ten-incher out of the water, it wriggled and tossed about like an acrobat. It took two hands to pin it down and unhitch the hook. Then I lined the wicker creel with wet grass and laid the fish inside.

Gosh, she was a beauty. I'd caught a lot of fish in my life, but that little trout was the prettiest, with speckles of gold, red, and blue and a belly that was bright orange. The fins really grabbed my eye—striped like orange, black, and white candy.

Back to business, I replaced my worm with a fresh one and got back to casting. My hope was to catch at least a half-dozen trout for supper. Wouldn't you know it? Just when I thought I was gonna slaughter them, they quit biting.

"They're wise to you," said a female voice from behind me.

"Huh?"

I turned around and saw a girl on a bicycle.

My eyes zeroed in and . . . *Shoot!* . . . It wasn't just any girl. It was that Indian girl from Grayburn Jackson's house again.

*How did she get here so quietly? And, what was her name? Anna? Ida?*

"It's Raina," she said.

*How did she . . . ?* "I knew that," I lied.

Her eyes left me and focused on the sound of a woodpecker hammering in the trees.

I looked at the woven wood baskets on the back fender of her bicycle, loaded again with small trees, their roots wrapped in wet burlap.

"What's with the trees?" I asked in my Minneapolis-hooligan voice. I reached for my cigarette pack to complete the image but realized they were in the truck.

She ignored me and continued studying the woods instead.

*Whatever*, I finally said to myself and went back to fishing.

"They're wise to you," she said again.

"I heard you the first time." I almost shouted but didn't. I flipped the bait out again and let it drift. Nothing.

"If you get in the water and walk slowly upstream you will get more bites."

"Are you going to pester me all afternoon?" I asked.

"No."

"Good." I flipped the bait in again and let it drift back close to the bank. Again, nothing.

"If you do walk up the stream, stay away from the beaver dam."

"Whatever," I said. I flipped the worm again but not a single trout showed itself.

I heard the rattling of the girl's bicycle as she rode off without saying good-bye.

*What was that all about? And what was that hooey about the beaver dam?*

With Raina no longer watching me, I pulled off my shoes and pants and hid them in the tall grass. Then I went right in wearing only my underwear and a shirt. It was hard walking with all the sunken branches, stones, and clams on the bottom. There were soggy parts too, where my feet sunk in and got stuck in the silt and muck. At each bend in the creek, I flicked out my worm and let it drift back toward me. In time I caught another trout, then another. I missed a few, too, but had fun battling those little scrappers.

I had been gone from the road for almost an hour and had four fish in the creel when I came upon what looked like the perfect spot. A big, round pool. Deep too, I figured. And the only thing between me and that perfect hole—a beaver dam. If ever there was a spot that looked fishy, this was it.

*Why was she warning me off from this place?* The light bulb went on. "She wants it for herself."

Slowly I moved toward the dam. More and more sunken branches jabbed at my bare feet. A few more steps and I would be close enough to cast out the bait. Then, suddenly, I felt the sensation of something sticking to my legs and ankles. Placing one hand on the beaver dam for balance, I lifted my right leg out of the water and . . .

"*Gaaahh!*"

They were leeches. Thick, black-and-brown bloodsuckers, and I don't mean just one or two. Thrashing and splashing, I made a one-man stampede toward the edge of the creek, where I hurled the pole and wicker creel into the tall grass and struggled to pull myself out.

"Dammit!" I screamed, kicking and trying to yank my feet from the muck. I was stuck and could feel more bloodsuckers latching on.

*Gotta get out! Shit!*

At last I grabbed a clump of grass and weeds in each hand and pulled hard enough to free my mud-anchored feet. I kicked and squirmed out of the stream and onto the bank, breathing hard. Only after calming myself did I dare to look down at my bare legs.

*Gawd!*

Each leg was thick with the bloodsucking bastards from the thighs on down—coated with them. There had to be a couple hundred, and each one was latched on tight with its suction cup mouth. I scraped one off with my fingernails and a trickle of blood appeared where the sucker had been.

*Son of a bitch!*

Out of desperation, I grabbed a small chunk of driftwood and started working it like a paint scraper. It hurt. *Damn!* But at least they were coming off, and in clumps. I plowed the faceless vampires like a thick layer of brown frost. With each handful, I tossed them left and right.

A few minutes into the nightmare and I had removed all except for the last ten or twelve, and went back to pulling them one at a time. I started insulting the last few individually.

"Get off me, you slimy bastard!"

My stomach took a queasy turn. Each bloodsucker came off with disgust on my face. As I tugged off the last of them, it felt like I was removing the fingers and toes of the devil himself. The last one was the biggest— a thick, black maggoty thing the size of my thumb. I scraped it off with the fingernail of my index finger and hurled it like a baseball.

My heart continued to hammer as I inspected those two horrible legs. They were speckled with suction bites and pissing blood. I splashed water on both legs to clean them as best I could, but it didn't stop the bleeding. At last I grabbed my gear and started walking through the thick brush until I was far enough from that beaver dam that I dared enter the water again.

At the county road, I found my shoes and pants and climbed out at the edge of the culvert. By then all but the largest bites had quit bleeding. Still, the sight of my legs almost sickened me and I slid my pants on to cover them. But now I had a whole new problem. My legs itched like hell.

~

Four small trout with our supper was better than no meat at all, that was for sure. Combined with potatoes, stewed tomatoes, and bread, it filled us up. Through the whole meal I scratched at my legs until Ham finally set down his fork.

"Did you get into poison ivy?"

"No."

"Well, what is it then?"

I rolled up my pants leg and revealed my collection of red dots and smeared blood. "Leeches. They swarmed me."

"That ain't good." He walked over to the cupboard and grabbed a red-and-white can of baking soda. "Try sprinkling some of this on your legs."

"Will that stop the itch?"

"Don't know. Worth a try, ain't it?"

"I guess so."

We piled the baking soda all over my leech-ravaged legs until they were as white as birch bark.

"How's that feel?" asked the old man.

"A little better," I lied.

"It's all I've got. I don't know how else to help you."

"I've got to stay busy," I said. "I'll go check on that new calf."

"Good idea."

I moved slowly up the lane and through the pasture, willing myself not to scratch my legs. The cow ignored me, grazing with her baby standing beneath her. The calf's legs were splayed out as she bumped her head twice against Momma's udder. In the grand scheme of things, maybe a thousand-leech attack wasn't the biggest event in the universe after all.

# Chapter 14

I slept like a dead guy but woke up itchy. One look at those blood-suckered legs in the lantern light and—*Urgh!*—what a nasty sight. Every suction bite had turned purple and grown to the size of a shirt button. Two or three and I could have shrugged them off. But what was a fella supposed to do when he had two hundred? I made my way to the kitchen and dusted both legs again with baking soda before stepping into my pants.

Ham walked into the kitchen and, between the two of us, we slugged down four cups of egg coffee. After that? You know the routine—climb, pitch, wheel, heft, pump, shovel, pull, and haul ten-gallon cans. I cranked the truck to life while Ham worked the throttle. Then I jumped in on the passenger side for another Sunday morning trip to the Milltown Creamery. The sky was bright and cloudless.

Just like before, a dozen or more farmers waited in line to unload their milk. Just like before, we positioned the truck in line with all the others and got out to mingle. All week long I had been sort of wondering about that kid with the deep scar in the back of his head. I looked around and spotted him right off in those same ratty clothes, with that same forlorn look on his face that set him apart from the crowd.

I walked over and tapped his shoulder. "My name's Milo."

His head snapped around and his eyes grew bigger while the rest of his face got smaller. His mouth almost disappeared completely, like both lips were drawn in by a string pulled from inside his head. He was afraid, that was certain, and the weird part was that it had nothing to do with my scar. What was it? Who was it? The answer came quick, in a voice that roared like thunder.

"Get back here, boy!"

The kid's mouth showed up again. "P-P-Pa says I can't talk to you," he whispered.

"Get back here, *now!*" The voice bellowed again and my eyes connected with the face of a bear. The thick, brown fur of the man's beard covered everything except his nose and dark eyes. The floppy brim of his gray felt hat darkened him further.

I watched as the boy took a few steps backward. Then he dropped his eye contact with me and walked quickly toward the Bear. The kid tightened up as he approached him—arms pulled in rigidly against his sides. It was like he was bracing for something. Then it came. A full-fisted punch to the boy's right ear. I watched as the kid dropped his head with legs quivering. He put his hand over the injured ear, then pulled it away and I could see the blood. Through it all, he made no sound.

A silence fell in among the gathering of farmers followed by murmurs of anger and a shuffling of feet.

"Don't you ever let me see you do that again, Albin!"

The new voice was deep, loud, and angry. It drew the attention of all the gathered farmers, especially me. I did a quick one-eighty and searched the crowd on tiptoes. There he was—a tall, thin fellow in his thirties wearing dirty coveralls like the rest of the farmers, with a shock of brown hair that went off in about ten directions all at the same time. His face was pale, the color of a pine board, but his eyes were blue, fearless, and wide open. The most impressive feature about the young man was his calmness. He seemed unintimidated by the Bear. Serious and unblinking.

"He's my boy and I'll smack him when he needs it," said the Bear.

"You do it again when I'm around and you'll find yourself on your ass with a broken nose."

A tense silence came with the staredown that followed. It probably only lasted five seconds, maybe ten, but to me, it felt longer than a red light at Hennepin and Lake. It was the Bear who finally turned away, and he made a big show of it too. He spat, snorted, and flicked away a cigarette butt before turning and pretending to watch something in the sky. That's when the smart-ass inside of me showed up.

"Real tough guy, aren't you!" I regretted the words just as quick as I said them.

Everybody was looking at me all of a sudden and that included the Bear, his son, and the man who had challenged him. I felt a hand on my shoulder. Ham's eyes were icy and his white beard jutted out, almost touching my chin. "Let's wait in the truck until our turn comes up," he said.

We got into the still-idling truck and closed the windows.

"You got a lightning rod up your ass this morning?" asked Ham.

"Huh?"

"That wasn't too bright, shooting your mouth off like that to Albin Zilstrom."

"Somebody had to," I said. The old man's comment really burned my toast.

"And somebody did. Vern Nygard took care of it. Next time, just let it lay."

"Sorry. It just came out," I said.

Truth be told, I was feeling less sorry with each passing second. I felt the blood rise up inside of me and I bit my lower lip. Ham and I both sat there quietly for twenty minutes and the whole time I wondered about the life of that kid who had a bear for a father. Was anybody *really* going to do anything to help him? For twenty long minutes, my conscience and the rest of my brain had a wrestling match inside my head. For those twenty minutes, my legs didn't itch.

By the time our milk cans were emptied, cleaned, and back in the bed of Ham's truck, we were both feeling better again. I realized that the old man was right—mostly. I still had my own sins to worry about, and everybody knew it.

So it wasn't out of spite when I told Ham that I was going to walk back to the farm. "I think I'll explore the town some more," I said.

"You peeved?"

"No."

"You coming home for dinner?"

"I'll just get something to eat here in town."

"You got money?"

"Yes."

"Suit yourself then. Can you be back at the farm by two o'clock? I need your help with something."

"I'll be there."

Ham nodded, climbed into the Ford, and rumbled up the highway.

When the truck was all the way out of sight, I started walking back in the direction of the village. The itch in my legs was back and I scratched them every few steps. At Gustafson Tractor and Implement I pivoted, crossed the highway, and found a goodish hiding spot between two bushes. That's where I settled in to spy on the German prisoner of war camp. I peeked between the slats of the snow fence at a white sign with black letters that stood above a narrow building.

From that large tent, I heard the clanking of dishes and the low murmurs of men talking. Minutes passed and nobody moved in or out. The door flap was tied open, but my angle was bad, and I saw nothing through it. The itch was still killing me. I bit my cheek, clamped down on my pants, and endured. What else could I do?

From my hiding place in the bushes, I scanned the rest of the camp. Three perfectly even rows of tents, all the color of canned peas. All around them, perfect order. No stuff on the ground. No towels drying on the stake-down ropes. No trash anywhere. Not even a bottle cap as near as I could tell.

Another ten minutes came and went, but still nothing happened. Suddenly, I heard a rising ruckus coming from the large tent and, just like that, men poured out between the flaps. One soldier with a hat different from the others stood in the middle of the chaos.

"*Antreten!*" he shouted.

The men continued to emerge, one after the other, and lined up in six long rows. While they got themselves organized, I noticed a few guys tucking in shirts and checking shirt buttons. Each man measured his position next to the one to his left, some by extending an arm and others just by eyeball. Their leader waited calmly while the lines grew straighter. Then he snapped his heels together.

"*Stillgestanden!*"

The command was loud, and the resulting thud of boots coming together was even louder. Next thing I knew, I was staring at a platoon of murderous Nazis standing at perfect attention and just an acorn's toss away. The sight chilled me like cold well water running down the center of my spine. I hunkered lower in my hiding place, my face still pushed up against the slats. My left eye was closed and my right eye glued to the action. And no, I wasn't scared. I was just worried a little.

More German words were blurted out by the gravel-throated commander. Everyone was paying close attention. Maybe he was giving the soldiers the plans for the day. I wasn't sure. Then, almost as quickly, the men were released to a more relaxed position, and their leader took roll call to make sure everyone was there. It took a while, but each soldier's name was read, and I heard names like Schwartz, Mueller, Hoffmann, and

Schmidt. As each was read from the commander's clipboard, the soldier matching that name shouted.

"Yah!"

When the roll call was done, the commander tucked the clipboard under one arm and shouted.

"*Wegtreten!*"

In unison, the entire group of soldiers snap-turned right and took three goose-marching steps straight toward me. *Christ!*

After the third step, it was as if they were all discharged from the army and a general commotion started up. My eyes flashed all around. Several Germans gathered in small groups, just talking, laughing, and lighting up cigarettes. Others headed to the small tents. Still others went back into the large one.

Then guess what took shape in the open space right before my eyes. A soccer game. I'm not kidding. It was a real European soccer game with the goofy-looking black-and-white ball and everything. Two makeshift goals were quickly rigged with poles stuck in the ground and bedsheets strung in between them.

As they lined up for the start, I counted eleven men on each side, the same number as in American football. Somebody made a sound like a whistle, and before I knew it, I was watching tenth-grade gym class at Washburn High. Just like when I had seen them at the railroad depot, it occurred to me again how young they were. Were they men or were they boys? *Shoot!* Half of them looked like they could have been my own age.

Up and down the field they ran—laughing, shouting—probably cursing. What seemed like a stupid game of luck at first turned out to be a sport of extreme skill. Where I would have kicked the ball as hard as I could, these young fellas handled it with finesse. They passed the ball sharply from one to the other and—get this—all that passing was done with their feet.

I studied one guy in particular who had skills none of the others could match. He looked like Joe DiMaggio, and so I started thinking of him in that way. When defenders came after the ball on his right foot, just like that it was back on his left. When a man slid his foot in the path he was going, he made the ball hop right over.

Then I gawped at something that almost turned my eyelids inside out. Another man kicked a high pass in front of the goal and DiMaggio ran toward it, not with his foot but with his head. He bounced that black-and-white ball right off his own noggin and it flew in a fast, straight line right past the goalie and into the bedsheet for a score. I'm not lying. I saw it myself and almost cheered, even though he was still a scum-sucking Nazi.

Shortly after the goal, one of the Germans accidentally kicked the ball over the fence right near my clump of bushes, and it rolled to a stop in a grove of pine trees. I just watched and stayed low in my hiding place. Partly it was because I didn't want to be found. But part of it was that I didn't want to help out a platoon of Nazis.

Then, fancy this, DiMaggio gave a quick wave to the guard, and the guard nodded. Next thing I knew, that speedy Kraut took a run at the fence and hurdled it in one try. He picked up the ball, then turned around and spotted me. He yelled something at his teammates, and they all walked straight at me. I was screwed. DiMaggio came at me from my side of the fence and about a dozen other Krauts came at me from the other.

Then I heard DiMaggio say something like, "*Willst du Fussball spielen?*" and I figured it probably meant "Do you want to die?"

All I could glean was that they were fixing to roll me up in the snow fence and beat me senseless with the steel goalposts. I took off at a full sprint, around the corner and north on State Highway 35.

I heard someone shout, you know, friendly-like, but I knew it was a trick and kept running. I ran all the way out of sight and then halfway back to Ham's place before slowing to a walk. By the time I got home, I was 50 percent pooped and 50 percent parched. I sat down in the kitchen to calm myself with a glass of cold water from the pump.

Then my legs started itching all over again.

# Chapter 15

I pumped three glasses full of well water and gulped them down, then shouted for the old man but got no answer. The weekend was only three-quarters done and it had already been a dilly. I'd pulled a newborn calf, been mauled by leeches, picked a fight with a bear, and got run off a soccer field by Nazis.

*Son of a bitch.*

While reaching for my pack of Luckies, I spotted a letter on the kitchen table and knew right away that it was from my mom. It had a Minneapolis postmark, a blue envelope, and a return address on Thirty-Seventh Street with my mother's swirly handwriting. It was my seventeenth birthday.

When I opened Mom's card, I could see right away that it was home-made. She had drawn a picture of a skinny dolt standing next to a blue convertible. I'm pretty sure the guy was supposed to be me and the car was supposed to be a 1941 Chevy Special Deluxe, because she knew I liked them. On the inside of the card she had drawn about a hundred little red hearts and written these words:

*To Milo,*
*Happy 17th Birthday!*
*I think you're wonderful!*
*Love, Mom*

There—right there—in that little message was the greatest thing about my mom. She never wavered in her love for me. Even after all the trouble I had caused, she stood firm at my side. Even though the Washburn High School principal had a special file on me about two inches thick, Mom always believed in my potential.

I saw another scrap of paper on the kitchen table and recognized Ham's choppy handwriting.

Meet me in the pasture.

## Ham

I stuffed my cigarettes into my shirt pocket with Mom's card and hustled out the door, worried about the newborn calf. When I got out there, the calf and its mother were nowhere in sight. What I found instead was my great-uncle Ham, all out of breath and wrestling with what appeared to be a medieval torture device wrapped around a barbed wire fence.

*What the hell? What is it?* I wondered.

"You know anything about fence repair?" Ham asked through a pink face and bloodshot eyes.

"No."

"Fair enough," he said. "I found this thing in the shed but can't remember how to work it."

"Maybe I can figure it out," I said.

"I sure would appreciate it." Ham showed me a portion of the fence where one strand of barbed wire was hanging loose and another strand had fallen all the way down. "Three cows got loose the other day and we need to get these wires tightened up."

I took the contraption from the old man's hands and studied the gadget from one end to the other. It was a weird-looking thing, but the operation seemed straightforward enough. Two sets of steel jaws, a ratchet bar, and a lever handle. My mental wheels started spinning and even created a picture in my brain on how it all worked. I showed Ham how to clamp the jaws on the two loose ends. Then I started ratcheting them toward each other with the lever. Slicker than snot. The whole works tightened right up.

Ham scratched his head. "Now we just gotta join them together so they don't come loose again?"

I grabbed the pliers out of Ham's pocket and made a V-shaped bend in each wire. Next, I hooked one over the other and twisted both. Guess what. It held. And with all those barbs, the wire wasn't going to pull back through no matter what.

"Now I've got an even bigger favor to ask," said Ham. "Could you tighten up the fence all the way around the pasture?"

I nodded, scratched my itchy legs, and squinted into the sun.

"While you're doing that, I'll go and check up on that newborn calf that you yanked into creation yesterday." Ham took three steps, stopped, and turned back around toward me. "You know what I think?" he asked.

"No. What do you think?" I answered.

"I think you're pretty damned smart."

I don't know what I was expecting, but it wasn't that. In just over a week I'd been called out for being a liar, a thief, and a selfish jerk by the old man, and each time he'd been right.

*Damned smart?*

I just stood there, glowing like the torch on the Statue of Liberty. Then I hefted the fence-mending contraption up over my shoulder and moved on to the next loose wire.

Two hours and a whole lot of clamping, ratcheting, twisting, and leg scratching had brought me all the way around to the last corner post on the pasture, and Ham was waiting for me with two brown bottles. He handed me one.

"Happy birthday."

"How did you know?" I asked.

"Blue envelopes with girly writing on them don't come in the mail every day," he said.

We each took a swallow of beer. I leaned on one of the fence poles and gazed out across the green pasture.

"Can I ask you a question, Ham?"

"Sure."

"Why don't you have a crop growing in the big field beyond the pasture? It looks like nothing but weeds out there."

Ham scratched his whiskers, looked away, and didn't answer.

"That is your land, isn't it?" I continued.

"Yes."

"You need a crop to make the farm work, don't you?"

"Sure do." He quartered away from me, staring at the horizon.

"Well . . . What is it then?"

Very slowly, the lifelong farmer of the land, Hjalmar Rehnquist, turned back to face me. "I just couldn't manage it this year."

"What do you mean?"

"What I mean is I'm damn near broke. The bank won't loan me the money for seed. My tractor and planter are both shot to hell."

"What?"

He shrugged.

"But if you don't grow a crop, what are the animals going to eat? And if you can't keep the animals, what happens to you?"

Ham dropped his head and I saw the white whiskers of his beard quiver. "As soon as that silo goes empty—it's over."

"Over? What does that mean?"

"It means the animals get sold and the land goes back to the bank."

"No! That can't happen! You love it out here!"

Ham shrugged.

"Where would you go? What would you do?"

"The Polk County Poor Farm," he said, his voice shaking.

# Chapter 16

For the next three days, my brain was like a jumble of letters from an anagrams game. They may have formed a few words, but no answers shook out.

For almost the whole entire week I'd been soaking in a pond of self-pity. Then come to find out the old man who had volunteered to rescue me needed rescuing himself.

While I continued to wrestle with the dilemma, I dipped a brush into a can of green paint and applied the finishing touches on the corn planter that I'd been working on between toilet cleaning, floor mopping, and garbage hauling for the past few days. I stood back and admired the final product.

"Looks good as new!" said someone behind me.

I turned around and saw Mr. Gustafson standing there with his legs apart and his arms folded over his chest.

"Took a long time to get through all that rust," I said. "Then I oiled all the moving parts and pumped fresh grease in the zerks. This thing should be good for another ten years."

Mr. Gustafson kneeled down by the planter and studied it. "Good work, Milo."

"Thanks."

Gustafson squinted and stared into my eyes like he was trying to solve a puzzle too. "How did you get so handy around equipment? I thought you were a city boy."

"I hung around shop class at Washburn High during lunch and after school. That and helping fellas work on their cars in the alleys." Mr. Gustafson was listening carefully and thinking hard about something. I could practically hear the grinding gears.

"Milo, do you think you could take apart the steering mechanism that you damaged on the Minneapolis-Moline tractor, fix it, and put it all back together again?"

"Yes, sir."

"Are you familiar with the parts inside a drive like that?"

"Steering shaft, bearings, worm gear, rear bushing. Reckon there's an oil seal or two in there somewhere."

Gustafson nodded. "How would you suggest we go about straightening the bent shaft?"

"On a shop press, if you've got one. Either that or use a vice and a big cheater bar."

"Forget the cheater bar. We've got a shop press," said Mr. Gustafson. The gears were really crunching now. I waited hopefully. He scratched his chin and squinted.

I took a chance and gave him a nudge. "I can do it, sir."

Gustafson nodded and then spoke. "I believe you can, son. Tell you what. You finish out the week working for Mr. Krankel and on Monday morning you can start working for Mr. Torkelson on fixing up the Minneapolis-Moline."

I could have pole vaulted over the moon. As Mr. Gustafson turned back toward the building, I remembered a question I'd been meaning to ask him.

"Mr. Gustafson?"

He stopped and faced me. "Yes, Milo?"

"Suppose a farmer hadn't planted his corn yet. Is it too late?"

His forehead filled up with wrinkles and he squinted at me again. "Well, that depends. Is he hoping to harvest a grain crop or chop it for silage?"

"Silage."

"Then there's probably still time."

"Thank you," I said, and neither of us spoke for a few seconds.

"You're welcome," said Mr. Gustafson.

By the time I cleaned the paint brush and put away the can of green paint, it was already eleven o'clock. I filled out my time card for the day and headed out the door, where my rickety bike waited alongside the building. Instead of going straight back to the farm, I couldn't resist the urge to ride past the German prison camp. Just like every other day, I rolled by the fences real slow and watched for movement on the inside. Just like before, everything was dead quiet. I wheeled across the highway and stopped outside the main gate. I had seen the sign before but read it again.

CAMP MILLTOWN

NO ENTRY WITHOUT PERMISSION

UNITED STATES ARMY

While I was looking over the tops of all those tents, a man walked out of the nearest one. He wore a snappy United States Army uniform made up of tan pants and a shirt that had three stripes on each shoulder. He also wore black boots, a brown belt with a shiny buckle, and one of those nifty tent-shaped hats that was situated a little off to one side. Upon seeing me, he paused.

"Hello there! I'm Sergeant Harrison. Can I help you?"

"Just looking, sir."

"There's nothing to see here, kid. They're all at work."

"At the canning plant?" I asked.

"Yep, mostly. We also have several groups working on farms."

"Ordinary farms?"

"Sure kid. Any farmer who needs help and can pay."

"Pay? I thought they were prisoners. Don't they have to work for free?"

Sergeant Harrison stepped closer to me and smiled. "That's not how it works."

"Why not?" I didn't get it. Here they were, a bunch of lowdown Krauts. If I had my way, I'd make them work their asses off, make them sweat like hell, and make them do it all for nothing on account of the rotten mess they started.

"You ever hear of the Geneva Conventions, kid?"

"No."

"According to the rules, these men get paid eighty cents a day for a full day's work. On top of that, the United States Army takes a cut. Bottom line is that the cost to the local farmers is just over a dollar a day, plus meals, for each prisoner."

I pondered that notion and scratched my head. "But what good is American money to a German prisoner?"

"We don't pay them in American dollars. We pay in something called camp scrip. They can spend the scrip on things like candy, cigarettes, books, writing materials, and the like, but it's useless anywhere else."

"Is that to keep them from having money if they escape?"

"That's part of it. They can also save the scrip in something like a bank account to be converted into German money when they return home."

I wondered about all that. What if Tom were captured? How would the Japs treat him? Would they pay him eighty cents a day to work on a farm—meals included? As you can imagine, I had my doubts. I'd read the newspapers. I'd heard all about the Bataan Death March.

"How would somebody go about signing up for help," I finally asked.

"Come back with your father," he said. "We'll get you on the schedule."

I decided not to tell Sergeant Harrison that my father was dead, my stepfather was in prison, and Ham was going bust. Instead, I nodded and shot a wave of thanks. Then I wheeled back to Milltown's Main Street.

Outside of Lindoo Drug, I flipped down the kickstand and took a couple steps toward the door. I even pulled a quarter from my pocket for another malted milkshake. Then something stopped me, and do you know what it was? It was knowing that twenty-five cents would buy me two hours of labor from a stinking Nazi prisoner—that's what.

Next, I went into Bimbo Grocery at Uncle Ham's request. I slid my quarter on the counter by the cash register, and old man Bimbo gave me a penny change and one pound of Maxwell House. Anyone could live without ice cream, but with our work schedule, coffee was a necessity.

My last stop was at Stenlund Radio. Before work I had dropped off my battery for a recharge by leaving it with a note on Stenlund's doorstep and hoping like hell that it wouldn't be stolen by some rounder. A metal bell jingled my arrival.

"Hello?" I said to the empty room.

A slightly disheveled man with a Charlie Chaplin mustache popped out from somewhere. "Hello back."

"My name is Milo Egerson," I said. "I dropped off a battery this morning, hoping you could charge it for me."

"Yes. I've got it right here." He pulled my battery out from under the counter and placed it next to the cash register.

"I'd have charged it myself except the electric company hasn't made it out to my uncle's place yet. How much is it?" I asked, reaching in my pocket.

He waved me off, shaking his head. "No charge for something like that. So, I've heard that you're Ham Rehnquist's grand-nephew. Welcome to the area. Have you enjoyed your stay?"

I pondered the past couple weeks. "To be honest, sir, it's had its ups and downs."

"Yes. Yes. It takes time to make friends in a new place, doesn't it?"

"Yes, sir. And I could have done a better job with my first impressions."

"I see. Well, that goes for all of us, doesn't it? I'm sure if you keep trying, you'll find Milltown and Luck to your liking. We've got our clinkers like every community, but mostly, both towns are stocked with fine folks. You'll see."

I nodded and walked over to a shelf where Mr. Stenlund had all his brand-new radio models on display.

"I've got a nice five-tube Crosley for a good price. Supplies have been limited, you know, but with the war winding down, our selection keeps growing. Do you like the new Bakelite shells?"

"You bet I do. They're cool. And I like the little Arvin 524 too. I read in Popular Science about the minitubes."

"How do you like the yellow color?"

"Swell!"

"I'll give you a good price."

"I can't afford it right now, but I'll probably be back. Thanks."

Lugging that heavy battery under one arm, I made my move to the exit. The bell jingled again as I swung the door open and closed it behind me. I placed the radio in the front bike basket and flipped up the kickstand.

Just as I was about to ride off, Mr. Stenlund came flying out the door with a piece of paper in his hand and a serious look on his face. "Young man?"

"Huh?"

"I'm wondering if you could help me out with something."

"What's that, sir?"

"How's your eyesight?"

"Good, I reckon."

"How's your hearing?"

"Fine."

"How would you like to join the United States Air Force Ground Observer Corps?"

"Umm . . ."

"We keep a lookout for enemy aircraft, Milo. It's serious business. I would like to make you the Deputy to the Chief Observer for the Milltown, Wisconsin, observation post."

"Who's the Chief Observer?"

If Mr. Stenlund were a giraffe, his head would have stretched above the treetops. As it was, he stood as tall as he could manage. "I'm the Chief Observer," he said.

"Well . . . I don't know, sir. You see I'm pretty tied up with helping my uncle and working for Mr. Gustafson at his tractor store."

"That's all right. You can choose your own hours. I could really use you, Milo. Seems that most folks around here don't take the danger of enemy air attack seriously."

"Well, we are a long ways from Japan."

Mr. Stenlund leaned in closer to me and lowered his voice to a whisper. "When they come, it will be through Canada and right over Lake Superior. Where do you think that will bring them?"

I imagined a map in my head. "Pretty close to right here, sir."

He nodded once, like the period on the end of a sentence. "Just one night each week, that's all I'm asking. What do you think, Milo? I need a good man like you. So does the United States of America. Will you do it?"

I felt like I was sprouting a lion's mane. "Well . . . when you put it that way."

# Chapter 17

I listened to *Beauty Banter* on my freshly recharged radio on Wednesday and Friday afternoons. Mom's coded message each time revealed no change at home. Everything was still fine and perfectly safe in the middle of the green range. Mr. Borsthagen was still making license plates at the Graybar Hotel. No threat for the time being.

Then Friday night rolled around, and with it, my first shift as Deputy Observer for the United States Air Force. Right at seven o'clock, following evening chores, I pedaled up to the front entrance of Milltown Public School, where Mr. Stenlund was already waiting.

He glanced at his watch. "Right on time. Are you ready?"

"I think so."

Mr. Stenlund unlocked the front door with a key and we both walked inside. Our footsteps echoed off the tile as we walked past empty classrooms. We climbed a set of stairs up to the second floor and then entered another room that was full of janitor supplies. I sidestepped a mop and bucket and a couple of disassembled desks before arriving at the bottom of a ladder that was leaning up against one wall.

"This is the way to the roof," he said.

At the top of the ladder, Chief Observer Stenlund turned the handle on a hatch door that he swung open to the outside. A cool clean breeze sifted through the dank room. I popped up and through the hatch, then found my footing on the gravel. Stenlund signaled me to follow him.

*Crunch . . . crunch . . . crunch.* We made our way toward the center of the roof, arriving at a six-by-six bunker surrounded by four-foot walls of stacked sandbags. From her seat on a bench inside the bunker, an elderly woman looked up at us from her knitting and smiled.

"Hello, Roger."

"Hello, Edith. I'd like you to meet the newest member of the Milltown Observer Corps, Milo . . ." Mr. Stenlund looked perplexed. "What was your last name again, son?"

"Egerson," I said. "Milo Egerson."

"Edith Quigley, this is Milo Egerson, our newest member."

A wreath of white, curly hair surrounded Mrs. Quigley's pink face. She blinked about a half-dozen times like she was trying to focus beyond my scar, then drew so close that I thought she might try to kiss me. I held my ground.

"You're Ham Rehnquist's nephew, aren't you?"

"Yes, ma'am."

"He told me you came up for the summer from Minneapolis. Is that right?"

"Yes."

"Have you been to any Minneapolis Millers baseball games?"

"Yes, ma'am, a few."

"Who's your favorite player?"

"Babe Barna. I've seen him hit two homers," I said.

"I liked Vern Curtis."

"Yes, ma'am. He's good too. They call him Turk. I think he's off the team now."

The old lady nodded and looked sad at the same time. "Off fighting the war," she said.

"Hopefully we'll whip the Japs pretty soon and they can all come back home. My brother, Tom, is in the Pacific somewhere, but he never writes."

"Goodness!"

Mr. Stenlund cleared his throat. "Edith, if I could interrupt for a few minutes to explain to our newest Deputy Observer how to conduct his station duties."

"Yes, of course, Roger."

For the next ten minutes, Mr. Stenlund spoke very seriously about my duties as a member of the Ground Observers Corp. He showed me a blue book called *Ground Observers Guide* and another one called *Aircraft Recognition*. It showed all sorts of silhouettes of bomber and fighter airplanes that our enemies might use to attack us from the north. He showed me the logbook too, and how I was supposed to sign in for my shift and where to record my airplane sightings. Last but not least, he told me where to find a two-way radio back in the janitor's room to call in any enemy aircraft sightings. Then he went on and on about staying alert at all times and using all of my five senses—blah, blah, blah.

Near the end of Mr. Stenlund's deadly serious presentation, Mrs. Quigley finally spoke up. "Roger! Stop it! You'll scare him!"

"Scare him or not, Edith. He's got to know the stark truth."

"You want the stark truth? I'll give you the stark truth, young man. We've been watching for three years and haven't seen a single airplane yet."

"None?"

"None. My advice is to bring a book of crossword puzzles."

Mr. Stenlund huffed and frowned. "When they do come, Edith, it will be a whole squadron. Milltown's big moment awaits us. Will it be of glory or shame? Everybody already knows about the Japanese and their surprise attacks."

Mrs. Quigley packed her knitting in a canvas bag and wobbled to her feet. "Maybe you're right, Roger. Either way, I'm through arguing about it." She turned and smiled at me again. "So nice to meet you, Milo. I would love to learn more about the places you've been in Minneapolis. Good evening."

"Good evening, ma'am," I said.

With that, she shuffled out of the bunker and over to the hatch and the ladder to the janitor's room.

"Can she manage the ladder?" I asked.

"Oh, don't worry about Edith," said Mr. Stenlund. "She could manage an anti-aircraft gun if we had one. Do you have any questions before I turn over the duties of the observation post?"

I shook my head. "No questions."

"One more thing," said Mr. Stenlund.

"What's that?"

He reached in his pocket and pulled out an oblong-shaped silver pin with a white circle in the center and the words "United States Air Force" around the perimeter. Underneath that was a small, blue banner and the word "Observer."

"What's this?" I asked.

"Your wings."

Chief Observer Stenlund pinned it to my shirt pocket and then saluted me. I'm not kidding. He saluted me just like a real military man. So, what did I do? I did what any halfway decent Deputy to the Chief Observer would do. I saluted him back.

After all of that I was on my own. So, was I bored? Nope, and do you know why not? Because from my post on the rooftop of Milltown Public School I could see everything—and I'm not even talking about airplanes.

Here's a list of my observations on my first night as Deputy to the Chief Observer for the Milltown, Wisconsin, observation post.

1. A card game went on past midnight in the kitchen of a house on Bank Street.
2. A lady on Third snuck out to her mailbox in her nightgown.
3. The scarecrow got off work from Lindoo Drug at nine o'clock and smoked a cigarette.
4. Melonhead at the Co-op station stole candy from underneath the counter.
5. That girl named Rosalyn and her boyfriend with the slick hair and two-tone wingtips were out and about too. They drove around in what must have been his daddy's Nash Ambassador coupe with the two-tone aqua-colored paint job. Up and down Main Street they went, making the circuit at least ten times in that fancy-pants car. When it got dark, they found a place to park behind the football field. I didn't care, of course. Stuck-up girls and their hotshot boyfriends could do whatever they want. Didn't make no never mind to me.

Using the electric torch under the seat at the observation post, I made my night's entry in the logbook under four columns.

| Name | Date | Hours | Observations |
|------|------|-------|--------------|
| Milo Egerson | June 15, 1945 | 7 p.m.–Midnight | None |

I looked through the pages and pages of entries in the book and learned that Edith Quigley was right. Nobody had seen any airplanes. It was a little bit creepy going down the ladder into the janitor's room and walking through the completely empty school at midnight. Once out the door, I reached in my pocket for the copy of the school key that Mr. Stenlund had made for me and turned it clockwise 360 degrees. I checked to make sure it was locked and it was. After that it was just a matter of twenty minutes riding the rickety bike to the accompaniment of a gazillion frogs and crickets. The usual left and right turns, then the wheel ruts, the shed and outhouse, Wonder Bread with jelly, a glass of water, four mousetraps, and bed.

# Chapter 18

It was an ordinary Saturday morning to start out. Two mice in the traps. Fried eggs on toast with *Chokladbiskvi* and Swedish egg coffee. Chores got done and a trip to the creamery took place without any drama. That's when the ordinary parts of the morning came to an end and my secret mission kicked into gear.

Ham was reading the Polk County Ledger at the kitchen table and drinking coffee when I approached him.

"Would it be all right if I borrowed the truck?"

"I reckon. You going to one of them monster movies again?"

"No. Just exploring the area, more or less."

"Is that code for you don't want to tell me?"

"Yes, sir."

"Fair enough. Just don't do anything crazy."

I didn't want to respond to that last comment because crazy was at the very nature of my secret mission that seemed very, very likely to fail. I was setting out on the gravel roads to introduce myself to the local farmers. Except for the Bear, I knew none of them. The scary part was that, even though I didn't know them, I was 99 percent sure that they all knew about me. My county-wide reputation for lying, stealing, and sass talking was well established in the community. I was the do-nothing-right smart aleck from Minneapolis. The rotten egg in the coffee.

In a way, my secret mission was a test for me. A chance to see how much guts I had to go knocking on those unfriendly doors. But in another way, it was a test for the locals, too. Just how willing were they to offer a second chance? Would they lend a hand to a scar-faced booger from the big city? And in doing so, would they help to keep Ham Rehnquist from going off to the Polk County Poor Farm?

Step one was the hardest. At each farmhouse, I had to present myself as the reformed hooligan in a humble and contrite manner such as not to get kicked off the property or shot. I had to shake off my attitude and come across as a decent kid for once. Well, guess what. Folks were nice, generally speaking, and a few even invited me inside.

Step two wasn't easy either, considering that I was showing up to ask for charity. Specifically, what I wanted was any leftover seed corn from their own planting that they could possibly spare. Well, a pretty large swath of the local farmers *did* have some seed corn leftover, and they had no hesitation about sharing it. This was especially true when I told them about the field full of weeds and how the bank was stonewalling Ham Rehnquist and all the rest. Yep, everyone who had some leftover seed corn flopped the partial sack right into the bed of the Ford truck. Some gave me food too. I ended up with a passenger seat full—a jar of pickles, a plate of cookies, and a half loaf of homemade raisin bread.

By virtue of not being home, even the Bear donated a partial sack of seed corn. Actually, it was his son who deserved the credit. He met me at the door with that gouge in the back of his head and a swollen ear that was turning purple.

"Wh-wh-what you want?" he asked as his eyes darted left and right. "Ain't you c-c-caused me enough trouble already?"

"Sorry," I said. "I'm Milo. What's your name?"

"Gilbert."

"Nice to meet you, Gilbert," I said. I reached out and he looked at my offered hand like it was a venomous reptile.

"What you want?" he asked again.

I took a deep breath and went into my well-practiced explanation of how I was looking for donations of leftover seed corn in order to help my great-uncle keep his farm going for at least one more year.

He still looked confused. "Wh-wh-what's that you want again?"

"Leftover seed corn. It's to help out Ham Rehnquist."

Gilbert hesitated and scratched his head, like it was the first time ever that somebody offered him a chance to make a decision. Then he stood up taller and his eyes opened all the way. I could almost hear his brain working. At last, a chance to decide on something for himself. A chance to show the world that he wasn't like his father. Well, let's just say he was all the way in on the proposition. From a nearby shed, he hefted a sack of seed corn into the green truck. Then he handed me a big purple thing the size of a softball.

"That's for your supper," he said.

"What is it?" I asked.

"Rutabaga."

By the time I got back to Ham's place, it was almost time for evening chores. I didn't see the old man anyplace and figured there was no sense tipping him off. I backed up to the shed, unloaded the sacks against a wall, and flopped a few old boards over the top. Likewise, I placed the food donations in mouseproof tins and hid them in the bottom shelves of the old wooden hutch.

"Come boss! Come boss!" I yelled. They walked slowly toward the barn. I made a beeline toward the silo.

~

I had finished my two weeks of misery working with Mr. Krankel and his toilets, mops, and wire brushes at Gustafson Tractor and Implement. My getting away from him and moving to a new assignment with Mr. Torkelson was like Friday escaping the cannibals in *Robinson Crusoe*. The main difference was that we both spoke English.

As you've probably already surmised, Mr. Torkelson was nothing like Mr. Krankel. For starters he assigned me to my own workbench next to his. Then he introduced me to his tools and told me that I could borrow any of them as long as I used them properly and returned each to its designated place.

After that he took me outside, and together we studied the mess I had made of the steering shaft, oil pan, and front wheel on the Minneapolis-Moline. Mr. Torkelson didn't judge me or chew me out. He knew that I'd been through that wringer already.

"How would you suggest we go about fixing it?" he asked.

"Well," I said. "I figured on using the shop press to make the steering shaft straight again. And while it's pulled out of the gear box, I could clean up the worm drive and the gears and bearings and such. I'd like to lubricate everything and put in some new oil seals."

"How about the punctured oil pan?" Mr. Torkelson asked.

"Would you be willing to teach me to use the arc welder?"

"I'm willing, if you're able."

"I'm able."

"Okay. Go on."

"Well . . . What I'd like to do with the oil pan is fashion a patch out of eighteen-gauge hot rolled and secure it with a fillet weld around the whole outside edge."

"That'll work," he said, twisting his mouth a little. I could tell that Mr. Torkelson had a different idea, but he didn't horn in, and I appreciated that.

"Then there's the popped tire," I said with a shrug. We both knew how easy that was to fix.

Mr. Torkelson gave me a friendly thump to the shoulder and nodded to my face. We walked back to the shop together for a lesson on how to safely use the shop press.

~

My welding lesson took place on Thursday afternoon. I'd already fashioned the steel patch by making a two-inch square on the shear press. I had flattened out the punctured spot on the oil pan too. Ready to go. In my mind it would be a ten-minute proposition—put on the welding mask and lay down a perfect weld. Come on. How hard could it be?

I got the answer to that question right quick. Very hard. Very, very hard, actually. Mr. Torkelson knew, and he had set up a special practice area using a couple of old, junky oil pans from scrapped tractors and several patches of steel similar to what I had made. His were round instead of square. *Whatever.*

Mr. Torkelson looked at me. "The first thing to do from here is make sure the metal surfaces are prepared for welding," he said. According to his instructions, I cleaned off all the oil and dirt. Then, using a grinder, some sandpaper, and my old friend the steel brush, I got everything as shiny as a newly minted dime. It took me an hour.

"I'm ready," I said.

"The parts need to be clamped together before welding," said Mr. Torkelson. He showed me what to do and I did it. That took another ten minutes.

"Ready," I said again.

He walked over and looked at me in my thin short sleeve shirt and ratty pants. "You'll need to wear some leather sleeves, gloves, and a leather apron," he said. He handed me the stuff and I put it on.

"It weighs a ton," I said.

"Beats learning the hard way," he answered.

At last it was time for Mr. Torkelson's demonstration on two pieces of steel lapped and clamped together.

"Cover," he said, and we both dropped our masks over our faces.

As he touched the welding rod to the steel, the black world behind the mask exploded with light. The steel edge of the sample patch melted at the same time that the welding rod applied a ribbon of new steel in a perfect line—a three-thousand-degree version of Elmer's Glue. He kept going halfway around the edge, then lifted the electrode, and we flipped up our masks. The result was a beautifully rippled, perfect weld.

"Damn!" I said.

"Now you try."

It took three hours, but I managed to screw up every practice piece that Mr. Torkelson had prepared. *Heck.* I could turn a wrench left-handed, upside down, and blindfolded—no problem. But this welding stuff? It was like art class or something.

It took a dozen tries but I finally did it. A good clean weld on my own square patch on the Minneapolis-Moline oil pan. It was fixed.

"I guess you're one of them now," said Mr. Torkelson.

"One of what?"

"Welders."

~

I could hardly wait to get to my job at Gustafson Tractor and Implement on Friday morning. The Minneapolis-Moline repairs were completed and I was proud of how they all turned out. After stashing my bike outside the shop, I walked straight to Mr. Gustafson's office.

He smiled when he saw me. "I hear that you did a bang-up job on the tractor."

"Thanks. I think it turned out swell."

"Mr. Torkelson says you're a pretty decent welder now."

"Yes, sir." I was oozing with pride.

Mr. Gustafson tapped his finger on a pad of paper and removed his green visor. "With you working so efficiently, the repairs cost less than my estimate. Looks like your obligation will be fulfilled by the end of this month. I hope you'll stay on through the summer. You've got a knack for this sort of work, and Mr. Torkelson has plenty to give you."

"Yes, sir. I would like that," I said.

"Outstanding!" Mr. Gustafson stood and reached out to shake my hand. "Go on now. Mr. Torkelson has an Allis Chalmers cracked open and I know he's looking for your assistance."

"Sure."

Mr. Gustafson kept smiling at me as I continued to stand there, shuffling my feet and wringing my hands.

"Is there something else, Milo?"

"Yes, sir."

"Sit down. What is it?"

I sat in the same wooden chair where I had my ass chewed off just three weeks prior. "Mr. Gustafson, I have a big favor to ask."

He leaned in.

"Could I borrow the Minneapolis-Moline and the corn planter?"

Mr. Gustafson rocked in his chair. "I assume that this has something to do with the question you asked me earlier about whether or not it was too late to plant corn."

"Yes."

"Are we talking about Ham's back eighty?"

"Yes."

"Is he in a bind with the bank?"

"Yes."

"When do you need them?"

"Tomorrow."

Luckily Mr. Gustafson was sitting down because his eyebrows might have busted the light fixture.

"Does Ham know that you're arranging all of this?"

"No."

"And you've got the seed corn?"

"Yes, sir."

Mr. Gustafson sat and stared at me for a long time, drumming his fingers. I studied his face, from the frown to the nose hairs to the wart underneath his left eye. He picked up a pencil and tapped it against an empty coffee cup.

"Can you help me, Mr. Gustafson?"

For another whole minute there was no response. He shut his eyes hard and opened them again. He ditched the pencil tapping and went back to drumming his fingers. At last he relaxed and looked at me again.

"Well, what do you say, Mr. Gustafson?"

"All hands on deck, lad. That's what I say. All hands on deck."

# Chapter 19

As Deputy to the Chief Observer for the Milltown Observation Post, I was up until past midnight before the big day. It was just like the week before. A card game on Bank Street, the scarecrow walking home from Lindoo Drug smoking a cigarette, and Melonhead at the Co-op station pretending to be tough and stealing candy from under the counter. I spied pretty Rosalyn again too, hand in hand with her boyfriend walking to his car. After that, they didn't waste any time. He drove her straight away to that dark place under the maple tree behind the football field. There wasn't any mystery about what they were up to either, because there was a little green glow coming off the radio dial. Rosalyn must have had an eleven o'clock curfew, because they buzzed out of there at ten minutes before the hour.

By the light of the battery-powered electric torch, I made my second entry in the logbook. Except for the date, it was the same as the first.

| Name | Date | Hours | Observations |
|------|------|-------|--------------|
| Milo Egerson | June 22, 1945 | 7 p.m.–Midnight | None |

∼

Not even that short night's sleep could have kept me from getting out of bed before five o'clock on Saturday morning. All the way through chores, I was keyed up and restless because I knew what was coming and Ham didn't. It probably sounds weird that I didn't tell him, but I was worried that a guy like Hjalmar Rehnquist might be too proud to take a helping hand. In the meanwhile, I could only wait. I was as nervous as a chicken in a fox den.

We were sitting at the kitchen table when I heard the sound of a large engine rumbling up the wheel ruts.

"Who could that be?" asked Ham.

"Mr. Gustafson, I reckon."

Ham looked out the window, then back at me. "Well, I'll be damned."

We both scrambled outside through the busted screen door, each one of us trying to be first through. When I prevailed, I found Mr. Gustafson driving the Minneapolis-Moline and pulling the freshly painted green corn planter, just as I had hoped. But that wasn't all, because right behind the MM there were two other tractors lined up, each pulling farm implements of their own.

"Mr. Gustafson, you came!" I yelled across the engine noise.

"Of course! I recruited Mr. Torkelson to bring another tractor and a plow. Then word got out and Mr. Hanson decided to chip in with his Farmall and a harrow."

I recognized Mr. Hanson from my seed-begging circuit. He shot me a wink and a nod.

All this while Ham was standing next to me saying nothing. His eyes darted from person to person, from machine to machine. Finally he turned and faced me with a quizzical look in his eyes.

"How are you fixing to plant corn when we ain't got no seed?"

"I made the rounds on Saturday," I answered. "Seed corn is in the shed."

I watched the old man for a clue, and it came in the form of pink cheeks and damp eyes. Ham gave me a solid whack in the shoulder. "You son of a gun. And I thought I was going to the Poor Farm."

"Not this year," I said.

Ham's eyes locked onto something at the end of the drive. "Who's that young feller at the end of the line with the Belgians?"

I spun around. "What?"

I hadn't noticed until that exact moment, but while Ham and I were yakking, a skinny kid had come up the wheel ruts on a contraption of unknown purpose pulled by the largest pair of horses I had ever seen.

"It's Gilbert Zilstrom," I whispered. Then I yelled. "Hey, Gilbert!"

Ham looked up to the sky. "God help us."

I ran down to him, offered my hand, and he shook it this time. "Thanks for coming!" I said.

Gilbert seemed half happy and half scared. He offered a little nod, then quickly looked back over his shoulder as if danger lurked in his tracks. While his head was turned, I got a good look at his purple right ear and the scar in the back of his head. At that moment it occurred to me that, maybe, Gilbert Zilstrom needed even more help than Ham Rehnquist.

"Does your father know you're here?" I asked.

"Not yet."

I didn't know how to respond to that, so I decided to change the subject. "What kind of machine is this?"

"S-s-sickle mower," he said. "You've got a hay f-f-field that needs cutting."

"We do?"

Gilbert nodded in the direction of Ham's southwest forty acres.

"Let's do it then," I said. "Come and meet the others."

We were a circle of six now—Mr. Gustafson, Mr. Torkelson, Mr. Hanson, Gilbert Zilstrom, me, and Ham. Seven, including Black Cat. The crow bobbed nervously on the old man's shoulder. She let out a single *Caw!* Then she flew to the top of the silo to keep watch.

With Ham's permission, Mr. Gustafson got everybody lined up with assigned tasks. As far as corn planting was concerned, it would be done in assembly line fashion. Mr. Torkelson would take the lead, pulling the two-bottom plow. Next, Mr. Hanson would come with his Farmall and that spiky thing called a harrow. Behind both of these contraptions, Mr. Gustafson would follow on the Minneapolis-Moline with the corn planter.

Mr. Gustafson looked at Gilbert. "You fixing to cut hay?"

Gilbert nodded.

Mr. Gustafson then looked at my great-uncle. "You okay with that, Ham?"

"So long as the lad don't get in trouble with his father."

Gustafson looked at Gilbert again. "You sure you want to do this, son? I reckon it wasn't your father's idea."

"Yes, I want to do this." Gilbert's jaw was set.

Gustafson squinted his eyes and nodded. "Okay, son. Have at it. If you're cutting, who's going to rake up the windrows?"

"I'll take that job," said Ham. "The hay rake is one piece of equipment that still works around here. Besides, it'll be good for Bullet and Smoke to get into their harnesses again."

It was all coming together like a football play. Now it was time to break huddle and step up to the line. Only one problem. I was still on the sidelines.

Just then we heard the deep-throated rumble of a large truck and the crunch of rubber tires on gravel. Black Cat made a ruckus from the top of the silo as the truck hissed to a stop. Mr. Gustafson, Mr. Torkelson, Mr. Hanson, Ham, and Gilbert all gawked, unable to grasp why a big green truck with a white star on the door was parked at the foot of the wheel ruts.

I walked down to the gravel road where Sergeant Harrison stepped out of the truck and waited in his uniform of tan pants, tri-striped shirt sleeves, shiny black shoes, and a cap shaped like a tent. We shook hands.

"Is your uncle okay with all this?" he asked me.

"I think so."

"What do you mean, you think so?"

"He's just finding out now."

Sergeant Harrison blasted me with a scowl. "Do you think that *now* might be a good time to tell him?"

"Yes, sir." I said. "Now would be a fine time."

Sergeant Harrison opened the back flap on the covered cargo bed of the army truck and four German prisoners jumped down. Out of the group, only one was smiling, and it was DiMaggio from the soccer game. He nodded at me and I nodded back. The other three stood around exchanging glances between Sergeant Harrison and my scarred face.

"Let's have a talk with your uncle," said the sergeant.

He signaled for the Germans to follow. I led the way.

"What's this all about?" asked Ham.

"My mom gave me some money when I left Minneapolis," I said. "I thought this would be a good way to use it."

"The work assignments are made already," said Ham.

"I thought that the prisoners could put in a garden," I said. "We're running out of canned vegetables in the cellar. Besides, I bought all the seeds."

Ham thought it over for a few seconds, then nodded sharply. "You're right, Milo. We do need a garden. You're in charge."

Mr. Gustafson, Mr. Torkelson, and Mr. Hanson marched off toward their respective tractors. Ham and Gilbert, likewise, walked away to get the horses lined up. Sergeant Harrison was halfway back to the truck when I shouted to him.

"Are you getting your rifle?!"

He turned to face me. "No, I'm going to check on the work assignments for some of the other prisoners."

"But who's going to guard these four?" I asked.

Sergeant Harrison looked me square in the eyes. "You're the boss, son. That makes you the guard, too." He got in the truck and drove off.

# Chapter 20

I was as good as dead and nobody cared.

Mr. Torkelson and Mr. Hanson were already up the lane and halfway to the eighty. Mr. Gustafson had pulled up alongside the shed and was filling up with seed corn. I looked for Gilbert and found him closing the gate behind his horse-drawn hay-cutting contraption.

"Shovels and spades are in the shed," Ham yelled to me while walking at a fast shuffle to the tack room in the barn.

Everybody was running on high octane. Everybody had a swell job. Everybody, that was, except me. I was the turtle on a fence post. I was the newborn calf in a pack of wolves. I was the unsuspecting patsy in a Boris Karloff movie.

"Jesus—Mary—Joseph," I said right out loud. At last, I found a molecule of courage and swallowed it down. Then I walked right toward the four prisoners.

I got it in my mind that those men might be from General Rommel's Panzers—a mean and ruthless bunch, according to the newsreels at the Boulevard Theater. I was sure they were a hard-boiled lot with three-fourths of them brainwashed to hate Americans and every one of them a bloodthirsty killer. They probably had special training too, and even with a rusty nail or a piece of wire, each one knew a dozen different ways for putting me in the grave. My left hand pressed against my thigh and felt the two-blade Remington jackknife in my pocket—like that was going to do me any good.

Left . . . right . . . left . . . right . . . left . . . right. I marched on to my own doom.

At about ten feet away from the Germans, I stopped. My knees shook. Heck with that. All of me was shaking. One of the Germans smiled and nodded, and that helped a little.

I motioned with my hand for them to follow me to the shed. As we walked up the wheel ruts, I heard them talking in German and my imagination had them plotting about where to dump my dead corpse.

I addressed the small group. "Anybody speak English?"

Three out of the four turned in the direction of DiMaggio and he made a "not me" face and put his hands in his pockets. I walked up to him anyway.

"You speak English?"

"A little," he said.

"We are going to make a vegetable garden below the barn," I said.

My words didn't register at all. Four blank stares gazed back at me.

I looked into DiMaggio's eyes and tried again. "Garden?"

"*Garten?*" he asked back.

"Yes, a big one."

I went into the shed and pulled out the packs of seed that I'd picked up at Twetten Hardware. All four of the men leaned in and studied the pictures of squash, beans, carrots, green peppers, sweet corn, and beets printed on the paper.

"*Ein garten!*" declared the blond-haired Kraut who couldn't have been much older than eighteen. Heads nodded all around. "*Ya! Wir werden einen Garten pflanzen!*"

Next came the part that I feared most. Handing out deadly weapons. I started with shovels placed in the hands of DiMaggio and Blondie, the least dangerous-looking of the bunch. They accepted the tools without comment. What I had left was another shovel, a hoe, and a garden spade that looked like a four-pronged bayonet. I handed the shovel to a man whose face smacked of a young Spencer Tracy, and the hoe went to the guy who reminded me of Son of Dracula. For obvious reasons, I kept the four-pronged bayonet for myself.

"Follow me," I said with a hand signal, and together we walked through the thick weeds, between the rusting skeletons of dead machinery. We kicked up some chickens along the way, and I noted a few hidden eggs. By the time we reached the former garden plot between the barn and the gravel road, all four Germans had identified the enemy. Thistles, quack grass, goldenrod, and burdock. The entire area was a weedy mess.

According to Ham, it had been two years since he had even attempted any sort of garden. Nonetheless, I could still make out the approximate shape of the huge rectangular plot and walked the perimeter for the prisoners.

"We pull out these weeds and turn over the soil," I said.

Blank stares met me once again. I grabbed a large clump of goldenrod by the base and yanked it right out of the ground. I then did the same with another and another. Once I'd cleared off a few square feet, I positioned the spade and drove it into the earth with the heels of my boots. As I pushed back on the handle, the brown, sandy soil popped loose and flipped over.

DiMaggio jumped right on it, giving out orders to the other three with finger-pointing, hand-waving, and more *achs*, *unds*, and *echs* than I'd heard in my whole life. In no time at all, they had figured out a plan for working in a line from the south edge of the garden plot to the north. With the sun pounding down and the temperature rising, the sweat poured off our chins and noses.

~

It was midmorning when DiMaggio approached me.

"Do you have water?" he asked.

"Yes, of course," I said. I trotted to the house and filled a metal pail at the kitchen pump. Lugging it back through the falling-apart screen door, I was relieved to see that the prisoners were still working hard and hadn't run off. I plunked the bucket on the ground and handed the tin cup to Spencer Tracy. Three times the cup made the circuit of five thirsty drinkers. The pail was empty in two minutes.

Black Cat started screaming from the top of the silo, and I turned to see another vehicle rolling up Ham's driveway.

*What the heck?*

Both doors opened on the rickety black pickup, and three people popped out. I swallowed hard. Ladies. Pretty ones.

All five of us watched, hawk-like, as the women moved toward the house. The Nazis chattered in German, their words full of excitement and punctuated with smiles, winks, and popping eyebrows.

"Keep working," I said. "I'll check things out."

As I stomped through the weeds toward the house, I no longer had any worries about escaping prisoners. All three ladies looked at me brightly as I stepped into the kitchen. They were pretty, all right. Especially the youngest one, a girl no older than me. I couldn't unhitch my eyes from her face. She had milky skin, strawberry lips, and golden hair that hung to her shoulders. Her eyes were bluer than blue and locked on mine.

"Hello," she said.

"Hi, my name is Milo."

The young one glanced at the other two women before facing me again. "I'm Betty. This is my mother, Mrs. Hanson, and over there is Mrs. Torkelson. We're the kitchen crew."

"Oh . . . I hadn't thought about dinner," I said, and it was true.

"How are the Germans working out?" asked Mrs. Torkelson.

I considered her for the first time. Maybe thirtysomething with blue eyes, an egg-shaped face, a pretty smile, and skin turned pink by wind and sun.

"Oh . . . They're fine, ma'am. Thank you for asking."

Next to speak up was Mrs. Hanson, a tall, thin woman with blond hair a little bit lighter than her daughter's and the same crystalline blue eyes. "You must be the boy from Minneapolis," she said. She held her head at a slight tilt and her lips made a flat line. Her arms were folded at her chest.

"Yes, ma'am."

She studied my face like a teacher might look at a suspected vandal. "I heard that you got into some trouble your first day in Milltown."

"Yes, ma'am. But I'm working it off."

"You had a little problem in Luck too, I heard."

"I paid my debt for that one too."

Mrs. Hanson produced a fake smile. "My husband likes you for some reason."

"I'm glad to hear that, ma'am."

"He thinks you showed initiative and a good heart trying to help out Ham Rehnquist like this. Ham's your uncle, is that right?"

I nodded and swallowed. "Yes, ma'am. My great-uncle."

"I like Ham," she said. "He's a good man, even though his farm is a bit of a jumble."

"I like him too, ma'am."

I glanced around the kitchen. The young movie star named Betty had been listening and watching me wide-eyed while Mrs. Hanson raked me unevenly through the mud. It didn't seem to bother her. Maybe she was okay with my having done some things. Maybe she was interested in a guy who'd been pulled through the wringer already and even carried some scars to show for it. Her pretty smile vanished when her mom plunked a ten-pound sack of potatoes onto the table in front of her. The clatter that followed was a paring knife tossed from the drawer.

Before heading back down to the garden plot, I took a few minutes to climb all the way up to the highest rungs of the silo for a look over the tops of the fields. When I got there, Black Cat sailed over from the maple tree and took her post next to me. The rolling waves of land practically glowed under a cloudless sky with two hawks circling overhead.

*God, no wonder Ham loves the land so much.*

My eyes zoomed in on the corn-planting crew, and it warmed my insides to see those three tractor rigs worked one behind the next, each machine clattering and occasionally belching black smoke as they crawled over the rise. The field of weeds was being converted just like a slow change of tablecloths. With the passing of the first tractor, two perfect furrows appeared. With the passing of the second tractor and the harrow, those furrowed clumps became smooth ground. Then, with the passing of that yellow Minneapolis-Moline, the shiny green planter dropped the kernels in rows exactly forty-eight inches apart, and the cover wheels put them to bed at the proper depth.

Out in the hayfield, another team was at work. Gilbert sat, straight-backed with his hands on two sets of reigns and his skinny butt bouncing in the cast iron seat with the sickle bar angled off to his right side. In front of him, the pair of reddish-brown Belgians walked in harness, each shouldering a black padded collar, straining at the chains that pulled the carriage and mower like they were giving a haircut to planet Earth. Behind Gilbert, and a couple of rows over, I could see Ham in his baggy coveralls and straw hat pulling the spinning tines of a hay rake behind his own pair of Belgians, Bullet and Smoke. The whole scene was one of productivity, teamwork, and beauty.

By the time I got back to my crew of German prisoners, I was as fearless as Ulysses. No more worries about a shovel and hoe revolt. No more keeping them separated from the four-prong garden spade. They had the garden tilled already.

We kept at it for another solid hour. Then a bell started clanging from the cupola on top of Uncle Ham's roof.

"Dinner," I shouted.

The Germans needed no translation.

~

Ham's old house wasn't set up for a crowd, but that's exactly what we had. When Mrs. Torkelson saw me and the prisoners loitering outside the screen door, she poked her head through and asked us to rig up some makeshift tables outside. Well, I puzzled over that one for a whole two seconds before the idea hit me. I signaled my gang of four Krauts, and we hustled single file through the weeds to the shed.

It took a few trips in and out of the shed, but in ten minutes' time the German prisoners and I had two old door panels laying end to end on sawhorses in the area between the wheel ruts. We then assembled benches from some old wooden planks that we positioned on inverted milk pails and stacks of brick.

The three men from the cornfield came walking down the lane at the same time Ham and Gilbert were rounding the corner of the barn. Everybody stood around with dirt and dust stuck to their pants, shirts, and faces. The Germans hung together in their own group.

As eyes darted and men shifted on stiff legs, it was like everybody was waiting for the same signal. It finally came with Mrs. Hanson stepping through the screen door to take charge.

"Find a place and sit down, everyone."

Mr. Gustafson, Mr. Hanson, and Mr. Torkelson all took off their hats and found places around the same door-sized table. With a nod from Ham, Gilbert joined him at the corn-planting table too. That left me and the Krauts staring at each other. I found DiMaggio's eyes.

"Please sit," I said, gesturing to the second door on sawhorses.

DiMaggio and Spencer Tracy took one side, leaving Dracula and Blondie on the other. I sat down next to DiMaggio in hopes of English-language conversation.

Mrs. Hanson started back inside but found herself wrestling with the busted screen door. She made it through and came back with a broom to prop it open. Then she turned her scowl on me.

"I'm counting on you to fix this door, young man."

"Yes, ma'am," I answered. "First chance I get."

The kitchen crew parade followed. First it was Mrs. Torkelson with a stack of white ceramic plates. Then came Mrs. Hanson with a tray full of water glasses. I watched the Germans as their eyes followed the women. Betty stepped out the door carrying one glass pitcher of water and another of milk. To say that the Germans liked Betty Hanson was to say that ants appreciated grape jelly. Each man grew an inch taller and I noticed Spencer Tracy even smoothing down his hair and trying to straighten his shirt.

The food came next. Fried chicken, mashed potatoes, gravy, peas and carrots mixed, two loaves of homemade bread, coleslaw, a block of butter, and an open jar of sliced pickles.

*What a feast!*

Mrs. Hanson cleared her throat and forced the corn-planting crew to quit their yakking. Suddenly, all was quiet. Folded hands fell into laps as steam rolled off the serving dishes. Mrs. Hanson turned next in Ham's direction, tipping her head slightly and lifting her eyebrows skyward.

The old man met her gaze and flinched. Then, realizing her expectation, he ran his claw through his white beard and made a mumbling sound before rising to his feet. His eyes moved from person to person, pausing briefly at each one, including the Nazis. He coughed once and began to speak.

"I want to thank you all for your work here today. It's no secret that I've been struggling to keep up on things recently. To be honest, I thought this might be my last year farming. Today, thanks to my grand-nephew Milo and all of you folks, it looks like we might be able to feed the cows and ourselves for at least another year. From what I can see, the corn team has got almost ten acres planted already. Milo and the men from Camp Milltown are close to having the garden put in, too. I want to thank Mabel Torkelson, Ruth Hanson, and her daughter Betty for taking care of us with this fine meal."

Ham turned to Gilbert next and gazed at him while the kid with the purple ear looked at his hands. "Gilbert Zilstrom here, I believe, deserves the biggest thanks of all. He came of his own free volition with those two fine Belgians. And he came knowing full well what his father might think of it."

Everybody except the prisoners squirmed a little when Ham came right out and put it that way. Folks understood what Gilbert was up against. Folks rooted for him on their insides but couldn't do much else. He was the boy who lived with the Bear, and everybody knew that it took a special kind of courage for him to wake up every morning and survive until sundown. And now he had volunteered for this.

Ham clapped his hands once and smiled through his whiskers. "Well, folks, that's about enough of my fancy words. Milo will now lead us in a prayer."

My stomach took a hard left turn. I went from being the hawk on a fence pole to the rabbit in the grass.

DiMaggio nodded and folded his hands, with the other Germans following suit. I looked at Mrs. Hanson. Her head was bowed too with her eyes closed. The only one looking at me now was Betty, eyes wide and mouth open. Maybe she knew that I would mess it up and just wanted to watch the train wreck. I took a breath and just went with whatever spilled into my head.

"God . . . Thank you for this meal that we are fixing to eat shortly. And thanks for the good weather so we can get the crops and garden planted before it's too late. We surely do appreciate all of these men and women helping us today. I reckon it's worked out better than any of us thought. Please keep Mom safe and bring Tom back home soon. Amen."

I glanced around the table and, like before, most of the Germans returned blank stares. DiMaggio responded with a nod. Mrs. Hanson smiled and Betty stared at me like I'd just conjured a genie out of a lamp.

"Eat it while it's hot, boys," said Mrs. Torkelson, and everybody did. The platter of chicken and steaming bowls of vegetables made the slow-motion race around the tables, followed by coleslaw, bread, pickles, and butter. Spoons, forks, and knives flashed in the bright sunshine. Betty Hanson refilled cups and glasses with coffee, milk, and water.

When everybody thought they were done, two pies showed up from the kitchen—one rhubarb and one apple—and they disappeared in a snap.

~

Before heading back down to the big garden, the German prisoners all lined up to thank the kitchen crew. DiMaggio did it in English. The others spoke their words of appreciation in German, but the message was just as clear.

The ladies stayed around through the afternoon, cleaning up all the dishes and even scrubbing the insides of the cabinets, the hutch, and the kitchen floor. At three o'clock in the afternoon, Mrs. Torkelson brought coffee and ginger cookies to me and the prisoners in the garden, and I watched as Betty Hanson and her mother headed out with another large coffee pot and a basket toward the fields. When Betty glanced my way, I waved to her and she waved back. Then her mother snapped some words at her, and she looked straight forward again.

The truck with the white star on the door showed up again right at five o'clock. The brakes squeaked and hissed as it stopped at the foot of the wheel ruts. When Sergeant Harrison saw us finishing up in the garden, he walked over.

"Looks like you survived!" he said.

"Yes, sir!" I answered, and both of us smiled.

The prisoners didn't need me to tell them that it was quitting time. They helped me return the tools to the shed, where I stacked them all into one corner. Back outside, in the sunlight, I found DiMaggio, Spence, Drac, and Blondie waiting for me, standing together in a tight row.

DiMaggio reached out for my hand and gripped it hard. After that I walked right down the row, exchanging handshakes and smiles with each of the men in my platoon.

"You did a fine job," I said, and indeed they had. The large, rectangular plot was, in fact, beautiful. A rich, brown blanket sectioned off in various regions with white string that were marked with empty seed packets on wooden sticks. It all looked very German.

# Chapter 21

We worked on Sunday too (all of us except for the prisoners and Gilbert). Mr. Hanson, Mr. Torkelson, and Mr. Gustafson were determined to finish tilling and planting the cornfield. After a trip to the creamery, Ham and I rolled up our sleeves and started moving stacks of hay into the barn using wagons, ropes, pulleys, hooks, and a couple of powerful engines named Bullet and Smoke. It was flat-out work. Five times harder than milking cows, three times harder than shoveling shit, and even tougher than pulling out a stuck calf in the middle of a moonlit briar patch.

At a little past noon, the ladies came back and set up shop in the kitchen again. It wasn't the same spread like we'd enjoyed on Saturday, but they served up chicken sandwiches, potato salad, and green beans. On top of that, they brought enough salt and ice to make vanilla ice cream for the whole crew.

Ham, Bullet, Smoke, and I had just finished putting all that hay into the loft when Mr. Hanson and Mr. Torkelson came in from the eighty.

"It's all tilled up," Mr. Hanson said. "Nils is about twenty minutes behind with the planting."

"I can't thank you enough," said Ham, now holding his straw hat in both hands.

"It's nothing at all," said Mr. Hanson.

"Our pleasure to help out," said Mr. Torkelson. "Besides, it was Milo here who brung us all together in the first place. Thank him."

Ham lifted his eyes to me. "I appreciate what you done here, Milo."

I gave a little nod.

Mr. Gustafson eventually made his way down the lane too, all sunburned on his arms and neck. We all sat for a few minutes sipping egg coffee in the kitchen. There wasn't much talking because folks were so tuckered—just the slurping of hot coffee and some discussion about the weather. With the seeds in the ground and the hay in the barn, it was time to wish for rain.

They left at right around five o'clock.

"Come boss! Come boss! Come boss!"

The cows walked slowly toward the barn and so did I. Uncle Ham followed—even slower.

～

Almost all night long, the rain fell. Nothing heavy. Just a soaking, steady rain. And over the course of the next two weeks, more rain fell, and the sun shone brightly between the showers. I watched with pride as everything came alive in slow motion—as those eighty acres changed from brown linoleum to a carpet with stripes of green. The garden popped, too, with rows coming up out of the ground about as straight as the steering shaft on a Minneapolis-Moline.

As a city kid, it had always been easy to ignore the work of people who tended animals and turned the soil. We looked down our noses at country folks—even using the word *farmer* as an insult. I hadn't shaken off those notions entirely but was beginning to think differently.

You know what else had turned the corner besides my attitude and Ham's prospects? My stature in the communities of Milltown and Luck. I didn't know it at the time, but my door-to-door pilgrimage through Polk County had yielded more than partial sacks of seed. It also made me friends.

Turns out, your average resident of the region had a predisposition toward kindness. So, when folks found out that I was hell-bent on rescuing Ham and keeping him out of the Polk County Poor Farm, it not only reminded them how much they liked Ham—it caused them to like me at the same time. My reputation as a lying, stealing hoodlum embarked on a bend that damn-near reached 135 degrees. Not a full U-turn but close enough.

Folks were even heard talking about me with chatter that included words like "responsible," "hardworking," and "able-to-turn-a-wrench." I was a reformation project in progress and people were actually rooting for me.

There were exceptions to my upgrade, of course. The Bear still hated me. And I could tell that Mr. Krankel still wished for another chance to shove my nose inside a toilet. The one that surprised me most, though, was that melon-headed kid at the Co-op station. While I was willing to forgive him for that sucker punch to the gut, he wasn't interested in any peace treaty.

~

We were into the second week of July when I found out for sure. I had pulled into the Co-op station on my way to Gustafson Tractor and Implement one morning just to top off the air pressure on my bicycle's rear tire. I hadn't even dinged the bell cord or nothing—just went straight to the air hose—that was all.

"You here looking for more trouble?" asked Melonhead, strutting out of the office with both thumbs locked into belt loops.

"No." I unscrewed the valve stem cap.

"Reckon you think you're hot shit, now—don't you?"

"No." I applied the brass fitting and gave it a two-second spurt of compressed air.

"What are you, scared of me or something?"

"No." I screwed the valve stem cover back in place.

"Yes, you are. You're scared that I'll whip your ass just like the last time."

"Anybody can throw a sucker punch," I said. "If we were in my back alley on Thirty-Seventh Street in Minneapolis, I'd drop you like a fifty-pound sack of shit." (Talk about your stupid things to say at quarter to seven on a Monday morning.)

"I got a back alley," said Melonhead.

Behind the Co-op Station, between stacks of worn-out tires and a rusted-out Model T, I got my first look at the slab of weed-laced asphalt that my rival called a back alley. I pocketed my Hamilton wristwatch for safekeeping. Standing three paces apart, we put up our dukes.

Melonhead stood flat-footed and waited for me to make the first move. I faked with my left and charged forward with a right hook. *Blam!* Just like that, the guy nailed me in the mouth. I stumbled backward.

Like an idiot, I opened my quickly swelling yap. "Lucky punch."

My pink-faced adversary didn't say a word; he just took up his stance with one leg slightly in front of the other and both fists positioned on either side of that fat little chin. Just like that, he waited for me.

What came next was something that I believe is referred to in boxing as a combination. I didn't see any of it, but it started with something like a wrecking ball to the center of my face. This was immediately followed by a cinderblock sensation to my jaw and an atom bomb to my left eye.

Did I fall down? You better believe I fell down. Like a fifty-pound sack of shit.

Melonhead gave me a kick to the ribs on his way back around the building to his post at the Co-op Station front desk. From my reclining position on the asphalt, I gently touched my hands to various parts of what was left of my face. I sat up and noticed a steady *drip—drip—drip* from my left nostril.

"That wasn't very smart." The female voice came from my left. I turned and dialed my eyes back into focus.

*Dammit-all! That Indian girl again.*

"What do you care?" I said, still wincing.

She said nothing.

"And what are you doing here?"

"Riding my bicycle."

The Indian girl's black bicycle looked like a forest on two wheels. The wooden saddle baskets were full of sapling trees sticking up in the air with the leaves all clumped together.

"Aren't you supposed to be catching rabbits?"

She shrugged. "That's my winter job."

"Of course. And what's your summer job? Planting trees?"

"That's one of them."

Neither one of us spoke as I maneuvered from a sitting position—to kneeling—to standing. As you can imagine, it took me a while.

"You need to fight better," the Indian girl said.

"Now, *there's* a brilliant observation." I spat blood at the nearest stack of worn-out tires.

"Most white boys from around here are on their high school boxing teams. It's a big sport in Polk County. They all know what they're doing. You, on the other hand, don't know what you are doing."

"Thanks for the pep talk."

She said nothing.

"So, they really teach boxing in Milltown High School?" I asked.

"Milltown, Luck, Frederic, Amery. They all have boxing teams. If you're going to fight them, try something else."

"Yeah—sure—and who's going to teach me? You? Your grandfather?"

"Lots of people fight better than you do. My cousin could show you a few things."

"Huh?"

"My cousin, Len. He knows how to fight the white boys. Better than you, anyhow." She straddled her bicycle and pushed off with one foot, disappearing behind the piles of tires.

Retrieving my watch, I checked the time. I was ten minutes late to work. With a shake of the head to clear the leftover cobwebs, I retrieved the bicycle and slowly walked it to the front of the Co-op station. The bell cord was laying right there, so I stood on the pedals and rode right over it. *Ding! Ding!*

I cranked hard on the pedals at the sound of Melonhead's feet slapping the pavement. He wasn't fast enough to catch me as I escaped to Gustafson Tractor and Implement.

# Chapter 22

For the rest of that morning and into the afternoon, my face got even more attention than usual. "What happened to you?" That was the most popular question asked in Milltown, Wisconsin, on July 16, 1945. I got it from Mr. Torkelson. I got it from Mr. Gustafson, and I got it from his secretary. Even the scarecrow at Lindoo Drug couldn't resist when I stopped in for a milkshake.

"What happened to you?" he asked flat out.

"I got in a minor scuffle with a very well-trained opponent thirty pounds heavier than me. That's what."

"Did you ding the bell cord at the Co-op station again?"

"Yep."

"Buck doesn't like that, you know."

"That's the whole point."

The scarecrow smiled.

"Hey," I said. "What's your name?"

"Herman Schrapp."

"That doesn't sound Swedish or Danish."

He laughed. "It's German."

I almost thought, *another damned Kraut*. I didn't though, because I wasn't prejudiced, like some people.

"My name's Milo Egerson," I said. I shook a couple cigarettes out of a pack of Luckies and placed them on the countertop. "That's for when you get off work."

Herman's eyes got big and he looked to his left and right. "What makes you think I smoke?" he asked.

"I'm a trained observer."

He looked at me with a sort of confused half smile and scooped up the cigarettes. Then he wandered down to the other end of the ice cream counter to take care of a lady who had just arrived with three little kids.

I put the pack of Lucky Strikes back in my pocket and looked around the room. Two old women nosed around the main part of the store. The druggist, in his white shirt and owl glasses, held up a brown bottle for a bald-headed man who appeared to be skeptical as to its contents. I turned and looked in another direction, and there, in a booth, was that pretty girl, Rosalyn, sitting with her super-duper boyfriend, Mr. Fancyhair Wingtip. A few weeks ago I would have wanted that pretty girl to notice me for any reason at all, including my bashed-in face. Isn't it weird how quick a guy can change his mind on things like that?

My thoughts were on a different girl lately, and I think you already know which one. Betty Hanson. I already told you about how pretty she was and about her smile and the sparkle in her eyes. On top of all that (and I know this is going to sound like a stretcher coming from a dolt like me), I think she liked me back.

I had one rather large problem with the whole idea of getting out of the starting blocks with Betty Hanson. Her mother—her hands-on-hips, eyeball-glaring, hater-of-my-guts mother.

As I headed for the exit, two little boys stood gazing at the colorful contents of the gumball machine by the door. I slapped two pennies on top of the glass bubble and kept on walking.

~

I got back to the farm at around half-past noon and strutted into the kitchen through the perfectly operating screen door. Yes, I had fixed the rickety thing, and I think you know why. (I had fixed it because Mrs. Hanson told me to fix it and because she's Betty Hanson's mom.) I slapped some butter between two pieces of bread and wandered back outside to see what Ham was up to as well as to admire those wonderful, straight rows of corn plants standing about ten inches tall.

Ham was nowhere in sight, but I heard a familiar sound. *Caw! Caw!* It was coming from the garden, so I wandered down there. Sure enough, there was Ham bent over a hoe, scraping weeds between rows of vegetables. His mouth was working too.

"What are you two jabbering about?" I asked, walking down the slope.

"Black Cat doesn't think I'm doing this right," said Ham, seriously. *Caww!*

"Do you need any help? Or will I just get in trouble too?"

Ham leaned on his hoe and looked up at me. "You know what you could do this week?"

"What?"

"You could cultivate the corn."

"Cultivate? What's cultivate?"

"It means get the weeds out between the rows."

"Oh." I looked at the hoe in the old man's hands and scratched my noggin.

"Not by hand, you numskull."

"Well . . . How then?"

"By riding the cultivator behind Bullet and Smoke."

"I don't know how to steer horses."

"I'll teach you."

"Couldn't we just borrow a tractor?"

Ham ignored me, already striding toward the tack room in the barn. Thirty minutes later I had a set of leather reins hanging over both shoulders, and my butt was in the iron seat of a contraption so rusty that I couldn't believe the wheels spun around.

"We'll do the first few rows together," said Ham.

Ham guided the horses to the edge of the field while I bounced on the metal seat. Once positioned, the horses already knew what to do, walking between the rows. The wheels of the cultivator also traveled between the corn rows so as not to crush them. With a hard push down on a rusty iron lever, the blades dipped into the soil and began slicing through the weed roots. A guy didn't have to be a genius to see that this was tricky business. A little too far to the right and those cultivator blades would be slicing corn. A little too far left—same thing. I was plenty nervous.

Ham taught me the commands and how to say them, loud but calm, to the horses. *Chee-yup* was the command to get them to go. *Gee* and *Haw* were the words for right and left. *Whoa* of course meant stop, and *Stand* was the word to—well—to get them to stand. Ham also showed me how the reins went through loops on the padded collars and attached to the steel bit that each horse held in its mouth. The actual pulling was done through chains that went from the horse collars to the cultivator.

*Give me a tractor any day.*

All the way to the other end of the field, Ham held Bullet's and Smoke's bridles together—the horses walked nice and straight, never leaving their rows. According to Ham's instructions, I pulled up on the lever to lift the blades. Ham and I maneuvered the horses and the cultivator so they were two rows over and pointed the other way.

"You walk with the horses this time," said Ham. "They need to get used to you."

Ham took a seat on the cultivator, and I gently touched Bullet's nose. Then I held onto the bridle just like Ham had, and we walked together back to the south. At the end of the field, we got them turned around again.

"You've got it from here, kid," said Ham. "Bring them in for water in an hour or two."

Up and down the field I bounced and rolled behind the rumps of those two big Belgians. Smoke and Bullet had obviously done this before because they settled right into the routine. The blades cut, the metal seat bounced, and the sunlight flashed in and out from behind the clouds.

I kept glancing at my watch after we had traversed the field a dozen times. Then, shortly before three o'clock, I pulled the lever and brought the horses back to the water trough. I ran up the steps to my bedroom and pulled my homemade radio and the battery out from under the bed. I checked the time again. One minute until three. I crossed my fingers, clicked on the switch, and hoped for a strong enough signal.

As usual, the show started off with a commercial, and this one was for Tootsie-Roll candy. "They're slam-jammed full of energy!" said the announcer. "And still just a penny." I listened close because I knew Mom's voice would be coming next.

"Hello everyone, and welcome to another edition of *Beauty Banter*. This is Hedda Egerson, your host, and today we're going to learn about how to give your hair a permanent, and I don't mean at the beauty salon. I mean a lovely, long-lasting permanent, done all by yourself in the comfort of your own home." For fifteen minutes I listened to my mom go on and on about how ladies could give their hair a lovely curl and a new glow in three easy steps.

"Without heat or electricity," she said. "All you'll need are some scraps of cloth, rubber bands, and a bottle of waving lotion to do the trick."

Mom's energy and excitement were a match for Cedric Adams, the radio master himself. I could see her pretty blue eyes as her voice sang across the airwaves. I got my thermometer decoder card ready because, after fifteen minutes, it was almost time. My right ear was six inches from the speaker.

"Once again, thank you for listening, ladies. And remember, beauty isn't just skin deep."

As Mom's voice went away and a Vegemite commercial came on, I scanned down the card for the sentence "Beauty isn't just skin deep." There it was, right in the danger zone.

Beauty isn't just skin deep = High yellow

I read the words again. Then a corn cob stuck in my throat and an icicle shot up my ass. All along, a part of me held out hope that Borsthagen would never get out. That hope was now dashed—shot, straight to hell. The bastard was on his way back. It wasn't for absolute certain, but it was certain enough. Once outside the gate at the Stillwater State Pen, he would be trying to find me.

I went back to the fields with Bullet and Smoke and bounced along on that cultivator until it was time for evening chores. It was a good thing those two horses knew how to stay between the rows, because ever since hearing the message from Mom, my mind was exploding like a fireworks show over Lake Calhoun—in a hundred different directions all at the same time.

It took the rest of Monday evening and all of Tuesday afternoon to get the entire eighty acres of corn scraped free of weeds. Bullet and Smoke were both dogged and so was I. With their heads hanging low, those two mighty Belgians walked slowly down the lane and made a beeline for the water trough. While they drank, I unhitched the cultivator and rolled it back into the shed. Then I got all their other gear put away in the tack room, and that included hauling those humongous padded collars that each weighed about a ton. I got the horses moved back to their stalls, brushed down, and fed. I wiped the sweat off my brow with my sleeve, then lit a ciggy and took a deep draw.

When I looked in the direction of the house, all I noticed was more trouble standing right next to Ham in one of the wheel ruts.

*Cawww! . . . Cawww!*

Yep. Black Cat had seen her too. That pesky Indian girl again, with her ridiculous bicycle full of trees. Peacock was rubbing against her leg and circling it. The old man nodded his head as the girl spoke to him. I ambled over.

"What gives?" I said to the Indian chick. *What was her name again?*

As usual, she didn't answer.

Ham turned to me with a pretty serious look on his face. "We've got a problem with the corn," he said.

I glanced at the field, then at the Indian girl, then back at Ham. "What?"

"It appears we plowed under several young trees that Raina had planted out there near the high ground."

I flashed another glance at the field, then back at Ham. "The pine trees are all still standing around Isabella's grave. What's the problem?"

"Raina's trees went beyond the pines."

I felt my jaw flop open. *Am I really hearing this?*

Ham continued. "She brought out some more trees, and I reckon now is as good a time as any to replace them around the knoll. She'll go out there with you, Milo. She'll show you what she wants done."

It was the most pea-brained notion I'd ever heard. "That's ridiculous. It's your own land, Ham. And you need the corn."

The old geezer set his feet and locked down his glare. "We need trees, too."

"What?"

"Raina needs places for her trees, and the edge of that knoll is a perfect spot."

It was lunacy times two. My brain spun through the details. First and foremost, tree-planting didn't pay. Any moron already knew that.

*What about getting out of debt? What about staying out of the Polk County Poor House?*

It was senseless, ridiculous, and stupid on its face. Ignorant too. Turning over perfectly good corn-planted ground for some lame-brained, Johnny Appleseed scheme that wouldn't even produce fruit.

Guess what I did for the next hour and a half. I ripped up perfectly healthy, freshly cultivated corn plants, roots and all—right out of the ground. Right behind me in the path of destruction followed the Indian girl with her narrow spade and that basket of little trees. Birch, pine and oak saplings, one after another going into the best patch of ground on the whole danged farm. I already thought it a hundred times, and I thought it yet again as I pulled out another healthy corn plant.

*This is just plain dumb!*

I walked back down the lane with her, but only because there was no other choice.

"Thank you for helping me," she said.

"You're welcome." I kicked a rock and watched it roll into the weeds.

"Your face looks better today."

"Yeah, well I'm sure that'll change once I cross paths with Melonhead again."

"You could beat him, you know."

"Yeah—and those cows could jump over the moon."

"You want that I should introduce you to my cousin?"

I looked at the Indian girl and could tell that she was dead serious. "What was your name again?"

"Raina . . . Raina Jackson."

~

After evening chores, Ham and I polished off another vegetarian meal because the canned meat was gone, and there were only so many live chickens we could spare. Do you know what a steady diet of peas, rutabaga, and Wonder Bread had done for me? Turned me into a rake handle—that's what.

I was going to bed hungry (again) and boy oh boy was that ever getting old. Ham and I discussed the options for putting some meat on the table, and they included things like shooting blackbirds and trapping skunks. If we would have had the ammunition, I'd have signed up for the blackbird idea.

# Chapter 23

The days of the week clicked by like dew drops falling off the roof eaves. By the time Friday afternoon came along, I had received two more messages from Mom during her Wednesday and Friday radio shows and they were both the same as before.

*High yellow!*

He was getting out soon, and I had two big questions. *How soon is soon?* And *What am I going to do about it?*

~

At the kitchen table before evening chores, I decided that Ham and I needed to have a Franklin D. Roosevelt–style fireside chat about a few things that had been bugging me like pebbles in my shoe. I poured two cups of egg coffee, placed one in front of each of us, and launched into topic number one.

"Uncle Ham?"

He slowly turned his head and gazed at me. "Yah?"

"What else can we do to keep the bank from taking your land?"

Ham let his head fall back against the wall and it made a hollow-sounding *clunk*. "That ain't exactly my favorite subject, you know."

"Sorry."

"Naw, don't be sorry. You're right to bring it up. The corn crop will fill the silo, but it won't get me caught up on the mortgage. I've been kidding myself, hoping I'll find a leprechaun and his pot of gold at the end of a rainbow. Truth is, even with the corn field planted, I'm running out of hope."

"Could you sell some of the land?"

"Cut up the land? No. We can't do that."

"Sure you can," I continued my pitch. "That cattail marsh in the southwest corner is good for nothing right now. Sell it to somebody who can afford to drain it. And your woods on the north end—same thing. Somebody could clear the lumber out of there and use it to plant more corn."

"Are you smarter than God, boy?"

I put up my hands, palms out. "I'm not looking for a fight."

"Well, you got one." Ham's eyes narrowed and his nostrils flared.

"I'm sorry," I said.

We both just sat and calmed ourselves. Then Ham softened. "I know you're just trying to help."

I nodded and listened.

"What I'm worried about, Milo, is someone coming along who doesn't care about the land other than what money they can make off it. Most people these days would drain that marsh in the southwest corner because it ain't producing a crop. Hasn't anybody seen the sandhill cranes nesting in that marsh? Have you seen them, Milo?"

"No."

"Same thing with the woods. And think about the small patch that Raina is bringing back to the knoll. She's replanting that high ground to oaks, pines, and birch, and that's a noble cause. Can you understand that?"

Ham was looking at me with a mix of certainty and desperation. His eyes burned soft and blue like twin kerosene lanterns on short wicks.

"It's hard for me to understand, Uncle Ham. How can you *not* manage the land for money?"

Ham worked the muscles around his mouth, but for a long time neither of us talked. At last, he licked his lips in preparation for what he was about to say and locked down his gaze.

"According to the bank, this land is an asset—just like my truck. The truck is a made-by-man thing that lasts twenty years and then gets hauled away for scrap. The land is a made-by-God thing, meant to be preserved forever. Do you follow me?"

"I think so."

Ham leaned in closer to me from across the kitchen table. "You and I have a duty to take care of that land while we live off it. That means keeping some of the beauty and wildness intact. We aren't the only living creatures living here, you know."

"Yes, I know."

"Some things are more important than making money."

"I know."

"And that's why we ain't never gonna drain the cattail marsh nor plant corn across the top of the knoll."

Ham's eyes and mine were locked. I tried to keep my mouth shut but just couldn't. "But . . . if the bank takes it, you lose everything and the next owner gets to decide."

Ham dropped his eyes but didn't answer. He let out a heavy sigh and his head bobbed like the drunk guy I had seen at the Northern Tavern.

"Maybe there is no good answer," he finally said.

I kept my mouth shut, for once. Ham took a sip of his coffee and brushed a few crumbs off the table to the floor.

*What now?* I wondered. The old man was so dug in on his notion of taking care of the land that he refused to make the changes that would take care of himself. Even the way he said those two words. *The Land—The Land—The Land.* It was like a religion to him or something. *Jeez!* It was just property. The old guy just didn't get it. Ham was too stuck in his ways to understand something as simple as progress.

Topic one had been a swing and a miss. I tossed the old man a stick of Wrigley's, then took a swat at topic number two.

"Uncle Ham?"

"Yah?"

"You know that kid, Gilbert?"

"Yah."

"What can we do to help him?"

"I don't know. I'm pretty sure the county is already keeping an eye on him and Albin Zilstrom. I hope so, anyhow."

"I think I'm going to go talk to him," I said.

"Albin Zilstrom?"

"Gilbert."

"How you planning to do that?"

"I don't know. But somebody needs to talk to him. He needs to save himself, somehow. And somebody might need to help him figure out how."

"That boy can barely speak," said Ham. "Let alone get along by himself."

"He did pretty well with you in the hayfield the other day," I said.

"Yah, he knows how to work. Knows his way around horses."

I shrugged. "Oh, well . . . I just wanted to see if you had any ideas."

It wasn't a swing and a miss, but it wasn't a base hit either. Something like a foul ball, I figured. My third topic was a doozy so I waited for a couple minutes to click by.

"Uncle Ham?"

"Yah?"

"There's one more thing that I'd like to talk about."

"You're really putting me through the wringer today, aren't you, boy?"

"Sorry."

"Well . . . Let's hear it."

"You know that man I'm hiding from—Mr. Wayne Borsthagen?"

"Yah."

"He's my stepfather."

"Yah, I figured as much." Ham crunched up the foil gum wrapper and rolled it into the center off the table. "What about him?"

"He's getting out of prison soon."

Ham studied me and scratched his beard. "How do you know that?"

"Got a message from Mom."

"Reckon that means we need to keep you hid."

"I wish it was that easy," I said.

"What do you mean?" A deep wrinkle appeared between Ham's eyes.

"My stepfather is crazy but he's not stupid. He *will* figure out where to find me. The only question is when."

"And then what?"

"And then he'll try to finish what he started nine years ago."

"Does this have anything to do with the scar on your face?"

I nodded.

"Ain't you scared?"

"Yes."

"You don't look it."

"I've spent nine years pretending I wasn't."

The old man took a deep breath and let it out. I lit up a cigarette and offered him one, but he shook his head.

~

I arrived at Milltown Public School just before seven o'clock and went inside using my key from Mr. Stenlund. It was an odd feeling walking through those halls and climbing the wide stairs all alone. Each footstep echoed like I was in a dungeon. I could almost feel the ghosts of dead teachers and principals watching my every step. Inside the janitor's room on the second floor, I kicked aside an empty paint can and climbed up the wooden ladder. The hatch popped open and bright sunshine blasted through. *Crunch . . . crunch . . . crunch.* I walked across the flat rooftop to the bunker.

"Hello, Mrs. Quigley."

"Hello, young man."

"Anything exciting happen this afternoon?"

"Yes! I finished a pair of mittens for my granddaughter." She held up the perfect pair of red-and-white striped mittens that reminded me of candy canes.

"Those are nifty, ma'am."

She smiled and packed her knitting supplies back into her canvas bag. Together we walked to the hatch and I held her knitting bag as she took her first two steps down the ladder. Suddenly she climbed back up.

"What's wrong?" I asked.

"I found something for you."

From her knitting bag she retrieved a stone about the size of a walnut and placed it in my palm.

"What is it?"

"It's an agate," she said. "I found it in all of these stones up here on the roof."

I studied the stone's swirly pattern, like vanilla ice cream mixed in with hot caramel. I held it up and let the sunlight shine through it. Nifty as hell.

"This is swell," I said to Mrs. Quigley. "But I thought agates only came from Lake Superior."

"Folks get confused about that all the time. There's plenty to be found all around these parts, and the Milltown School roof is as good a place to look for them as any." She cackled and slapped my shoulder. "I thought of you right away, young man. An agate like this is lucky. That silly uncle of yours could probably use some of that luck about now. Maybe you could too."

"Yes, ma'am. I think we both could."

Mrs. Quigley proceeded down the ladder and I closed the hatch.

*Just how much does Mrs. Quigley know about me and Ham?*

Night fell with a pink glow blending to turquoise in the western sky as the lights of Milltown blinked on one at a time. Just like all the other nights, the Milltown Observation Post delivered no airplanes but, as usual, there were things and people to see. The card game started up on Bank Street at the usual time. Melonhead stole candy bars from under the counter again. A German scarecrow named Herman Schrapp took his stroll down Main Street and discretely lit up another cigarette. Then, along came Mr. Fancyhair Wingtip and Rosalyn in that Nash Ambassador coupe. I didn't give a rip about that dandy and his father's fancy car. I didn't give a rip about Rosalyn neither.

# Chapter 24

I rode out to the southwest corner of the Zilstrom farm and flopped my bicycle in a thicket from where I could study the place. Small, white, two-story house. Unpainted barn. Red brick silo with a wood slat roof resembling a Chinaman's hat.

I scratched my head. How was I going to talk to Gilbert without alerting the Bear? Several notions crossed my mind. I could stay in the thicket and watch for my chance. I could crawl on hands and knees, then sneak into the milk house. I could even make a dash for the silo and establish a lookout post at the top. In the end, I just did what Humphrey Bogart woulda done. I walked up the driveway and knocked on the front door.

I heard a clatter inside the house and prepared myself not to run away—legs planted shoulder-width apart, hands glued to my hips, and facing straight forward. Gilbert's eyes flashed from around the door when it swung slowly open. They were bright green but wreathed in purple and black. *Jesus God!* Suddenly I understood why he hadn't been to the creamery in over a week.

"Wh-wh-what do you want?"

I forced a smile. "I just came by to talk, Gilbert. And, thanks again for your help cutting Ham's hayfield."

He ignored my words, stepped out on the wooden planks of the front stoop, and craned his neck in the direction of the barn and silo. "M-m-my father don't like you much."

"Can I come inside for five minutes?"

His whole face was one big question mark around that collection of bruises and scars. He stared at me for a long time. Then, with one more glance at the barn, he held the door open and signaled me inside with his hand.

"Five minutes. Th-th-that's all."

"Can I sit down?"

"No."

It wasn't much of a conversation, because the talking all came from me. I started off with a load of pure bullshit about how much I admired the looks of their farm and kept it going with more fancy talk about his knowledge of agriculture and his skill with the horses. Seeing no response but occasional glances out the window, I went on with a string of stupid questions.

"Do you go to the movies much?"

No response.

"Do you like baseball?"

Nothing.

"When do you figure Polk-Burnett will get the powerlines strung up?"

Nothing again. Strike three.

Finally, I kicked my own ass and told myself—*just get to the point!*

"Gilbert," I said. "Is anybody helping you?"

That earned me a steady gaze. "Are you talking about my Pa?"

"Yes. Is anybody helping you?"

"Some people from the county been here, twice. Nothing come of it, though."

"You want me to talk to the police?"

"You better not!" Gilbert's eyes blazed and his whole body went stiff.

"Okay . . . Jeez."

"You g-g-gotta go now," he said. With his hands and eyes, he urged me out the door, his face shielded by a thin layer of phony toughness. I paused between the door jambs for one last-ditch try.

"Do you like fishing?" I asked.

That seemed to hit a nerve. "I been known to f-f-fish sometimes."

# Chapter 25

Back at the farm, we had eggs and rutabaga for supper and canned tomatoes with rutabaga for breakfast on Sunday morning. I loaded milk cans
into the truck and we puttered off with yet another delivery for the creamery. As usual, we got in line and chatted with a few locals. I spotted the
Bear and he stared at me with flamethrower eyes until I turned away.
Gilbert was nowhere in sight. Ham took possession of a milk check and,
based on the way he shoved it into his pocket, I could tell it didn't amount
to anything.

Instead of going immediately back to the farm, the old man surprised
me by pulling in at Stokely's. The canning factory hissed, rattled, and
threw off steam like a caged demon. I thought it was all pretty keen, but
we weren't there as tourists. Ham backed his pickup to a large pile of spent
pea vines and signaled me to pitch them into the truck bed.

"What's this for?" I asked.

"What do you think?"

I felt a little bit like a hobo scrounging a free meal at the city dump as
I pitched them into the truck. When it was loaded, I looked around and
was glad to see nobody watching our mild act of desperation.

Back home we dumped the pea vines at the base of the silo for the
cows to eat later. Before going in the house, Ham scrabbled up enough
pea pods from them to fill a small bowl. They would boil up later on the
Monarch Malleable as a side dish with today's noon meal of—you guessed
it—rutabaga.

We ate right outside on one of the makeshift tables left over from the
corn-planting party. I watched as Ham pushed his nose in a brochure,
squinting to read the fine print. In the weeks I'd known him, the old man
had never been much of a reader, so I leaned over to see what was so interesting. When I saw bold letters spelling out the four words AGRICULTURE
AND LAND CONSERVATION, I turned away and rolled my eyes.

*Studying more ways to go broke.* That's what I figured.

It took Black Cat flying down from the top of the silo to get Ham to pocket the brochure. With the crow waiting patiently for food scraps, the old man finally relented and tossed her a few leftovers. I spotted Peacock sneaking toward the barn, looking for a mouse dinner.

"I'll be taking the truck for the afternoon," said Ham. "Going to Balsam Lake to visit an old friend. You weren't gonna see no picture shows today, were ya?"

"I'm low on money," I said. "Might head up there for another reason, though."

"What's that?"

"Raina Jackson." I shrugged. "She's helping me with something."

Ham shot me a wide-eyed look. "You fixing to hitchhike?"

"I'll just ride the bicycle."

Ham's eyebrows popped. "You strong enough to go that far?"

I snorted. "If a seventy-five-pound Indian girl can ride a bike loaded with trees all over the whole county, I'm quite sure I can cover the distance in half the time."

"Knock yourself out, boy."

Together, we washed and put away the dishes. Then Ham grabbed his straw hat and whistled for Black Cat, sparking the crow to fly to his shoulder. I gave the truck a crank start and shot them a thumb's up. Off they went, down the wheel ruts and south on the gravel.

That was my cue to hit the road, too, in the opposite direction. I tapped out a Lucky and put a matchstick to it, then breathed in a long healthy draw. "Piece of cake," I said to myself before straddling the rickety bike and heading off.

With a steady south wind, the ride into Luck was easy, but I still needed a drink because of the heat. Remembering a certain water spigot on the back side of the depot, I spun in that direction and leaned the bike against the building. With my hand on the valve and my mouth right under the spout, I gulped down about half of Big Butternut Lake.

I strolled to the front of the depot and watched a worker latch three boxcars to a northbound freight. The enormous black steam engine hissed and popped like an angry bull. The engineer looked out his open window at me and my ready-for-the-scrapheap bicycle.

A crazy notion hit me all of a sudden, and I looked back up at that engineer. "Race you to Frederic?" I said.

You should have seen him smile. "You're on, kid."

I checked my Hamilton—1:43. Then, quick as a grasshopper, I jumped in the saddle and started pumping like a crazy man. I was flying, or that's how it felt at least, on that first mile of the seven-mile sprint. There was an engine inside of me and my legs and feet were the rods and pistons. The road beneath me was a gray blur.

I glanced again at the time—1:49. I was six minutes in, and by my figuring, I had two miles behind me and five yet to go. The train whistle let loose with two long blasts, and I knew it was leaving the station. I heard the slow thrusts of the pistons and glanced back just as the sky over the Luck depot started filling up with black smoke.

"Go! Go! Go!" I shouted to my legs as they pushed the rickety bike another mile. A white barn stared me down. A fence row flanked with day lilies flew by like so many orange streaks. I looked back again. *Ha-Haa!* I was even further ahead than before.

I kept it going best I could, my legs now feeling twinges of pain. Drops of sweat on my face had turned into rivers. Still, through it all, I kept the crankshaft inside me churning round and round. I checked the time again and figured myself halfway.

My legs paused and the bike coasted as I gasped for breath. I coughed and spat the gob into the weeds. The sound behind me was getting louder and louder. *Chuffa—chuffa—chuffa—chuffa—chuffa—chuffa.* It was a cadence that I'd heard a thousand times before—but this time it was personal. The steam locomotive was coming up hard on my right, almost even now.

Just like that, it was over. The wolf pack, at last, had caught up to the leg-weary deer. As the train took the lead, approaching the underpass beneath the highway bridge, the engineer's face came into view. He cupped his hand and shouted from the window.

"Nice try, kid!"

By the time I crawled into the Frederic station, the north-bounder had already disappeared. None of the stragglers at the station paid any notice as I coasted up to the platform, dropped the bike, and flopped to the ground.

Lucky for me, the Frederic Station had a water spigot, too, and I sucked down a good portion of Coon Lake this time. For fifteen or twenty minutes, I just sat in a shady spot. When I was breathing easy again, I enjoyed another cigarette. What was it those Lucky Strike ads said again?

*Smoke a Lucky—to feel your level best!*

It took me another hour, including three or four wrong turns, but I finally managed to find Grayburn Jackson's house. Just like last time, he stepped out to greet me before I could even knock at the door.

"You came back. I'm pleased," said the old Indian with the weather-beaten face. He looked at my rusty steed and smiled. "And you're taking on some of Raina's traits, too, I see."

I chuckled. "Yes, sir." I leaned the bicycle against the side of the small house, and Grayburn signaled for me to come inside. Nothing had changed since my last visit. Snow shoes in the corner. Raina's blanket woven out of rabbit-fur strips. I touched the soft fur again with my right hand.

"You like it," said Grayburn. "I remember that from last time."

"Yes, sir," I said. "Is Raina here?"

"Outside. She'll be back soon. You want tea?" he asked.

"That would be good," I answered.

"English or Chippewa."

"Chippewa." I could hardly believe my own voice.

Grayburn walked into the kitchen, making the tea himself this time. Just like before, it came out orange in color and steaming, in a plain white cup. On a separate saucer he had placed several brown lumps of maple sugar.

"Thank you," I said. I dropped one of the lumps in the tea and stirred it until it was dissolved. We sat facing each other, quietly sipping.

"Raina tells me you've been in some fights."

"A few."

"There's some warrior in your face."

"Yes, sir. You said something about that last time."

"So, you're going to meet Len today?"

"I guess so."

"Good idea."

We sat with our tea for a while. Then the back door leading to the kitchen swung open and clunked back shut. Raina peeked around the corner to see who was there.

"Hello," I said.

She said nothing back. Didn't even smile. Then, to her grandfather, she said, "I will take him to see Len when you are finished."

Grayburn nodded. Her eyes met mine again, but only briefly. Then she ducked back into the kitchen and left me sipping bitter tea with the old

Indian. It took me a while, but I downed the whole thing, and with only a single lump of maple sugar this time. There was plenty of time to think as nobody talked. Gradually, another bitter taste took root inside me. The one planted there by Mr. Wayne Borsthagen.

~

Raina's cousin's house was a one-room tar-paper shack, tucked away fifty yards off the gravel road and surrounded by jack pines and scrub oak. A rusty trash bin still trailed a few wisps of white smoke, and at least two dozen brown bottles lay scattered around its perimeter. What lawn there was amounted to trampled dirt and unmown grass with ferns creeping in around the edges. Just standing there made me feel crawly, like an entire army of wood ticks had been waiting all summer for somebody like me to show up.

Raina knocked on the door and we waited. When it opened slowly, a small, thin Indian emerged in a blue flannel shirt and brown pants. He couldn't have weighed any more than a hundred and ten pounds. His eyes were only half open, and he gave his head a little shake as if trying to wake himself. So . . . this was the great fighting coach who was going to help me beat Melonhead? I was not impressed.

Len looked me over for a few seconds, then returned his eyes to Raina. "This is him?"

"Yes," she said.

The slender Indian scowled. Being unimpressed apparently went both ways.

"Follow me," he said. We walked behind the house and came upon a large stack of firewood and an ax lodged into a tree stump. Beyond that was a flat area of ferns surrounded by trees.

"Raina tells me that you were fighting with your fists against someone taller and heavier."

"That's right," I said.

"Those Milltown boys and a lot of others around here are good boxers. You can't beat them that way."

I nodded. "It didn't help that the guy had thirty pounds on me."

"You making excuses already?" His scowl deepened, and his eyes flashed with ire. I decided to shut my mouth and keep it shut for a while.

My pint-sized Indian fighting coach took a step back and said, "Come at me. Punch me or take me down. Your choice." He stood facing me, legs apart. Arms at his sides.

I looked at Raina and she nodded.

*Whatever.* I took a breath and stared down at the scrawny Indian. *Jeez, how do I go about this without flattening the little shrimp?* I thought it through and finally decided to fake a jab at his face and then pop him with a couple soft punches to the body. I put up my dukes and got ready.

I bobbed forward, back, left, and right, then charged. Something happened very quickly that I couldn't really describe other than by telling you how it ended, with me falling flat and hard on my back and a fist coming down fast and stopping about an inch from my right eye. The Indian held it there for a long time. His scowl was gone, replaced by a silent snarl.

*Son of a bitch! What was that?*

I started getting up, but as soon as I moved, he dropped a knee into my chest. At the same time, he pulled back with his fist and brought it down, coming up just short again, but then pushing it slow and hard into the area of my cheekbone. I didn't move after that. Didn't talk either. For ten or fifteen seconds he hovered over me with that knee in my chest and that fist pushing down on my face. There was no doubt in my mind what came next if I even twitched. At long last, the scrawny Indian stood and stepped back. He said nothing at all.

I got up and brushed myself off. "What did you say your name was?"

"Len Jackson."

I pointed to the spot on the ground I just stood up from. "What was that just now?"

"A little bit of everything."

"Where in the world do people fight like that?" I asked.

He shifted his weight from one leg to the other and paused, contemplating my worthiness. "Different places. Some near Balsam Lake."

"Do you think you could show me a few moves like that? Maybe slow it down to half speed so I can see what the hell it is you're doing?"

Len Jackson looked into the face of Raina. Whether or not he would teach a dirtbag like me was apparently up to her. My eyes flashed between the two of them. Time passed. More time passed.

The girl finally nodded. "It's okay, Len. He helped me plant trees."

The lesson went on for another full hour, and by the time it was done I had a ripped-off sleeve, a mouth full of dirt, and three fresh welts on my already-messed-up face. I learned stuff though, especially about using the enemy's weight against him and trying to get him to make the first move. There was also a big emphasis on pounding the hell out of a guy once he went to the ground. I'll say this about the fighting methods of that scrawny Indian, Len Jackson—they weren't gonna be in any high school boxing manuals.

I was tired, beaten, filthy, achy, and hungry all at the same time. With my shirt sleeve already hanging there by two threads, I ripped it all the way off and shoved it in my pocket. Imagine what I looked like after that. I waved good-bye to Len and Raina, and together they watched me wobble down the gravel road on my rickety bike. I hadn't gone far, maybe twenty yards, when I realized the south wind had picked up and was blowing smack dab in my face. All that, and I was still sixteen miles from home.

*Swell!*

# Chapter 26

On Monday morning I worked hard on a couple of different projects for Mr. Torkelson. My first two hours were spent refurbishing a manure spreader that must have been made for George Washington. It needed new chains and sprockets all the way around. Then, for good measure, I welded some new tines to the shit flippers. My second job of the morning was swapping out a gas tank on a 1938 Case Model C. It took a full hour to get the old, corroded tank removed, one minute to insert the new one, and another hour to put everything back together again.

When the church bell clanged eleven times in a row, I wiped my hands on a shop rag and approached Mr. Torkelson with a question. He was filing a fresh edge onto a sickle bar blade, so I waited for a pause in the action. When he finally glanced up at me, a grin came across his face.

"What can I do for you, Milo?"

"Mr. Torkelson, are you aware of the old Briggs & Stratton engine collecting dust and spiders in the set-up shop?"

"Yeah . . . I reckon that's the one we pulled off an industrial-sized lawn mower. We were thinking about giving it to the scrap metal drive."

"Could I have it?"

He scratched his head and squinted. "What the hell for?"

"Well, sir. I've just about worn myself out riding Ham's rickety bicycle all summer. My idea is to convert it into a motorbike."

Mr. Torkelson's face lit up. "Now there's a nifty idea. Check with Mr. Gustafson. He'll probably let you work on it after hours."

"Thanks!"

I cleaned my face and hands in the bathroom sink and combed my hair with my fingers. In the mirror, the same old Minneapolis scoundrel glared back. The inescapable scar hadn't gone anywhere. Melonhead's contributions were still visible in my swollen lip and purple-tinted left eye. Three newly issued welts from Len Jackson rounded out the collection. Not exactly the best look for an unannounced visit with the boss, but there was no other option.

Mr. Gustafson had his nose in some papers and was wearing his green visor when I tapped at the office door.

"Come in, Milo. I've been meaning to talk to you."

"I have a question for you too, sir."

"You do, eh? All right, you go first."

"Mr. Gustafson, would you have any objections to my taking the Briggs & Stratton engine that's gathering dust in the set-up shop? I want to convert Ham's old bicycle into a motorbike. I already talked to Mr. Torkelson about it."

"What did he say?"

"He liked the idea. He said that with your approval I could even work on the project after my regular work hours."

"Fine with me."

"Thank you, sir." My heart swelled up. Project Lightning was ready for takeoff. Then I realized that Mr. Gustafson was still staring at me.

"Now for the other matter," he said.

"Yes, sir?"

Mr. Gustafson drummed his fingers on his desk, looking me over.

"I've been keeping my eye on you, Milo. Been taking a few notes on you too. Do you know what I've noticed?"

*Gulp.* "What's that, sir?"

"That you're a decent young man."

My mouth opened a crack, but nothing came out.

"Milo, when I asked you to own up to your mistake a couple months back, you swallowed your pride and did it. When Mr. Krankel loaded you up with shit jobs like I asked him to, you tightened your belt a notch and did them. Now we've got you doing real mechanic's work for Mr. Torkelson, and danged if you ain't swatting the ball out of the park."

I was starting to fluff up like a rooster.

"Young man, all of that has been very admirable. But what really impressed me is how much you've helped Ham. That man was going belly up. Hell, maybe he still will. But you've changed things for him and at least the old Swede has a chance now."

I blinked three times and my face softened into a closed-lipped grin.

"Son, I'm jacking up your hourly wage from 45 to 52 cents an hour. That's fifteen percent in just short of two months. On top of that, I did a calculation on your progress working off your debt. With everything you did on the Minneapolis-Moline, I'm pleased to tell you that you have fulfilled your obligations as of the beginning of last week. You'll be getting a pay envelope this Friday. Now, how does that feel?"

"Real good, sir," I said just before breathing again.

Mr. Gustafson stood up from his desk, walked around it, and shook my hand. "Keep up the good work, Milo."

"I sure will."

The rickety bicycle's wheels may have touched the ground on the way home, but I don't know when. All afternoon and clear through evening chores, Mr. Gustafson's kind words played over and over again in my mind. I cracked three eggs and fried them on the Monarch Malleable range. I cleaned all the dishes and mopped the kitchen floor. Hell, I even took another bath behind the shed.

All of that was swell until the sun went down, and the only light on the farm was a flickering kerosene lamp on top of the dresser in my bedroom. That's when I started thinking about *you-know-who* again and hearing strange noises outside my window.

~

The arrival of daylight and hard work had a way of tamping down my fear.

After chores, I worked extra hard from seven to eleven at Gustafson Tractor and Implement, then shifted gears to Project Lightning. Not surprisingly, the Briggs & Stratton engine wouldn't run. I cleaned and gapped the spark plug but it still wouldn't fire. Oh, well—no sense getting all bogged down and frustrated. I shifted gears and fixed up a bracket to mount her above the rear wheel. Then I figured up a scheme for making a clutch using belt friction.

By three in the afternoon I was back on the ice cream circuit, and as a fifty-two-cents-an-hour man, I saw no need to scrimp. Herman Schrapp made me a super-duper, chocolate-cherry, extra-everything malt that nearly overflowed the tall glass.

As long as I was on a winning streak, there was one more thing I had to do. At the pay phone in the corner of Lindoo Drug, my nickel clanked through the slot and the receiver made a crackling sound to my compressed ear. The operator connected the call according to my request. Then I waited through one ring. Another ring. Another.

"Ruth Hanson speaking."

"Hi, Mrs. Hanson, this is Milo Egerson. Do you remember me from Ham Rehnquist's farm?"

"Yes."

"Ma'am, thank you again for the fine food that you and the other ladies made for us. It was delicious."

"Is that a reason for your call, young man? To discuss my cooking?"

"No, ma'am. I mean, yes, ma'am . . . well, actually, that was just one of the reasons."

"And the other?"

"Could I speak with Becky, please, ma'am?"

"You may not."

Those three words had the same effect as a branch snapping back on my face. Mrs. Hanson's branch wasn't enough to completely knock me off my feet, but it stung. Not knowing what else to do, I sucked in some air and gave it a second try.

"Mrs. Hanson, I'm just hoping to invite her to see a movie at the Frederic theater. I'm an excellent driver and I'm earning fifty-two cents an hour now at Gustafson Tractor and Implement."

"I'm fully aware of what you are, young man. Isn't it true that you're a proven thief?"

"Umm . . ."

"And a destroyer of private property, specifically one large yellow tractor?"

"Yes, but . . ."

"Have you ever told a lie?"

"Yes."

"Do you smoke?"

"Yes."

"Have you ever used the Lord's name in vain?"

"No, ma'am. I would never do that."

～

All that week, I spent as many hours as possible working at Gustafson Tractor and Implement. Turning wrenches and welding steel acted like a sort of balm for my wounds. Just like the USS *Arizona* at Pearl Harbor, some things get sunk and stay sunk. That's pretty much how things were now with me and Betty Hanson—sunk.

On Tuesday, I greased up some wheel bearings and put a new magneto on a trade-in Farmall. On Wednesday, I welded a fix for a busted-up silage chopper. On Thursday, Mr. Torkelson worked with me putting a new clutch into a 1932 Allis-Chalmers. As you can imagine, I was learning a ton, and it helped me to not think about certain people.

In the afternoons of all those same days, I put an hour or two of my own time into Project Lightning. It went kind of slow, because just getting that old Briggs to run was like convincing a road-killed pheasant to flap its wings and fly again.

Maybe you're wondering about the messages I received Monday, Wednesday, and Friday afternoons on the *Beauty Banter* radio show. All three days they were the same as the week before.

Beauty isn't just skin deep = High yellow

# Chapter 27

Milltown and Luck both had blackout drills scheduled for Friday night, and when I got to the bunker on the school roof, Mr. Stenlund was already pacing the gravel. As usual, Edith Quigley sat and knitted. Her hands and needles clicked and whirred like a machine as they produced a large set of long underwear this time.

"Those look warm," I said.

Mrs. Quigley smiled. "Deer hunters swear by Quigley long johns." She paused to look me up and down as if determining my size. "I accept custom orders, ya know."

"But I'm not a deer hunter."

"You're a farmer. Some of them even wear my long johns to bed."

"How do you know that, Mrs. Quigley?"

She tried to jab me, but I was too quick for her.

Mr. Stenlund interrupted our antics, clearing his throat and tapping at the cover of a book that he wanted me to notice. "Milo, are you ready?"

"You mean for the blackout drill? I guess so."

"Before dark, I would like you to read this manual about your duties and those of fellow citizens during the drill. The sirens will blast at precisely ten o'clock. After that, everyone will have five minutes to get inside and douse the lights. Cars and trucks must pull over and shut off their lights, too. Pedestrians moving toward shelter are not allowed to smoke. And, above all else, people must obey the Air Raid Warden during the drill. Understand?"

I nodded. It all seemed straightforward enough. "Who's the Air Raid Warden?"

Mrs. Quigley let out a chuckle as she packed up her knitting supplies.

Mr. Stenlund shot her an annoyed glance, then stood up straight and looked at me. "I am the Air Raid Warden," he said.

"Pretty keen, Mr. Stenlund! You're Chief Observer and Air Raid Warden—both!"

His chest expanded, his eyes squinted, and the corners of his mouth transformed into a General MacArthur frown. He took his eyes off me and gazed north. Only then did I notice the patch with the word "Warden" sewn to his shoulder and the silver whistle dangling from a lanyard around his neck.

Stenlund tapped my shoulder with a folded paper, then handed it to me. "Use this map if the bombs start to fall. Take notes of everything—good and bad."

"I thought it was just a drill?"

"It is, but you never know. Any questions?"

"I guess not."

"No more guessing, young man. Lack of knowledge results in fear. Fear leads to panic."

A sense of duty surged through me. "I'm on it, sir." I delivered a crisp salute.

Mrs. Quigley, for her part, had had enough. She rolled her eyes, waddled toward the roof hatch, and started down the ladder.

Mr. Stenlund and I stood there looking out upon Milltown's rooftops until Mrs. Quigley disappeared from sight. Only then did Stenlund reach down behind the sandbags and lift the two hidden helmets. Each one was painted white with a chin strap, canvas lining, and full perimeter rim to shed falling debris and shrapnel. On the front of each helmet, the Civil Defense Air Warden insignia glistened—a red-and-white-striped triangle inside a blue circle.

"Wear this tonight, Milo. Just in case." Mr. Stenlund put on his helmet and I did the same, strap and all. I nodded and he nodded back. Then he did an about face and walked to the hatch.

As soon as Mr. Stenlund had disappeared down the ladder, I ditched the helmet behind the sandbags and unfolded the map. Every single fire hydrant and street light in Milltown was marked. Every manhole. Every tree. The Air Warden's post was at Mr. Stenlund's radio shop, and the bomb shelter symbol was at the feed mill. Some symbols on the key didn't actually exist yet. These included bomb craters and demolished buildings. I folded up the map and tossed it in the direction of the helmet.

It was 7:15. Almost three hours until dark. I picked up a handful of small stones from the gravel and chucked them one by one, wishing I'd brought my radio or something to read. That's when an idea slammed me. I walked to the hatch and snuck down the ladder.

In the gloom and silence of a summer Friday evening, the Milltown Public School library oozed spookiness. About a half-dozen tables occupied the center, surrounded by bookshelves on three sides. On the fourth side stood a librarian's desk, perfectly cleared except for a green blotter, quill pen in a stand, ink well, and a rectangular white block of wood with *Miss Gerty* painted on it in swirly letters. I imagined a pretty lady looking at me from the chair. I turned toward the shelves, all identical, painted black and about six feet tall. Some had numbers on the sides. Others, letters of the alphabet. Not knowing what else to do, I pointed myself toward the letter *T* for Twain and came out holding *The Adventures of Huckleberry Finn*.

*What next?*

The path was clear for me to simply swipe the book. Back at Washburn High, a year ago, that's exactly what I would have done. But that was before I met Hjalmar Rehnquist, Henrick Jesperson, Mr. Gustafson, Betty Hanson, and her mom.

I would check out the library book like a student should—good and proper. By looking at the card on the inside cover, I could see the names of all the kids who had read *The Adventures of Huckleberry Finn* before. It was like reading roll call for the Swedish army, with all of the Petersons, Olsons, and Johnsons. I spotted the name of the German scarecrow, *Herman Schrapp*, scrawled in pencil on a line dated October 1944. Then two more lines below his autograph, the handwritten name *Rosalyn Magnusson*.

She had written her name in blue ink, all swirly, girly, and perfect next to the date, April 19, 1945. It didn't matter to me that that pretty girl with the hotshot boyfriend had read the same book I was fixing to read. I didn't give one rip.

I took the book over to the librarian's desk and sat down in Miss Gerty's chair. It made a loud creaking noise that stopped me for a second. Removing the cover off the lady's ink well, I picked up the quill pen and dipped it in.

*Milo Egerson*          *July 27, 1975*

Just like that, I marked the card and placed it in the center of Miss Gerty's desk. I wiped off the tip of the quill pen on my pants and put the cover back on the ink well.

Back in the bunker of the Milltown Observation Post, I plopped myself down in the loose gravel and settled my back against the pile of sand bags. Then using my index finger for a guide on the first line of chapter 1, I started reading.

*You don't know about me without you have read a book by the name of The Adventures of Tom Sawyer; but that ain't no matter. That book was made by Mr. Mark Twain, and he told the truth, mainly. There was things which he stretched, but mainly he told the truth.*

That's how chapter 1 started out, and I was already snared like one of Raina Jackson's rabbits. I settled in for the next three hours, shirking my duties as the Deputy to the Chief Observer for the Milltown, Wisconsin, observation post. I didn't look around for enemy airplanes. I didn't wear the helmet or study the map neither. If Mr. Stenlund had seen me, he'd have plucked my wings on the spot.

I kept on reading *The Adventures of Huckleberry Finn* and pretty soon started remembering the tale from a long time ago. I liked the parts about the Mississippi River, a place that brought memories of home. I especially liked the boy, Huck, who smoked a pipe and got pegged early on as a troublemaker. These thoughts led to others, and pretty soon my mind had drifted across the Pacific Ocean to another sandbagged bunker. Like Huckleberry Finn, I wasn't much when it came to religion and praying. Nonetheless, I set the book down and put my hands together. I arranged my fingers and thumbs so that all of them were pointing up. I shut my eyes.

*God in Heaven, please bring Tom home and let him be safe.*

~

It was ten o'clock sharp when the promised sirens started wailing like a choir of demons. That was my cue to shut off the battery-powered electric torch, fold down the corner of the page, and give Huck Finn a rest.

One by one the lights blinked out up and down Main Street. Bank and Bering Streets, too, and all five of the avenues. Cars pulled over and doused their lights. Neon bar signs dimmed to black. Even the yellow glow from the Co-op station went dark. I lifted my eyes to the northern horizon in the direction of Luck. The faint glow slowly darkened.

The hooded headlights of a single car moved slowly along Fourth Avenue and turned right onto Highway 35. Warden Stenlund had completed his duties in Milltown and was now making his way toward Luck. I reached down behind the sandbags and pulled up a white helmet with the red, white, and blue insignia on the front. I put it on my head and yanked hard on the strap.

# Chapter 28

Waiting to get the final word on Mr. Wayne Borsthagen was tough duty. As long as he was stuck behind bars at the Stillwater Prison, I was safe. Part of me kept hoping for a miracle. Maybe a judge would add another five years to his sentence. Maybe another convict would beat him to death with a lead pipe.

In the meantime, all I could do was wait and keep myself busy, and there were plenty of distractions beyond chores and my job. I learned how to shoot Ham's .30-30, for one thing. I took two more fighting lessons from Len Jackson, for another. My biggest diversion, though, was still my scheme to combine Ham's rickety bicycle with the Briggs & Stratton engine.

The big day for Project Lighting came on a Saturday with the final turn of a three-quarter-inch wrench. I stood back and admired the finished product, realizing that the only thing left was to clean her up and apply a fresh coat of paint.

I started in with my old friend the wire brush, removing layer after layer of dirt and rust on what was once a bright-turquoise paint finish. As my scrubbing reached the chain guard, a row of slanted black letters appeared. Unbeknownst to me, this bike already had a name—STAR-CHASER.

I had never been superstitious, but there was no sense messing with fate. Even though it would mean extra work, Star-Chaser's name would be preserved along with the rest of the paint job. That meant a trip to fetch Miss Gerty's ink well from the Milltown Public School library and another trip to Twetten Hardware for turquoise-blue paint. Very carefully, with one tiny paint brush and one bigger one, Ham Rehnquist's old bicycle got her old good looks back.

With Ham and Black Cat watching, I stood back and admired the result.

"Looks like a fine machine," said Ham.

The raspy *Caw* from his shoulder felt like an insult.

I nodded toward the old man and glared at the crow.

In my mind the newly motorized Star-Chaser was way better than fine. She was a marvel. The engine gleamed shiny and black with fresh paint. The flywheel hung off the side, connecting to the rear wheel with a separate pulley and belt. The carburetor sat on top and a separate gas tank was strapped beneath the crossbar. I let out a low whistle. She was a rocket ship all right, a rocket ship on two wheels.

"Let's see it go down the road," said Ham.

Ham held the bike steady while I strung a starter rope around the flywheel and gave it a yank. Then another. Then another. Then another. At last, on the fifteenth or twentieth pull, she caught and putted to life. I let her warm up and fiddled with the choke and throttle before getting in the saddle. With the push of a lever on my customized idler pulley, the belt tightened up on the drive sheave and carried the bike forward. Star-Chaser chugged down one of the wheel ruts and picked up speed on the gravel road past the cattail marsh. I turned her around and came back.

"How's she run?" asked Ham.

"Swell!"

Ham reached out to me holding something in his claw hand. I focused my eyes and realized that it was a pair of goggles, the kind with glass lenses protruding out from a leather mask and an adjustable strap on the back. They were the real thing, just like the air force pilots wore—nifty as hell.

"Thanks, Uncle Ham!"

"Try them on."

I did, and Black Cat started bobbing with excitement. I looked at myself in the reflection of the kitchen window.

*Crackerjack!*

"Okay if I take off for a while?"

"You got plenty of gas?"

"Yes."

I was down the wheel ruts again and past the cattail marsh like a flash. After a left onto paved asphalt, I bumped up the throttle to two-thirds of max. Wind rushed through me and bugs bounced off my goggles, face, and chest.

*Yessss!*

My heart found a whole new tempo, jumping from Mozart to full-blown jazz. People looked at me from passing cars. I could almost hear their words.

*There's that clever young man from Minneapolis who built his own motorbike.*
Flying up State Highway 35 with my back arched and my head low, I
blasted into Luck. Two short toots from a train whistle greeted me as I
slowed near the depot. There it was again. The same Soo Line train that
whipped my ass last time. Same engineer, same tender, same everything.
The engineer looked at me like I was the headless horseman and he was
Ichabod Crane. I disengaged the slip-belt clutch, braked to a stop, and
stared back through the lenses of my goggles.

"Nifty rig!" shouted the engineer.

"To Frederic?" I shouted back.

His eyebrows jumped. "You better give me a mile head start this time,"
he said. "Wait until our caboose is out of sight."

I nodded back. The rematch was on. Just for show I juiced the throttle,
and the engineer let off a shot of steam. The train left the Luck depot and
rolled north. Pulling a short string of about twenty empty hopper cars, it
accelerated quicker than I thought. Onward it chugged, toward Duluth.
*Chuffa—chuffa—chuffa.* Faster and faster it picked up speed while I sat at idle.
Finally—finally, the red-and-white caboose disappeared behind some trees.

Star-Chaser took off like a pebble launched from a slingshot. She had no
speedometer, but I didn't care. The engine had power to burn and it didn't
take long before I was zipping past somebody's white-haired grandma in
an old Dodge sedan. After that, it was a farmer in a Model BB Ford truck.
Then guess what came up on my front fender. A Cadillac, one of the big
ones, with the powerful V12. I pulled up alongside slow enough to give
the driver a thumbs up and a wink through my goggles. He returned a nod
and the *A-O-K* sign, making a circle with his thumb and index finger. I
zoomed past.

At the crossing where the tracks passed beneath the highway bridge, the
train was still ahead of me, but not by much. He was pinning the throttle
and so was I. It was a matter of simple mathematics. At the speed Star-
Chaser was going, the race was mine. I cruised into town prepared to take
the checkered flag, but then—oh no—a traffic jam. How could there be a
traffic jam in Frederic, Wisconsin, of all places? It was backed up a block
and a half from the intersection of 35 and Oak.

I screeched to a dead stop. *Nuts!*

"Let's go! Move it!" I shouted like a fool.

The train's whistle blasted again. *Son of a buck!*

The finish line was just three blocks away, and I was fixing to lose unless I took desperate measures. With the clutch disengaged, I hammered the throttle to let folks know I was there. The Briggs roared like a lion. That was all the warning the city of Frederic was gonna get. I juiced the throttle again, darted between parked cars and jumped the curb to the sidewalk. For fifty feet my path was clear. *Clunk—clunk!* I was off the sidewalk, through the intersection, and heading left onto Oak with the depot in my sights.

Another double blast of the train whistle just about shook the whole town. A hellish mix of white steam and black smoke boiled above the treetops. I kept the throttle pinned for the final fifty yards, then side-wheeled into a skidding stop just as the locomotive roared into full view.

We were looking for each other, me and the Soo Line engineer. When we finally locked eyes, he offered a nod and his face opened up into a toothy smile. What happened next came with a flip of his wrist and elbow. The engineer launched a silver object spinning though the air and bouncing in the vicinity of my feet.

I picked it up. A silver dollar—the real thing. The Goddess of Liberty on the front. American Eagle on the back.

~

Not surprisingly, Grayburn Jackson wasn't very impressed with me and Star-Chaser when we rumbled up his lane.

"I liked it better when you came quietly," said the leather-faced guy.

My visit started with yet another cup of Chippewa tea and a chat in the living room, where a hot breeze drifted through the open windows. Grayburn did most of the talking, asking a lot of questions about Ham and Black Cat.

Raina was there too, but like always, she preferred to listen from the doorway to the kitchen. It was a weird friendship, if you could call it that, with me visiting with her grandpa while she hovered in the background like a hawk. Whether it was drinking tea with Grayburn or practicing fighting with Len, that girl preferred to watch and not speak. Then on the rare occasion that she did say something, it always came with a wallop. Remember when she warned me to stay clear of the beaver dam? Remember when she spoke with Ham about her grove of saplings? Some people are quiet but powerful, and I was getting to know one of them—slowly.

My final lesson from Len Jackson came that same afternoon. He battered me again. *Could a guy learn from a book once in a while?* I had to admit, though, that at least I had made some real progress. For every two times that he flung me hard to the ground and dropped a fist an inch from my face, I once was able to grab an arm or leg and hurl him down just the same. The three key points hadn't changed since my first lesson. Get the other guy to make the first move. Use his own weight and speed to throw him down. Don't let him up after he falls.

Today's lesson ended with me heading home with a new collection of welts and scrapes on my face and body. But to my immense satisfaction, my scrap-iron, pocket-sized instructor didn't come out of it scot-free. He had a fat lip, a mouth full of dirt, and a purple lump above his left eye. We gazed at each other and he offered a slow nod.

During the walk back from Len's shack to Grayburn's house a strange thing happened—Raina Jackson almost smiled.

"He likes you, you know," she said to me.

"Who does?"

"My cousin, Len. He likes you. He says there's some raccoon inside you."

"What's that mean?"

"You ever see a raccoon fight another animal?"

"No."

She shrugged.

I shrugged back. *Wacky Indian girl.*

Back at Grayburn's place, Raina just stood back from the motorized Star-Chaser like it was a wicked thing that didn't belong.

"You want to go for a ride?"

"No."

Slowly she walked toward the front door, then turned around, watching me put on my goggles and get ready to start up the Briggs. I felt something in my pocket, reached in, and pulled out the agate that Mrs. Quigley had given me. Just like before, I held it out in the sunlight between my thumb and index finger, studying the nifty orange and white stripes.

A notion hit me and I looked at Raina. "This is for you." I tossed it in her direction and she caught it one-handed. She turned the stone and studied it in the bright sunlight like I had. Then she looked at me awkwardly.

"It's an agate," I said. "It's like vanilla ice cream and caramel swirled together and froze up in a stone for all time. Sort of feels alive, doesn't it?"

Her eyes sharpened and locked on mine. "That's because it *is* alive."

I squinted at her, puzzled by what she had just said.

"Do you know the word *Manitou*?" she asked.

"Mani-what?"

"*Manitou.*"

"No."

Raina actually smiled. It wasn't big, but it was powerful. Then she walked inside the house and closed the door without looking back.

*Manitou?* What the heck was *Manitou*?

I shook my head like it was full of bees. That Indian girl had me more confused than ever. I wrapped the rope around the flywheel and the engine started with one pull. Maybe I didn't understand Raina, but at least I was getting to know my way around my motorized Star-Chaser.

# Chapter 29

Ham and I had just finished chores on Sunday evening when we dragged ourselves into the kitchen to wash our filthy hands and get ready for supper. Ham pulled a covered dish out of the Monarch Malleable, where it had been warming while we worked. Imagine my surprise when my eyes landed on a pork roast surrounded by rutabaga and peas. The broth was bubbling and smelled like heaven.

"Thanks, Uncle Ham," I said. "Was pork on sale at the grocery?"

"I didn't buy it," he said.

From the look on the old man's face, the puzzle pieces fit together. I pressed my face against the glass of the kitchen window and focused my eyes on the pig pen. One sow lay in the mud where we used to have two. The pigs weren't there to be pets. I knew that much. I poured two glasses of milk and reached for the Wonder Bread and butter.

"Uncle Ham?"

"Yah?"

"You ever hear the word *Manitou*?"

"Yah."

"What is it?"

"You should probably save that question for Grayburn Jackson."

"What's the big secret?"

"It's an Ojibway thing."

"I already figured that much."

"It's an Ojibway spirit thing."

"Spirit?"

"Yah."

"I gave an agate to Raina and she said something about it being alive. Then she asked if I knew the word *Manitou*."

"For the Ojibway, there is a spirit inside of everything—both living and dead."

"Even a stone?"

"I reckon."

"I don't understand."

"And Raina wouldn't say anything more?"

"No."

"You'd best have a talk with Grayburn Jackson."

~

I wandered outside to get away from the heat still pouring off the Monarch Malleable and filled my lungs with summer air. The sky shone turquoise blue, and a light breeze whispered through the maple leaves. For no particular reason, I walked over to the silo and climbed the steel rungs all the way up to the very top.

The cows and horses made a pretty picture on the lime green pasture. The corn stood belt-high, reflecting diamonds from their dagger-shaped leaves. I shifted my gaze to the garden, still organized in perfect rows that made me think again about DiMaggio, Spencer, Blondie, and Drac. Maybe it was almost like bragging, but I felt proud knowing that I had something to do with it.

At the high point of the cornfield, I allowed my eyes to focus on the pine grove shading two graves. The leaves on the birch and oak saplings around the perimeter fluttered and shimmered in the sunlight. Maybe it was okay, after all, that Raina got to replant all those trees. I let my eyes drift to the cattail swamp and from my elevation could see muskrat houses and the family of sandhill cranes that Ham had talked about. Maybe the old man was right not to drain that marsh just to create more cropland.

Satisfied, I climbed back down and walked back toward the machine shed where Star-Chaser seemed to be calling my name. There was more than an hour of daylight left.

*Why not.*

Without asking Ham, I pull-started the engine, rolled down one of the wheel ruts to the gravel, and accelerated toward Highway 35. I passed through Milltown slowly, then zigged east and south on the back roads until I came to a body of glistening water that was curved in the shape of the letter *C*. The swimming beach and diving platform looked familiar from my first weekend drive with Ham.

"Half Moon Lake," I said right out loud, feeling like a local.

Other than the beach, the lake was bordered by trees and farms. On a small point I spotted a lone fisherman. I engaged the slip clutch on my idling motorbike and rode in the guy's direction.

I shut off the engine. "Hey, Gilbert, is that you?"

He turned and faced me, eyes wide. "Wh-wh-what you doing here?"

"Riding my motorbike." I extended my arm and gave a couple taps to the Model F. "What do you think of her?"

"It's okay."

"How did you get here?"

Gilbert pointed in the direction of some trees, and I glimpsed his speckled gray horse looking at me with a mouthful of grass.

"Are the fish biting?" I asked.

He pulled up a rope with two walleyes and a dozen panfish all strung through the gills.

"Do you mind if I watch?"

"N-n-no law against it."

It wasn't the warmest invitation I'd ever received, but I sat down in the tall grass anyhow. I pulled a timothy stem and chewed it while looking over the water. Other than that, I just breathed in the smells of the lake and listened to the nighthawks overhead.

"Gilbert, what are you going to do with your life?"

"Stay here and f-f-farm, I reckon."

"You ever think about getting away from your father?"

Gilbert glanced at me sharply, then cast his worm and bobber again. "I ain't got an uncle like you do. I ain't that l-l-lucky.

I laughed right out loud. "Oh—so *I'm* the lucky one, is that it?"

"Yes," said Gilbert. "And d-d-don't laugh at me no more."

"Sorry."

For a few minutes I watched Gilbert fish. He twitched his bait, drawing it in slow half turns of the fishing reel. When the cork bobber went all the way under, he pulled back and set the hook. The fish dashed for a sunken tree branch, but Gilbert was too quick for that old trick, and a hand-sized bluegill sailed right out of the water and into the grass. A minute later, the fish was on the rope with the others and a fresh worm was soaking in the same spot.

"Gilbert, can I tell you a secret?"

He looked at me with an open mouth and searching eyes. I must have had a certain look about me, too, because he even reeled in his bait and bobber, set down the pole, and sat next to me. I gave him the short version, but it was enough.

"When is he getting out of prison?" Gilbert asked.

"Don't know, exactly."

"You g-g-gonna tell the sheriff?"

"Once we know for sure that he's been let out. Ham says that the sheriff can't do anything before then anyhow."

"What you gonna do if he finds you?"

"Don't know. What are you gonna do about your father?"

"Don't know that either."

"Seems like we both got a problem."

Gilbert nodded and stared at me hard. "Seems so."

The sound of diesel engines and tires on gravel interrupted our chat. Five large army trucks—greenish gray in color, canvas covering the cargo area, and a white star on each door.

Gilbert and I hunkered down in the grass and observed what must have been the entire population of Camp Milltown climbing down from the trucks. As usual, they wore work clothes with *P* and *W* markings on each shirt and pair of pants. Of the dozen or so guards, maybe half of them had rifles, and they stood back a ways from the group. One of the other guards spoke to a man who must have been the German leader, wearing a brown shirt and a cap. He gave directions to his men. Do you know what that big crowd of over a hundred prisoners did next? They took their clothes off right down to their underwear and made a run for the lake—that's what.

I watched Gilbert almost as much as I watched the Germans. His eyes darted like a rabbit in a coyote pack.

"It's okay," I said. "Don't you remember them from Ham's farm?"

"Yes, but they was just four. This here looks like f-f-four hundred."

I shrugged and smiled. "Do you know how to swim?"

"That ain't funny," said Gilbert.

Just like that I started kicking my boots off and peeling my shirt over my head.

Gilbert shouted a whisper. "Are you crazy?!"

"Maybe. But when are you going to get another chance to swim with a gang of murderous Nazis? It'll be something for us to talk about when we're old men."

"If we live that long."

"Come on, Gilbert—take a chance. You get one life. Then you're dead."

"Th-th-that's what I'm worried about."

Despite his fears, Gilbert squirmed out of his boots and clothes almost as quick as me. We both slipped into the water at the weedy shore and dog paddled toward the big group. Once we got mixed in—hell—we could have been Nazis just the same as the real ones. At first we just swam and splashed around, keeping everything except our heads below the water. But when the Krauts started climbing the floating raft and going off the diving board, well, how could I resist?

"No!" shouted Gilbert as I scrabbled up the side of the raft.

Two guys in front of me jabbered in German while I waited. The Krauts each did a plain old swan dive. Then it was my turn. I looked at Gilbert before turning around backward on the board. His eyes were as wide as sliced apples.

"Backflip!" I shouted.

My jumping muscles must have been supercharged with energy because I ended up doing a one and a quarter, right onto my back. *Smack!* The sting was like landing on a hornet's nest. When I came up, a dozen Germans were all laughing and looking at me. I locked eyes with Spencer Tracy.

"*Der Gartenbauer!*" he shouted.

DiMaggio came swimming out of nowhere. Then Blondie. Then Drac.

"How are you coming here?" asked DiMaggio.

I pointed to shore. "By motorbike." Then I looked toward Gilbert. "He rode a horse."

DiMaggio threw his head back and laughed. A whole circle of Germans started laughing. Heck—we all were. Well . . . all except Gilbert.

With so many swimmers mixed together and all looking the same, the guards didn't know the difference. We did the usual teenage boy stuff, roughhousing in the shallows. We dunked each other, raced one another, and even tossed each other in the air. We had some chicken fights with me on DiMaggio's shoulders and Drac riding on Gilbert's. After that we all went off the diving board a bunch more, and by the time we'd finished, even Gilbert was doing cannonballs.

The sun was below the horizon when one of the guards blew his whistle and it was time for everybody to get out. By that time most of the Germans knew about our being there and many were keeping an eye on us.

"Just stay in the water," I said to Gilbert.

"But we'll get in trouble."

"You'll get in more trouble if you swim to the other shore and walk away from those trucks."

And so we just stood there until a guard approached the water's edge and waved us in.

"We're Americans," I shouted.

The guy glared into our faces. "Get in here!" he yelled.

We waded in toward the beach, and by then, three other American guards were also standing there waiting. Two of them were holding rifles and none of them looked happy. The tall one, a soldier with two stripes on each shoulder, started yelling. "Who the hell are you and what do you think you're doing?"

"I'm Milo and this is my friend, Gilbert. We were swimming."

"Don't smart off!" the guard shouted.

The man pushed his gun crossways against my chest and I stumbled backward, almost falling. I felt a surge of blood rush into my face. Without thinking about it, I got set in the ready-to-fight position that Len had taught me behind his tar-paper shack. I was on the verge of doing something stupid when two things happened at once.

First, Gilbert stepped in between me and the guard, facing him straight on with his hands hanging down. "You'll have to go through me," he said without stuttering.

The guard snarled and got his rifle butt ready to smack Gilbert. Then

. . .

"Back off, Corporal!"

The voice came from the trucks, and as soon as my eyes locked down on the source, I recognized Sergeant Harrison. He was peeved, and I figured we were in for it, but instead of going after me and Gilbert, he grabbed the rifle out of the tall guard's hands and ordered him into one of the trucks before turning around to face me again.

"This is the second stupid thing I've seen you do this summer, young man."

"Sorry, sir."

"Don't 'sorry' me, smart ass. What's the big idea?"

"We just couldn't resist a swim with the Krauts, sir."

With every single member of Camp Milltown watching Sergeant Harrison's back, Gilbert and I were the only ones who could see his face. His eyes softened and he moved in closer before speaking again in low tones.

"Ninety-nine percent of these young German soldiers want nothing more than to wait out the war and go home. But . . ."

Gilbert and I looked at each other, then back at Sergeant Harrison. "But what, sir?" I asked.

"But there's the one percent."

"The one percent?"

"The real Nazi believers. The ones who still believe in what Hitler stood for. The ones who wouldn't think twice about killing a Jew or a Negro. Are either of you boys Jewish?"

I made a face. "I ain't no Jew." I turned toward Gilbert. "You a Jew, Gilbert?"

"I ain't nothing," he said.

For a moment nobody spoke. Sergeant Harrison's eyes darted back and forth between me and Gilbert. His face was furrowed and unsmiling. "Do you boys know what separates good and evil in these men?"

Gilbert and I shook our heads.

"A thin line."

We said nothing.

"Most of these young men are just like you two, and yet they fought for Adolf Hitler. What if you were in their shoes? What if you were eighteen years old and happened to be born in Germany? Would you have fought for Adolf Hitler?"

We said nothing. Neither one of us even moved. It was something I didn't even want to think about.

"From now on, I want you boys to keep some distance from these prisoners. You understand?" said the Sergeant.

"Because of the one percent?" I said quietly.

"That's one reason," said Sergeant Harrison.

"Y-y-yes, sir," said Gilbert.

# Chapter 30

On Monday morning, August 6, I rode Star-Chaser to work on the usual roads but kept my head down when I passed by Camp Milltown. It wasn't that I'd lost my curiosity about the prisoners. I just didn't want to be seen by Sergeant Harrison.

Back at Gustafson Tractor and Implement, everything felt normal again—even good. I spent the first ten minutes showing off my motorized version of Star-Chaser. Mr. Torkelson loved it and even took it for a little spin. Mr. Gustafson gave me the thumbs-up sign when he walked by. Mr. Krankel turned up his nose, of course, still sore that he couldn't make me scrub toilets anymore.

After seeing what I had done with the Briggs & Stratton, Mr. Torkelson gave me a new assignment, and it was a doozy. A farmer had trailered in a 1936 Oliver tractor that had been nearly destroyed in a machine-shed fire. He was hoping we could save it. The wiring was fried. The rubber hoses were all ruined. Even the paint was almost all burned off. *Gawd*—other than still having the general shape of a tractor, it looked about as dead as a sunbaked worm.

Mr. Torkelson said the best thing to do was to take everything apart, figure out what was okay and what wasn't, and then paint things fresh and put them all back together again. I felt a little bit like Dr. Frankenstein getting ready for surgery.

Just then, Mr. Gustafson walked into the shop carrying his Philco radio in his hands and a worried look on his face. "President Truman is going to speak to the whole nation," he said.

Mr. Gustafson plugged in the radio right there in the shop, and while the tubes were warming up, Mr. Krankel came in and joined us. Even Miss Dunn, Mr. Gustafson's secretary, stepped into the room.

"What's it all about?" asked Mr. Torkelson. "Are we invading Japan?"

"Don't know. We'll just have to listen," said Mr. Gustafson.

Mr. Krankel said nothing. Miss Dunn knitted her fingers.

The next voice we heard was President Truman.

*"A short time ago an American airplane dropped one bomb on Hiroshima and destroyed its usefulness to the enemy. That bomb has more power than twenty-thousand tons of TNT . . . It is an atomic bomb."*

An atomic bomb. *Jesus—Mary—Joseph!* I had heard talk about a bomb that used the same mysterious power that held the protons and neutrons together inside an atom. Lots of people had heard whispers about it. The big fear to America was that the enemy might figure it out first.

With President's Truman's words, we now knew that the bomb was real. And most important of all—America had won the race to figuring it out. We had created an atomic bomb and dropped it on top of Japan. Only one single bomb had ruined a big city. Suddenly, it seemed like the world was a boulder balanced on top of a thimble.

The president continued talking, and the five of us silently stood there and listened. But not all of my brain was engaged in the bomb talk. Part of it wondered how this mattered to my brother, Tom.

∽

It was half-past noon when I washed my rusty hands with Lifebuoy soap and walked outside with my head still churning about those two huge words—*atomic bomb*. It should have been easy to smile about a big victory like that. Mr. Torkelson even said that it could save our soldiers from a bloody invasion. He seemed certain that it was the best thing for the world. So did Mr. Gustafson. So did Mr. Krankel. I wasn't so sure about Miss Dunn, because I had observed the look on her face before she walked back in the office.

I pushed Star-Chaser down the sidewalk to Milltown's Main Street and parked it at Lindoo Drug just as Herman and Rosalyn came walking outside.

"Did you hear about the atomic bomb?" she asked me directly.

"Yes."

"What do you think it means?"

"Don't rightly know. Maybe it will end the war quicker."

Rosalyn stepped closer to me and looked me straight in the eyes for the first time since my first day in town when I was such a know-it-all smart ass. "Is it true that your brother is fighting in the Pacific?"

I kept my eyes locked on her and she didn't even look away. "Yes," I said. "His name is Tom."

"I hope he's okay," said Rosalyn.

"Me too. We haven't heard from him in a while."

Rosalyn gave me a gentle smile and put her soft hand on mine. "Don't worry. He'll be fine. You'll see." Just as quickly, she pulled it away. Something that felt like atomic power flowed through me, and I wanted to reach out and get that hand back for a little longer. Then an idea hit me, and before I could stop myself, the words spilled out.

"Would you like to take a ride on my motorbike?"

Rosalyn's eyes sparkled like two glass doorknobs on Summit Avenue. "Oh—no. I couldn't," she said, but her sly grin said *maybe*.

"Come on." I patted on the steel plate over the top of the engine with my hand. "There's even a place to sit."

Rosalyn squinted and tipped her head to the side, pretending to be cautious.

"You can ride sidesaddle if you want." I waved her over and she came.

"Is it safe?"

"Are you kidding? I'm the safest motorbike driver anyone's ever seen. Never had an accident in the life of this machine, and that's been a whole two days."

Rosalyn laughed and gently shoved my shoulder. Then she looked at Herman for an opinion. He winked and nodded. That was all it took.

The engine started up with a single pull and puttered smoothly at idle. I pushed back my hair and strapped on the aviation goggles. With Herman's help, Rosalyn took her seat on the steel plate above the rear fender and I felt her grip my belt with both hands.

"You ready?!"

"Yes!"

I revved the engine a couple times without engaging the clutch. With a roar from the Briggs, we were off like a dart from a blowgun.

In a straight line, right down Main Street, we flew. A man and woman stopped to gape from the steps of the hotel. Mr. Schick at the Mobil station shot us a wave. It seemed like everybody and their brother had stepped outside to watch the spectacle. At the Co-op station, Melonhead tried to skewer me with his searing glare so I fought back with a grin and a high-pitched howl. That's about the time that Rosalyn started hooting right along with me.

When we turned around at the feed mill, I decided to really let loose. "You ready for some *real* speed?" I asked.

"Yes!"

Rosalyn's grip tightened on my belt. I feathered the clutch.

We must have set a new speed record for the feed mill to Lindoo run, because everything passed by in a colorful blur. I slowed for a stop, and Herman Schrapp helped Rosalyn off the bike. She was still smiling. I was too.

Two things happened at almost the same time in the moments after that ride. The first was Fancyhair Wingtip showing up. The second was him grabbing Rosalyn by the arm and marching her, practically dragging her, across the street and into his car.

"Stop it, Donny! You're hurting me!" Rosalyn yelled.

That was all I needed to hear. I sprinted after them, and just as Wingtip was shoving Rosalyn into the passenger seat, I grabbed him by the shirt collar and yanked him away from her. He spun and faced me.

"Why don't you try picking on somebody your own size?!" Those were my words even though Wingtip had six inches and fifty pounds on me.

"Why don't you mind your own business," he said.

After pocketing my wristwatch, I stepped hard on the toe of his polished shoe with my grimy boot and took three steps back. I stood with my legs apart and shook out my arms, leaving them dangling at my sides like Len had taught me.

"You looking for a fight, city boy?"

"I ain't running from one."

My rival screwed up his face till it looked like a scrunched-up tobacco pouch and put up his dukes in a boxer's pose. Slowly he moved forward with measured steps and I countered by moving back the same amount. He threw a jab but missed. He threw a hook and missed again. Finally, with both fists flying, he charged. It was exactly what I was waiting for.

I dodged the punch and immediately grabbed the guy's shirt sleeve with my left hand while spinning and hauling my right arm over the same shoulder. I spun, threw my hip into him, and over he went. *Thump!* Hard into the pavement. Instinctively I knew what came next, and it was a haymaker directed at Wingtip's nose. I should have nailed him but pulled up short instead, holding my fist against his face like I was ironing it.

You can probably guess what happened next. With his free left hand, he punched me square in the schnoz. Then, while I was shaking out the cobwebs, he punched me again. The blood started flowing as I toppled over onto the pavement. Wingtip stood up and brushed off his clothes.

"Next time don't try writing a check that your body can't cash," he said.

I heard him slam the car door and rev the engine on the Nash Ambassador coupe. There was Rosalyn in the passenger-side window. Her lovely smile was gone, swapped out for an open mouth and sad eyes like she had just seen a rabbit squished on the roadside. It was no way to impress a girl. I knew that much.

Wingtip spun his tires and roared off. Just like that, pretty Rosalyn and her laugh were gone.

～

Ham wasn't home when I got there. Just as well. I pumped a glassful of water and swallowed it in two gulps before checking my face in the bathroom mirror. *Dang!* Just when my lumps from Len and Melonhead were going down, my nose was swelling up like an overripe plum.

I unpocketed my watch and realized that it was getting close to three o'clock. Clomping up the steps, I retrieved my radio and battery. Through the corn I marched toward the crest of the knoll.

As usual, WCCO came in loud and clear at 830 on the radio dial. I listened to an advertisement for Aunt Jemima Ready-to-Mix Pancake Flour. *"Just add milk and water,"* the southern lady said. *"So tender, so delicious, so easy to digest."*

Once the commercial was done, Mom's voice came through the speaker as she launched right into the *Beauty Banter* topic of the day—creating mysterious and beautiful eyes. I listened as she went on and on about mascara and how to put it on properly. She talked about eyebrow makeup and how dark colors like charcoal were all the rage. She even suggested that ladies put a dab of olive oil on each eyelid for crying out loud, and I had no idea how that could look pretty.

Finally, the show dwindled down toward the final message, and I leaned in with an ear almost touching the speaker. Her voice got quieter than usual as she thanked her audience for tuning in. Holding the code sheet in my left hand, I waited for the clever words that would wrap up today's show.

Then she said them and—*oh my God, they weren't even in code.* She just blurted the words, speaking to me like we were sitting at the kitchen table of our second-floor apartment on East Thirty-Seventh.

"Be careful, honey. He's out."

My heart started banging inside my chest like a jackhammer on the corner of Franklin and Blaisdell. I didn't need the decoder card to see the color red on the thermometer. Would he find me? Was he up here already? *What now?*

# Chapter 31

Every square inch of ground around Ham's house looked like the perfect hiding place for Mr. Wayne Borsthagen. The weeds, grass, and thorn-bushes had all grown waist-high. Wild grape vines had crawled all the way to the eaves and halfway up the roof. On top of that, several pieces of junk farm equipment lay scattered between the house and the gravel road. *Crap!* Any killer worth his salt could sneak right up in full daylight.

I ran to the machine shed looking for something that could cut down a jungle. What I wanted was some sort of motorized, self-propelled sickle-bar outfit. What I came back with was a scythe—a six-foot-long wooden handle attached to a curved knife blade as long as my leg. It looked exactly like the thing the grim reaper carried in my *Tales of the Crypt* comic books. I took a couple practice swings, then got to work.

Was it hard? You better believe it was hard—like pretending to be Tarzan without the muscles.

It took an hour and a half just to hack down a twenty-foot-wide perimeter around the house. I only stopped three times to sharpen the blade. It was amazing how much gumption I could muster when it came to saving my own skin from a monster.

At five o'clock, I called in the cows and switched to chores. That's when my brain started working overtime, too. My terror-soaked thoughts fell into two buckets.

1. How do I survive?
2. Will Mom be okay?

The notion of hopping a freight train or hitchhiking back to Minneapolis crossed my mind, but it was too late in the day. I pondered the pay phone at Lindoo Drug, but according to the time, Herman Schrapp was getting ready to lock the door and stroll down Main Street smoking a cigarette. Besides, I didn't know if I had enough money for a long-distance call anyway.

For the next half hour, I went back to swinging the scythe. Then I heard the clanks, rattles, and familiar *tick-tick-tick* of Ham's old Ford, and I ran to meet him.

"Where were you? I was worried."

He looked at my face, my sweaty shirt, the scythe in my hands, my swollen nose. His eyes scanned the freshly cleared ground and the places where all the wild grape vines had been chopped down.

"What's this all about?" he asked.

"Just a few precautions."

～

It was an hour past sunrise on the seventh of August when Ham and I walked into the Polk County Sheriff's Department office in Balsam Lake. (Mr. Gustafson had given me some time off to attend to what I had described as *family matters*.) Anyhow, there we were, squirming in hard wooden chairs in a windowless lobby, waiting for the sheriff.

"He should be arriving very shortly," said a thin, bespectacled woman at the reception desk.

A half hour later, the door opened to a jangling sound, and a tall, gray-haired figure ducked into the room. The sheriff was lean but bent. His face was deeply creased, and more so on the left side than the right. Everything about him seemed out of plumb. His grin. His shoulders. His nose. Even his belt hung at an angle from the weight of a holstered six-shooter that could have anchored a sailboat on Lake Minnetonka.

"Morning, Ham! Long time no see."

"Morning, Sven. I'd like you to meet my grand-nephew, Milo Egerson."

He smiled and reached out with an oversized hand that swallowed mine. I didn't smile back.

"What brings you two in this morning?"

"It's about the boy," said Ham. "He's in danger."

The sheriff studied my face for a moment before returning his attention to Ham. "I'm listening."

Ham looked at me. "You want to tell him?"

I scooted my chair up close. "You see this knife cut on my face?"

"Yes," said Sheriff Nelson.

"It's what put my stepfather into Stillwater Prison nine years ago."

"Go ahead," said the sheriff.

"My mother sent me to stay with Ham this summer for fear of what he would do when he got out. Turns out that he has just been released."

The sheriff looked out his office door to the lady behind the reception desk. "Marge, this is going to require coffee."

~

Before starting again, Sheriff Nelson asked one of his deputies to come in and take notes. Deputy Heddon was a chubby, chrome-domed guy with a scrunched-up face and a mustache. (Basically, a walrus in brown pants and a white shirt.) The deputy leaned over the top of a notebook, licked his pencil, and nodded back to the sheriff. Four mugs of coffee threw up steamy plumes from each corner of the big wooden desk.

Sheriff Nelson looked at me and smiled. "Start at the beginning, son."

I spilled it all, except for the coffee.

The story began with me talking about what little I knew about my real father. He was a tall, lean man with a freckled face, wavy brown hair, and a big, easy smile. I knew that part because Mom still had a picture of the two of them together on their wedding day in 1924. Dad worked at the big hydroplant on the Mississippi generating electricity for Northern States Power. According to my mom, it was a good job, and they were even planning on buying a house. In 1926 my brother, Tom, was born. That little baby brought joy to their lives. Mom had said those were the best days for her and Dad.

I looked around at the three men, all listening intently.

"What came next?" Sheriff Nelson asked.

"All the bad stuff," I said.

"Go ahead."

I looked in Uncle Hjalmar's blue eyes and he looked back at mine and nodded.

"Well, as you know, the depression hit."

The deputy nodded.

"Then in January of 1930, two other bad things happened. The first was Dad getting killed. A car skidded off the road on a snowy morning and hit him while he was walking to work."

"I remember that," said Ham.

I nodded and sniffed.

And the second bad thing?" asked Sheriff Nelson.

"I got born."

"Hey now!" said Ham. "There's nothing bad about a child being born."

"Well, it's when everything went south for Mom. Husband dead. Depression getting worse. No money coming in. Then on top of that, she had an extra mouth to feed—mine."

"Then what?" asked the sheriff.

"Well, with no job, no husband, and hardly any money, Mom got kicked out of her apartment on Franklin Avenue, and for a couple of months we just bounced from place to place. It was a scary time for Mom with two little boys and not knowing where to go each night. Then one day, just to get out of the cold, Mom stepped inside a shop on Thirty-Seventh Street, which turned out to be a beauty parlor for ladies. The woman who ran the place took pity on us and let us stay and warm up as long as we wanted. Mom got to talking to the lady about how she was looking for a place to live and also about how much she knew about fixing up hair and putting on makeup—lady things like that. Well, with a stroke of good luck for once, Mom got herself a job there and rented the apartment right above it, all on the very same day."

I looked at Ham, Sheriff Nelson, and the deputy. All three nodded for me to continue.

"For several years, we got by pretty good, right through the middle of the Great Depression. Tommy and I both started going to elementary school. We had plenty to eat and a warm place to sleep at night. But then Mom started seeing a man."

"The one who became your stepfather?" asked the sheriff.

"That's right. Now, it wasn't surprising that a man was interested in my mother. She was about the most beautiful woman in Minneapolis, after all. Men always tried to sweet-talk her, but she was good at brushing them off. The man who became my stepfather was different. He was a big, strong guy with dark hair, dark eyes, and all the rest. Do you know what Cary Grant looks like?"

"Yes," said Deputy Heddon.

"Mr. Wayne Borsthagen looked something like that, so you can imagine why Mom liked him. At first, Tom and I liked him too, because when he visited my mom, he would always bring us pieces of Bit-o-Honey candy. So, my stepfather had all these things going for him and a good job too, since he worked in one of the flour mills down by the Mississippi."

"Did they get married?"

"Yep, pretty quick too, and just like that there were four of us piled into that little apartment above the beauty shop on East Thirty-Seventh. That was in 1936. For about a year and a half, everything went pretty well. He slowed down on the Bit-o-Honey treats, but Mom still liked him. She would cook beef pot roast on Sundays. They went to movies and even dancing sometimes. Once Mr. Wayne Borsthagen even took us to a Minneapolis Millers baseball game."

"Why do you call him that?" asked the sheriff.

"Call him what?"

"Mister."

"Oh—Tommy learned that the hard way for both of us."

"How's that?"

"Tommy started calling him Daddy and it didn't turn out well."

"How do you mean?"

"Tommy got a slap across the face and was told, 'I ain't your daddy, you little shit. From now on I want you to call me Mister.'"

The sheriff nodded and Ham's eyes went wide. Deputy Heddon was scratching out notes at the speed of light.

"What happened next?" asked Sheriff Nelson.

I took a deep breath and continued. "Well—our happiness started washing away pretty quick. Then things really turned south when Mist . . . I mean Borsthagen lost his job. For a couple months he pounded the streets looking for work but kept coming up empty. I guess there just wasn't much need for unemployed flour mill workers in the depression, even for a man who looked like Cary Grant. He was in about his third month of being unemployed when it really started getting to him. He was especially bothered that now Mom was making all the money for the family, like he was just a bum or something. That's when he went off in a bad direction—actually, lots of bad directions—and all at the same time."

"What do you mean?"

"For one—he started hanging out at the flophouses and bars on Washington Avenue and drinking booze with what little money we had left. Then when the money ran out, he started borrowing from bad men he met at those bars. These were the kind of men who would threaten to hurt him if he didn't pay it back. Do you know what I'm talking about?"

All three men nodded slowly.

"Then his worst choice of all, he started working for those bad men."

More nods.

"When that last thing happened, Mom knew he was a goner. Borsthagen wasn't just working for crooks anymore. He *was* a crook. After a while, he turned into one of the men who did the hurting on people who couldn't pay back the money they borrowed. He broke people's legs and smashed their fingers. He got so used to beating people up every day that . . ." My voice was starting to break, and I was embarrassed.

"Go on," said Ham. He placed a hand on my shoulder.

"He started practicing at home."

I looked up at the ceiling and wiped a couple tears from my eyes. So much for being a tough guy from the alleys around Washburn High.

"Do you want a glass of water?" the sheriff asked.

"No thanks."

"Do you want to keep talking?" asked Ham.

I nodded and continued.

"Mom didn't know what to do," I said. "She thought about getting a divorce, but even that took money, and we didn't have any. She wanted to take me and Tom and move somewhere else, but we had no money for that either. Week after week, she was getting beat up worse and worse. In order to not get caught, Borsthagen only hit my mom in places where it wouldn't show, if you know what I mean."

I looked at the men around the table and all three heads nodded.

"Then things got really, really bad."

"What do you mean?" asked the sheriff.

"He threatened to kill her if she didn't keep quiet."

I clamped my eyes shut to keep them from leaking but it didn't work. The tears were running down my cheeks. I gave up trying to wipe them away.

"We pretended everything was normal and sometimes a few days would go by without anything really bad happening. Mom kept on working in the beauty shop because it was the only thing holding us together. My stepfather's drinking never ended. And the beatings? Well, as you can imagine, they never ended either."

Ham nodded.

"Eventually, Mom kicked him out and had the locks changed. It didn't stop him though. He'd just bust up the lock and get back to beating up

Mom again. One day, after my stepfather kicked in the door, Mom decided not to take it anymore and fought back. From the kitchen drawer she pulled out a long knife and held it out for protection, but even that wasn't enough to stop my stepfather. He threw a chair at her and got the knife away. Then, in about two blinks, he had that knife right under her chin and I was sure he was going to kill her this time. Well, Tommy wasn't home, so the only person who could do anything to stop Mom from getting killed was me. I was just a little kid, but I grabbed my stepfather's arm—the one that held the knife—and started screaming and crying to make him stop.

"Next thing I knew, I was tumbling backwards on the floor, and by the time I looked up again, Mr. Borsthagen was standing back from both of us, still holding that long-blade knife. I looked up at my mother, and she was looking at me, more scared than ever. My stepfather was looking at me too, but instead of raging with anger, his mouth was hanging open and his hands were trembling. I didn't know what happened until my face started stinging. I put my hand up to it and it came away all bloody.

"My stepfather threw the knife and ran out the front door. Mom called for an ambulance and wrapped my head in a water-soaked towel. Three days later I was back home with stitches all the way across my face.

"Borsthagen got arrested and put on trial because of that. For almost two whole days, my mother told the whole story to the judge and jury. She talked about trying to keep him locked out, but how he kept breaking in and beating her over and over again. I wasn't there for that part, but she said it was awful. Then when Borsthagen's attorney stood up to ask her questions, it got even worse. A lot worse. He twisted all the stories around and made it seem like everything was Mom's fault."

I paused there to let that important point sink in with Ham, Sheriff Nelson, and Deputy Heddon.

"Your mother's fault?" said Ham. "That don't make no sense."

"I know it doesn't," I said. "But according to Mom, that lawyer was so tricky and used so much fancy talk that he had the men of the jury all nodding and agreeing with him. She said that it felt like *she* was the one on trial, if you can believe that."

I paused again to let that last comment sink in again.

"Go on, Milo," said Sheriff Nelson. "What happened next?"

"That's when I climbed up on the witness stand."

Ham and Sheriff Nelson leaned in during this part of my story and all three cups of coffee went cold and untouched. I could tell that they were imagining the scene in that courtroom. "There I was, a little freckle-faced kid with a knife cut and stitches going all the way across his face looking scared and shivering like a baby bird. Just like any other little seven-year-old kid, I wasn't that smart. All I knew how to do was tell the exact truth and after that . . . Well, after that, all the fancy talk in the universe couldn't keep the jury from pegging him as guilty."

The sheriff held the tips of his index fingers together and spoke softly. "You were the key witness then, weren't you, son?"

"Yes, sir. That's what my mother told me."

"And how did your stepfather react when all of this was taking place?"

"He went off like a keg of dynamite. First his face turned bright red and then he started yelling like a crazy man. He kept screaming, 'He's lying! He's lying!' For a second, I thought he was going to jump right over the table and grab me by the throat."

"What did the judge do?" asked Ham.

"He told the bailiff to restrain my stepfather and take him out of the courtroom."

"And then?"

"It took three men to wrestle my stepfather to the floor. And before they had both legs and both arms, Mr. Wayne Borsthagen looked up at me and he mouthed two words without actually saying them. I don't think anybody else in the room caught those two words, but I did."

"What words were those, Milo?" asked the sheriff.

"*You're dead.*"

All three men froze up like they were statues made of ice. "Go on," said the sheriff.

"Well, like I said, he mouthed those words. Then he did it again, and just to make sure I got the message, he made a slashing motion with his finger across his throat—like this." With my index finger I made a pretend knife and brought it across my own throat.

Ham's head dropped forward, eyes to the floor. The sheriff nodded slowly and kept his eyes locked on mine. "And he was convicted?" said the sheriff.

"Yes, sir. Nine years at Stillwater."

"Anything else?"

"Just the birthday cards, sir."

Ham and Sheriff Nelson looked at each other. Deputy Heddon's pencil scratched nonstop.

"Birthday cards?" said Ham.

"Sometimes he sends me a card on my birthday. Not every year," I said. "But often enough."

"What do they say?"

"Oh, they don't say anything. No name, no words, no return address."

"No message at all?" asked Sheriff Nelson.

"Oh, there's a message, all right. Each card has a pencil sketch of the same thing."

"What's that?"

"A knife."

All three men looked at each other.

"Did you get a card like that this year, son?" asked the sheriff.

"No, sir. I was living with Ham during my birthday. The only card I got came from my mom. And besides . . ."

"Besides what?"

"Besides, I knew that this was the year he was fixing to deliver his birthday wishes in person."

Ham took a deep breath. "I wish you'd have told me these things sooner."

"I've spent nine years trying to forget."

# Chapter 32

The sheriff assured us that his department would do what they could. He asked Deputy Heddon to get a picture of Borsthagen from the Stillwater Prison so he could post it on the bulletin board. He also promised to have the deputies keep a close watch on Ham's farm as they traversed in and out of Balsam Lake on their patrols of Polk County.

To be honest, it sounded to me like damn near nothing. I know that I wasn't being fair, but in my mind I had visions of undercover officers setting up stakeouts and nonstop patrols circling Ham's property. What I really needed was an armed guard, but I knew that wasn't coming.

The bottom line was this: when it came to saving my skinny neck from Borsthagen's knife blade, Ham and I were mostly on our own.

Back out on the sidewalk after the meeting, Ham looked at me. "Let's go over to Twetten's."

"Twetten Hardware? What for?" I asked.

"Locks, hasps, angle iron, timbers, nails, and screws."

"Reinforcements for the house?"

"Yep. Did I forget anything?"

"How about a box of shells for the .30-30?"

We bought all the supplies on credit and loaded them in the back of Ham's Ford. After that, we both walked across the street to Lindoo Drug. Ham ordered a cup of coffee from Herman Schrapp. I moved to the pay phone in the corner and called a number that I had memorized since I was six years old.

The telephone jangled once, then it jangled again and again. *Come on, Mom. Answer.* At last it came—the prettiest voice that belonged to the prettiest lady that ever lived in Minneapolis or anywhere else. My knees almost buckled. Tears leaked out of the corners of my eyes and I mopped them up with my shirt sleeve.

Once we got past that telephone hug, it was time to ask some big questions. Yes, my stepfather was out of Stillwater Prison as of Monday afternoon. No, she hadn't seen him. Yes, she thought I was safe staying with Ham. No, I shouldn't come home to Minneapolis. Not yet, anyhow.

Just like that, my coins ran out and so did the telephone operator's patience. The phone shut off, and all that was left were a few static clicking sounds in my ear.

~

We worked all day Tuesday and most of Wednesday, me and Ham.

While I finished hacking down weeds with the scythe, he worked behind Bullet and Smoke to get all those rusting hulks of farm machinery dragged behind the barn. The goal was to open up our view of the farmstead so that nobody could sneak up on the house.

Our next task was to build an impenetrable barrier. Thirty fence posts around the house and a dozen loops of barbed wire all met up at a padlocked gate. To top it off, we rigged up a bunch of old-fashioned cow bells to work as an alarm system. Black Cat was part of the alarm system too, of course—our sentry at the top of the silo.

Once the yard work was done, Ham and I got busy reinforcing the house itself. Every first-floor window was fortified with steel bars. We reinforced both entry doors with planks until they were each three times the original thickness. The regular hinges were swapped out with heavy duty barn hinges forged out of seven-gauge steel. Double deadbolts were installed, and we even added one of those barricade bars like they used in some of the shoot-em-up cowboy movies.

The final addition was Ham's idea while we were taking an egg coffee break in the kitchen. His eyes were on the .30-30 standing up in the corner by the Monarch range.

"What's the use of the rifle if we've got no openings to shoot through?" he said.

"Beats me," I answered. "What did Davy Crockett do?"

"Gun ports!"

Using a hand auger and a keyhole saw, I cut rectangles out of Ham's four walls, one for each direction of the compass: north, south, east, and west. Each port was a couple feet wide and about five inches tall. I fixed them each up with a slide board too, so that they could be opened or closed in a jiff. For the final test, of course, I grabbed the .30-30 and poked it through one of the openings. My eyes squinted down on the sights, allowing my imagination to take over. There he was, Borsthagen, charging toward the house just like the maniac in *Wild Horse Phantom*.

~

Fortunately, my exhaustion was more powerful than my fear, and I slept straight through until Ham shook me awake at 5 a.m. Chores scared me a little, especially the part where I had to walk beyond the gate, cross the yard, and climb inside the silo.

After breakfast I was faced with another frightful task—leaving the farm and going to my job again after two days off. I started up Star-Chaser and rumbled down one of the wheel ruts, stopping at the end to look both ways. Every cornfield, every wood lot, every thicket seemed to have sprouted eyes and fangs.

The quickest way to Milltown was a left turn from the driveway. Turning left was what I always did. It was the obvious and sensible thing to do—the direct path. Smelling an ambush, I turned right with plans to zigzag after that. Left turn—right turn—left turn—right turn—right turn again and into the parking lot at Gustafson Tractor and Implement. I wasn't about to park Star-Chaser outside, neither. I hid her in the back corner of the set-up shop. My heart thumped like a big bass drum, and the rest of me tingled with numbness.

What I needed was a distraction, and there it was. The 1936 Oliver. Combined with egg coffee and Lucky Strike cigarettes, that old tractor would keep me from going plum crazy—or so I hoped. The near impossibility of reviving that burnt-up shell of a machine was enough to keep any mind from wandering. I rolled up my sleeves, located a set of wrenches, and dove in.

Guess what else distracted me on that Thursday back at work. Another atomic bomb. Yep—three days after the first one, President Truman made the almost identical announcement again. Another Japanese city destroyed—Nagasaki this time. Maybe I paused for ten seconds. Then I went back to packing grease into a wheel bearing.

~

For the rest of that week and most of the week following, I tiptoed around, trying my best to transform into the invisible man. Never once did I cross

Main Street. Not a single time did I gawk through the window at Stenlund Radio. I didn't buy groceries or walk inside Lindoo Drug. Hell, I never even dinged Melonhead's bell cord—and that was really saying something.

My life had transformed into a slow, boring waltz to the rhythm of a three-step beat.

*Chores-work-sleep—Chores-work-sleep—Chores-work-sleep.*

That was the dance that kept me going. I still listened to Mom's voice on WCCO but for a totally different reason than before, because the days of coded messages were over. What I wanted to hear now was the reassuring voice of my living, breathing, always-cheerful mom.

∿

By the time the third Friday in August came along, I was beginning to wonder if my fears had been overblown. Gosh—maybe nothing was going to happen. Maybe Mr. Wayne Borsthagen's threats had been just a puff of warm steam. Maybe he was content to be back roaming the streets of Minneapolis drinking beer at the bars on Washington Avenue again.

During the week, while my nerves had started to calm down about my stepfather, another thing happened. Japan surrendered. The atomic bombs had worked. There would be no bloody invasion. But the best part was that it meant Tom was coming home—and soon.

The end of the war meant the end of my duties at the Milltown Observation Post, of course, but Mr. Stenlund asked me to work one more Friday night shift.

"They haven't signed the surrender papers yet," he said. "We'd best guard the northern flank for another week."

∿

After evening chores I took another roundabout path to Milltown and ditched Star-Chaser behind some bushes at the school. I looked up and down the street before unlocking the door and walking inside. I made sure to lock the door again behind me.

Walking through those silent, dusky halls had always given me the creeps, but lately it was scarier than usual. Every open doorway could be a hiding place. Every turn in the hallway, an ambush. I tried to avoid making any sound, but in an echo chamber like Milltown Public School, that was damn-near impossible.

Inside the janitor's closet, the ladder was already in position, and the roof hatch partly open. I climbed through and crunched across the gravel. Mrs. Quigley's white curls showed up like a surrender flag above the sandbags.

"Hello, young man."

"Hello, Mrs. Quigley."

"Any sign of your stepfather?"

"You know about that?"

"This is a small community, young man. Everybody knows about that."

"We haven't seen any sign of him. Ham thinks he's just glad to be out of prison—thinks maybe he hopped a freight train to California."

Mrs. Quigley packed up her knitting and doddered over to the roof hatch where she disappeared down the ladder. I placed *Huckleberry Finn* on the chair in the observation post and slowly turned myself around, studying my surroundings in every direction. As you can probably imagine, I wasn't watching for enemy planes. My radar tonight would be fixed on one single target and nothing else—Borsthagen. Maybe Ham had him riding a boxcar to California, but I wasn't letting down my guard.

After a few minutes of looking up and down the village streets, it occurred to me that my stepfather might be doing the same thing. What if he had learned that Friday nights found me alone on the dark rooftop of Milltown Public School from seven until midnight? The notion chilled me enough that I decided to do something about it. For the next fifteen minutes, one sandbag at a time, I built a pile that must have weighed half a ton on the hatch cover that led to the ladder. Some people might have thought I was being paranoid. But some people had never met Mr. Wayne Borsthagen.

Not wanting to show my face anymore until after dusk, I hunkered down inside the remaining sandbags and cracked open *The Adventures of Huckleberry Finn*. I tapped out a Lucky, struck a match, and climbed aboard Huck's raft on the Mississippi.

It took a while, but darkness came, and when it did, I rose up from the seclusion of the bunker and walked to the edge of the roof to improve my view of Milltown's streets. They looked the same and they looked different. As always, voices and laughter bubbled up through the trees as folks enjoyed a summer evening with their friends. Just like every other Friday night, cars rolled slowly up and down Main Street under the bright glow of the electric lights.

But there was another part of the night that I was just noticing for the very first time—the dark shadows. Behind every fence, a long, black band. Same thing inside the nook of every doorway and along the back side of every house. Behind every bush, every tree, every parked car—a shadow. And with every slice of darkness, a hiding place.

I was observing things that had eluded my eyes before. A dog chained to a garage back door. A woman pulling clothes off a line in an unlit backyard, two kids smoking cigarettes beneath the low branches of a spruce tree.

At shortly after 10 p.m., the usual Nash Ambassador coupe showed up in that same dark place under the same maple tree behind the Milltown Public School football field. Ever since my ride with Rosalyn on the back of Star-Chaser, she wasn't an afterthought to me anymore. I had heard her laugh with joy. I'd felt her hands on my waist. I had been on the receiving end of her sweet smile. Did I like it that Rosalyn and Wingtip were steaming up the windshield of his daddy's Nash under the green glow of the dashboard light? Hell no, I didn't like it. But, at least for tonight, I had bigger things to fret about.

Through all of those three hours of darkness between nine o'clock and midnight, I kept my radar whirling at full power. My dials were tuned. My frequencies properly set. All of my observation skills were zeroed in on the same goal—finding a creep who resembled Cary Grant.

Midnight finally came, and with it, my written log entry read the same as every night before.

| Name | Date | Hours | Observations |
| --- | --- | --- | --- |
| Milo Egerson | August 17, 1945 | 7 p.m.–Midnight | None |

It took an extra fifteen minutes to unload all of the sandbags that I'd stacked on the roof hatch and put them back in their places on the observation bunker. Jeez—what a ballbuster. At last it was time to climb down the ladder and head back home for a few hours of shuteye before morning chores. I yanked open the roof hatch and dangled my legs into the opening before it hit me.

*Gaaaahh!*

The ladder.

It was gone.

# Chapter 33

I was trapped.

Jumping down meant stepping into an ambush. But if I didn't jump down, I was stuck on the roof, and Mr. Wayne Borsthagen had all night long to figure out how to climb up there and finish me off. I slammed shut the hatch cover and started throwing sandbags on top of it again.

Five minutes later I had the thing loaded with so much sand that King Kong couldn't have busted through. I stood back and considered the pile. My hands twitched. My whole body was soaked in sweat.

*What now! What now!*

I grabbed *Huck Finn* and made a dash for one corner of the roof, where I lay on my belly and looked down. Just as I had hoped, a long drainpipe led to the ground. I tossed the book down first, then gripped the drain pipe with one hand and swung my legs over. Any other day of my life, I'd have been chicken to wiggle off that high roof and shimmy down a rickety old pipe. But this was no ordinary day. Today, the question wasn't: *Can I do it?* The question was: *How fast?*

Crouched and leaning over Star-Chaser's handlebars, I blasted for home. From the machine shed I dashed across the yard and through the door, slamming it behind me. A glance at my watch—12:29. I threw both deadbolts and wedged in the barricade.

～

Sleep didn't overtake me until sometime past 3 a.m. and the next thing I knew, Ham was thumping me in the shoulder.

"Coffee's ready."

I shook my head, trying to loosen the rust. At the hand pump in the kitchen, I splashed my face with cold water before stumbling to a chair.

Ham slid a steaming mug under my nose. "Did something happen last night?"

I nodded and took a hot slurp. Then, for the next five minutes, I told the old man about the school roof and the ladder.

"But why would he take away the ladder?" Ham asked. "If he wanted to get you, all he had to do was wait for you to climb down."

I had no answer and was miffed at the old man for trying to put a lid on my fears. Ham hadn't been there. He hadn't seen what I saw. He hadn't felt what I felt.

After I gulped down three boiled eggs, two slices of bread, and another cup of coffee, Ham signaled me to follow him at the door. It took a couple minutes to unlock Fort Knox. Then, with Ham holding the .30-30 deer rifle across his chest, we legged it to the barn. Nothing happened. Everything seemed normal. But who really knew?

My first task was pitching silage. That's when fear grabbed my belt and held me firmly to the floor. The dark inside of that silo was the best hiding place on the whole farm—another trap—just like the school roof. Not only that, but I had left the pitchfork inside from the day before.

I took a minute to drum up some courage. The animals still needed to be fed, after all. Not knowing what else to do, I put a baseball-sized rock in my pocket and headed up. When I reached the opening, I fired the rock inside like a hand grenade and listened for any noise. *Clunk!* No other sound emerged. I popped my head inside. All clear.

All through morning chores Ham carried the .30-30. It was an odd feeling. A war zone kind of feeling. *Jeepers! What was next? Helmets and bayonets?* When the milking was done, I dragged the ten-gallon cans one at a time to the milk house, making sure to duck my head whenever passing a window. So far, so good.

Calf feeding came next. I took a moment to ponder that little guy I helped pull into the world because he wasn't so little anymore. The calf was 120 pounds by Ham's reckoning and only a week or two from outweighing me.

That was it for chores. Ham waited for me to get behind him so we could step outside together with the rifle and make our move. It was almost time when I heard Black Cat hollering from the top of the silo.

*Caw! Caw! Caw!—Caw! Caw!*

"We better be careful," I said.

He nodded and took a deep breath. Like a couple of soldiers, we pushed open the milk house door and scanned the yard.

*Caw!—Caw! Caw!*

Slowly we patrolled the whole perimeter of the barn, but we came back to the starting point with nothing. We scurried across the yard to the house, and I unlocked the kitchen door. When I glanced back at Ham, he was aiming the rifle.

*Boom!*

The .30-30 jolted hard into Ham's shoulder and he stumbled a little before finding his footing. I looked in the direction that he had fired but didn't see anything. Ham signaled me to go inside, and I backed through the kitchen door with the old man right behind. As soon as he was through, I shut it. *Clunk!* I threw both deadbolts. *Clack! Clack!* Ham grabbed the barricade bar and wedged it in place.

We both stood there gasping for breath and looking at each other. "What was that all about?" I asked. "Did you see him?"

"No."

"Why did you shoot, then?"

"If he is out there, I wanted to give him something to think about."

~

For two hours on that Saturday morning, I walked back and forth through the house like the caged bobcat in the Como Park Zoo. I tried reading the funnies in a stack of old newspapers but got bored. I cracked open *Huckleberry Finn* again but couldn't focus my brain. At last I yanked out my radio and battery from under the bed and dialed up WCCO and Cedric Adams. As usual, his friendly voice calmed me. First the weather report, then the farm markets, then news from around the world. President Truman had announced that it was just a matter of weeks and the Japanese would sign the formal surrender papers. I couldn't wait to see Tom.

Fed up with my own skittishness, I started to believe what Ham said about the ladder. Maybe I was just seeing ghosts.

"Do you reckon I could go to the movie house in Frederic?"

"I don't see why not, so long as you take the back roads and don't run into you know who."

I slathered two pieces of Wonder Bread with jelly and swallowed them down. Then, with Ham standing next to me holding the .30-30, I fired up the Briggs & Stratton, engaged the clutch, and took off slowly down one of the wheel ruts. I was just about to hit the gravel road and goose the throttle when I came upon Ham's beautiful cat. There was no mistaking the patchwork fur of white, brown, and black. Yep, it was Peacock alright—dead, in the middle of the road.

"Ham!" I yelled. "Come quick!"

I kneeled down next to the cat and ran my hand across her fur. Still warm. The most likely cause was that she'd been hit by a car, but I had my doubts. There was no blood, so I knew she hadn't been shot, bitten, or stabbed. Just then, I noticed a faint streak of oily dirt in Peacock's white fur. It wasn't just a random splotch either. The stain had a distinct shape—a man's bootheel sort of shape. When I lifted the limp body, I felt something else—the crunching of broken bones.

*That son of a bitch!*

The old man lay the .30-30 down on the gravel road and took Peacock into his arms. "Sweet mother of God," Ham whispered. He hugged the limp form and closed his wet eyes. The tears leaked out anyhow, running down his whiskered cheeks as he began to mourn the loss of his dear companion. I thought Ham's knees might buckle, so I put my arm around him to hold him up. For a long time we just stood there.

Slowly, like he was a hundred years old, Ham moved toward the house. I picked up the .30-30, lifted Star-Chaser out of the gravel, and followed. Just short of the door, a gust of anger hit me and I spun. I pressed the rifle butt against my shoulder and aimed it at the empty sky.

*Boom!*

The blast thundered through the fields and echoed off the distant woods.

~

I scrapped my plans to go to the movies and stuck around the house with Ham instead. We wrapped Peacock's body in a clean towel and placed her in a wooden crate that once held bottles of soda pop. After that, Ham slumped into a chair at the kitchen table while I dropped an egg and a scoop of coffee grounds into a pan and stirred them up.

The gentle *tap—tap—tap* at the kitchen window damn-near launched me through the ceiling. I grabbed the .30-30 and dove to the nearest gun port, shoving the barrel through the slot. My eyes searched for the shape of a monster gripping a six-inch blade. What I found instead were two small feet in moccasins.

*Raina Jackson.*

I went through the lengthy process of removing the locks, bars, and barricade to open the kitchen door and waved her in.

"How did you get through the barbed wire," I asked.

"The gate was open."

Raina walked in and looked at the box that held Peacock. She glanced at Ham, knelt down, and ran her hand across the cat's side. She sat down at the kitchen table next to Ham, and for a long time nobody spoke.

"I've got a bur oak if you'd like it," she said.

Ham nodded. "For up on the knoll?"

"Yes."

Up through the chest-high corn, we slowly walked toward the knoll. Ham led the way, cradling his dear cat in both arms. Raina followed carrying the sapling tree, while I brought up the rear, shouldering the shovel and the .30-30. From the pasture, the cows and horses all watched. Sunbeams warmed our shoulders and bounced flickers of light off the corn leaves. From the top of the silo, I heard a single *caw!* With the beating of wings, Black Cat swooped in and took her spot in the funeral procession, on Hjalmar's right shoulder.

~

That afternoon, Ham and I took another drive into Balsam Lake to see the sheriff. Just like last time, we had to sit around for a half hour before he clanked through the door and spotted us.

"This can't be good," he said, waving us into his office.

Ham's head was still hanging from the loss of Peacock.

"Something happen?" asked the sheriff.

"Somebody killed my cat," said Ham.

I told the story from there, explaining how Black Cat was making a ruckus from the top of the silo, and then I found Peacock on the gravel road. I made a big deal about the boot mark, too, and told the sheriff it would be just like my stepfather to kill somebody's pet for the fun of it. Then I went on to tell Sheriff Nelson about the ladder and the roof hatch at the Milltown Observation Post. There it was—proof positive. What more did he need to put every deputy on the case and sweep the entire county for the creep? I leaned back in my chair and waited for him to speak.

He took a deep breath and let it out slow. "That ain't much to go on, fellers."

I snapped to vertical. "What do you mean by that?"

"Dead cat in the road. Ladder moved during the night. That ain't much."

Now it was Ham's turn to straighten up and lock eyes with the sheriff. "Peacock wasn't hit by no car. I can tell you that. And that ladder to the school roof didn't move all by itself. You gonna help us or ain't you, Sheriff?"

Nelson paused and considered us both, switching his eyes from one to the other and back again. He dug a lump of tobacco out from under his lower lip and dropped it in a trash can behind his desk.

"Did you see anybody?"

"No," said Ham. "Didn't have to. The shape of his boot heel stomped into Peacock's white fur is as good as a fingerprint. What more do you want?"

Sheriff Nelson opened both palms to us and nodded. Then he rubbed his chin. "Maybe you two should move out of there for a few days. Head up to Duluth."

Ham snorted. "I've got animals to tend to, sheriff. You know that."

"Maybe the young man should catch the train back home to Minneapolis."

"No," I said. "That puts my mom in danger."

The sheriff nodded and made a squiggly line with his lower lip. "I reckon it's up to you two fellas to decide. In the meantime, I can double our patrols on the roads around your property and I'll send a man out this afternoon to search the place."

I looked to Ham for his reaction. He nodded slowly. "I guess that'll have to do. We can't expect you to camp out in my front yard."

~

A black-and-white car with a star on the side door showed up just as Ham and I were fixing to cross the wheel ruts for evening chores. The man introduced himself as Polk County Deputy Harding. He was a forty-something guy, built like a potato with basset-hound eyes—not exactly Dick Tracy.

The deputy followed us across the yard and into the barn. While we were milking and feeding animals, I noticed him snooping around the edges of the walls of the barn and sticking his nose in the milk house and tack room. He walked the edges of the garden too, searched the machine shed and even the outhouse.

"Find any clues?" I asked as we walked back in the direction of his car.

"No, but I'll drive by a couple times during my patrol tonight. If you see a pair of slow-moving taillights, it's probably me."

Ham reached out to shake his hand. "Thank you, Deputy. We'll take all the help we can get."

The deputy drove off. Ham and I entered through the gate of our barbed-wire fortress, and I made sure it was locked up tight this time. I did the same with the locks on the kitchen door and threw the barricade bar back in place. Salt pork, rutabagas, and green beans from the garden made up our supper, but it didn't have any flavor.

Just before nightfall, Ham and I took the .30-30 with us as we made one last trip to the barn to check on the animals. Ham released the cows to the pasture, but the calf was still in its pen, and the last remaining pig was happily buried in mud. Bullet and Smoke stood in their pens, and we tossed them each a fresh armful of hay and a scoop of oats.

As we stepped back outside, Black Cat flew down from the silo and landed on Ham's shoulder. She touched her bill to his ear before flying to the top of a maple tree. All was good and proper—secure for the night.

That's when I spotted what appeared to be a scrap of paper fluttering in the breeze right next to our barbed-wire fence. Normally, I wouldn't have noticed a tiny scrap of paper blown in by the wind. But today, given everything, I walked over and picked it up.

One side of the paper was white and waxy, like a candy wrapper. I turned it over and eyeballed a red-and-gold rectangle with blue letters at a diagonal.

*Bit-o-Honey.*

# Chapter 34

I decided not to show the candy wrapper to Ham because at least one of us had to get some sleep. By the light of the kerosene lantern in my bedroom, I looked it over closely and even sniffed the slippery waxed paper before setting it on the nightstand. It was fresh all right, still smelling of almonds and taffy.

Laying on my bed and staring up at the ceiling, about a million memories ran through my mind of that old apartment on Thirty-Seventh Street in Minneapolis. I heard outside sounds like honking horns, sirens, and snowplows. My memories included inside sounds too—a ticking clock, the jingle of the telephone, Bing Crosby singing on the radio. But they also included Mr. Wayne Borsthagen sounds—sounds that started with heavy feet on wooden steps, creaking floorboards, and Mom crying in the night.

Through the bedroom floor I heard a familiar *skree-clack* . . . *skree-clack* . . . of the pump handle in the kitchen as Ham got himself a drink of water. The old man's shuffling feet migrated into his room. The door thumped shut.

I got out of bed and walked to the window, lifting the sash to let in the cool night air. Along with the breeze, a chorus of crickets became the main show, singing to an audience of one through my open window. The scurrying of a mouse followed the edge of my bedroom and disappeared inside a wall. I thought about our beautiful cat, Peacock, and tried to wish her back. An owl cried from the distant woods. *Whoo-wh-whoo. . . whooo-whooo!* Next came a whip-poor-will with its sing-song voice. I fell back into bed and turned on my side, thinking about Huckleberry Finn. My breathing slowed, my eyelids dropped, and I drifted along the dark wooded banks of the Mississippi.

~

It must have worked. Somewhere, somehow, sometime during the night I must have fallen asleep, because I sure as hell remembered the moment I woke back up. The first thing was the sound—a crackling roar. Next came the smell—a rasp of smoke inside my nostrils. My eyes snapped open to bright-yellow light pouring in through the window.

*God!—No!*

I tumbled out of bed and crawled fast to the window. *Jesus!* Huge flames leaped out of a gaping hole in the barn roof. The orange tongues licked at the sky and a tornado of fire swirled around the silo. More flames reached out of the barn windows on each end of the loft. And then there were the sparks. Swarms of them in cahoots with the flames, spreading high above the barn roof.

I guess it was movement that snapped me out of my trance, because my attention shifted suddenly to the side door at the base of the barn. There he was: the son of a bitch—the bastard—the goddamn creep responsible for it all. I looked directly down upon his lanky form and that Hollywood face. Borsthagen just stood there in the light of Ham's burning barn, looking back at me. It was bad enough that my eyes were locked with the monster, but then it got worse. He smiled.

I jumped to my feet and made a dash for the stairs. "Fire, Ham! Fire, Ham!" I kept right on screaming as I blasted down the steps. "Fire, Ham! Wake up!"

"What? What?!" The old man trundled out of his room.

"The barn's on fire! I saw Borsthagen!" I shouted.

"Who?"

"My stepfather! He set the barn on fire!"

Together, Ham and I scrambled for the door. I got there first, yanking out the barricade bar and unlatching the deadbolts. We flew into the yard as the heat tried to hurl us back. I shaded my eyes with both hands. If ever there was a time when a guy needed a telephone, this was it. My mind spun through the options.

"Should I ride into town for help?"

No answer came from Ham, so I tried again.

"Should I run and get the neighbors?"

Still no answer.

"Should I start pumping water into buckets?"

Ham's eyes practically bulged from their sockets and remained locked on the orange flames.

I screamed in his ear. "Ham! Tell me what to do!"

"We've got to save the animals!"

I followed him to the gate and helped him unlock it. Then the old man took off at a wobbly trot across the yard. I didn't see my stepfather anymore but figured him to be right inside the barn door.

"Ham, it's a trap! Wait for the rifle!"

I dashed back inside the kitchen, grabbed the loaded .30-30 and a lantern, then sailed back out the door just in time to see Ham entering the barn. A river of black smoke poured out before the door closed behind him. Seconds later, I was through the same door, but the heat and smoke immediately knocked me to my knees.

"Ham! Where are you?!" I yelled.

No answer.

The panicked cries of horses pierced the darkness and I knew that Ham must have crawled their way. *Lordy*, the smoke was thick. It hung from the ceiling like an upside-down fog—like a special invitation from the devil. I moved along on hands and knees, sliding the rifle along with my right hand and holding the lantern out in front of me with my left. Without that lantern it would have been complete blackness. Did Ham know to stay low to the floor? Was he lost? Did the smoke get him? Did my stepfather slice the old man's throat?

I detected movement and stopped. "Ham, is that you?"

The human form lifted its head and lantern light reflected off a pair of eyes. I had hoped to see Ham's eyes, a soft blue. *Damn*—these were bolts of lightning. And those teeth—a monster's snarl in the center of that movie-star face. It was the same look I had seen nine years ago. The look that he had flashed at me from across the courtroom as they hauled him off to the Stillwater pen. His words came next and he hissed them like a snake.

"You ready to die now, boy?"

"Not today, asshole."

My stepfather recoiled slightly and his eyes narrowed further. "Ain't you learned yet to call me *Mister* . . . *boy?!*"

Without thinking, my mouth fired back. "Hey, *Mister* . . . Screw yourself!"

He lifted an object with his right hand, pressed a button, and—*Click!* A five-inch steel blade reflected, mirror-like, in the lantern light and got larger as Borsthagen crawled in my direction.

I don't remember thinking about it, but somewhere in that moment I clicked off the safety and pulled the trigger on the .30-30. My ears barely detected the blast, but my eyes watched the wooden corner of an animal pen explode into pieces. A cloud of dust and wood splinters momentarily blocked my view. When it cleared, Borsthagen and the knife were gone.

I scanned to the left and right. Hell, for all I knew, he had gone vertical. The notion hit me that wherever the creep was hiding, he now held the advantage. I couldn't see him, but he could see me. With that thought, I doused the lantern. *Shit!* Talk about scary. I was living *Webster's* definition of the word.

Once again, my ears heard the cries of horses. Where was Ham in all this? I took one crawling step in the direction of the horse pens. Then another. Suddenly, the whole world broke loose from above.

It started with the loud *crack* of a breaking timber and was followed by a thunderous *whoosh!* Through the collapse, I ducked my head and curled up into a ball, barely breathing through the crook in my elbow. When I opened my eyes, it wasn't dark anymore. I was alive and not even buried, but surrounded by fire.

It was the floor of the hayloft that had collapsed, of course, but by some sort of miracle the part directly above me had stayed intact. The end of the barn with the horse pens was now a heap of rubble and flame.

"Ham! Uncle Ham! Haammm!"

I coughed and gagged and coughed some more as I moved a short distance to where the two Belgians, Bullet and Smoke, should have been. It was the heat that pushed me back. Huge flames swirled all around and they appeared to be growing in strength. Ham was probably dead with the horses. And my stepfather? I didn't know. I made a fist with my right hand and realized that it didn't hold the .30-30 anymore. There was only one thing to do, and my brain yelled it to the rest of me.

*Get out!*

My only chance was to move away from the collapse, toward the cow stanchions, and find the door leading to the pasture. The other direction swirled with fire.

The path to the stanchions was choked with black smoke, but what choice did I have? I plunged back into inky darkness.

I coughed and hacked through it, instinctively dropping lower and lower to the floor until I was slithering on my belly. My fingers found what must have been the manure gutter, and I dropped into the trough. Even in that lowest of low places, the air was still unbreathable. On my belly, I slithered through the slime. *Keep going! Keep going!* I ordered myself as I held my breath the whole time.

All of a sudden, I heard what sounded like a weak, bleating call.

A calf. *My calf!*

I knew at that moment exactly where I lay and reached up blindly for the latch to his pen. The gate swung open and my hand found one of those little hooves again. He knew which way to run, all right, and the path led right over the top of me. On hands and knees, I followed right out the open door—like the calf was pulling *me* this time.

In lurching steps, I stumbled into the pasture before falling again. My crawling from that point carried me all the way out of the smoke and into clean air. A few yards more and—*flop*. That's as far as I got. Coughing, hacking, spitting, more coughing. I was out, but would I live or die?

I remember puking in the clover. That was all.

~

Over and over again, something cold smacked me hard in the face. Finally, my eyes popped open and focused on Sheriff Nelson. Another whack with a water-soaked rag brought me closer to a place between drowning and full consciousness. I heard the sheriff's voice.

"That's enough, Edgar. He's awake now."

The man he had called Edgar leaned in to study my face, and I studied him right back. He had dimpled cheeks, a big, round nose, and black soot all over everything. The only colors I could see were the blue of the man's eyes and the yellow stripes on his raincoat. Even his fireman's helmet was black.

I turned quickly to the sheriff. "Where's Ham?"

"We're still looking," said Sheriff Nelson.

I squirmed sideways and brought myself to my hands and knees. The fire still burned over a pile of rubble that no longer resembled a barn. In the pasture, all eight cows and a calf, but no horses. No Bullet, no Smoke, no pig even—and no Uncle Ham. I keeled back over on my side and cried like I was four years old.

# Chapter 35

The sun had risen by the time Sheriff Nelson set me down in his office chair and asked his secretary to place a long-distance telephone call to my mom. The sheriff spoke first, telling her everything that had just happened. The fire, Uncle Ham, my stepfather. After those first five minutes, it was my turn. As exhausted as I was, me and Mom talked for a long, long time—a half hour maybe; I don't know. She cried during parts of it, and so did I.

After that, Mom and the sheriff spoke again, and I listened as they decided what to do with me. If Borsthagen survived the fire, there was no telling what he would do next. Staying in Ham's farmhouse was out of the question, but moving back into Mom's apartment on Thirty-Seventh Street in Minneapolis might be even worse. It seemed that anywhere I went, I would be a sitting duck.

In the end it was decided that I would stay with Sheriff Nelson himself. He and his wife would move me into their own home.

That same morning, a whole bunch of other things happened. First, Mr. Hanson came over to Ham's farm and adopted all eight cows and my calf. Somehow they had room for them, even though it meant a ton of extra work until the Hjalmar Rehnquist estate got sorted out. Next, Sheriff Nelson and his wife moved me into the spare bedroom at their house in the Village of Balsam Lake. They had electric lights, an electric stove, a ceramic bathtub, and no mice.

Mrs. Nelson took care of me like I was a special guest. Good food, clean sheets, Ivory soap, *Movieland* magazines, and WCCO whenever I wanted it on a plugin radio. It was pure luxury, but I was so heartsick about Ham's death that I couldn't enjoy it. All during that time, we took precautions against *you-know-who*. The house doors and first-floor windows were kept locked at night, and every deputy was on special alert throughout the neighborhood.

For the next three days, I stuck like glue to Sheriff Nelson, splitting my time between his office and the passenger seat of his patrol car. One day we stopped at the blackened ruins of what was left of Ham's farm and watched as workers sifted through the ashes.

"Once they get through the rubble, these men will try to recover Ham's body," said the sheriff.

"Don't you think it was all burned up?" I asked.

"Could be. With luck they'll find something."

The sheriff then took me through Ham's house so I could gather my stuff. It was sad walking through and taking one last look at everything. The kitchen hutch, the hand pump, the wash basin, the Monarch Malleable range. From my old bedroom, I looked out at the silo, the field of chest-high corn, the cattail marsh, and the wooded knoll. I grabbed my battery-powered radio and kicked a mousetrap into a corner.

~

On Thursday morning, as soon as we walked in the side door at the Polk County Sheriff's Department, I knew something was up. The secretary drilled me and Sheriff Nelson with a look like she had the world's biggest secret. Deputy Heddon was waiting outside the sheriff's office, practically twitching.

"Is there something I should know about?" asked the sheriff.

"Yes, sir," said the deputy. "May I sit down?"

The sheriff signaled me and Deputy Heddon to a pair of wooden chairs, then settled in behind his desk. "Well . . . Let's hear it."

"The men from the fire department completed the search, sir."

"And?"

"The bones were badly burned but the search crew believes that some of them were human."

I snapped to attention and Sheriff Nelson leaned forward in his chair. "One or two sets of human remains?"

Deputy Heddon sat erect in his chair. "Hard to say, sir, but the men found more than just charred bones."

From his pocket, the deputy pulled the blackened remnants of a knife. Most of the handle material had been burned away, but the five-inch blade was intact. "It's one of those gangster switchblade knives, sir. Just like Milo described it."

"Is that the knife you saw, son?"

I studied it for two seconds. "Yes, sir. That's the one."

"And you say it was with the charred bones?" asked the sheriff.

"Yes, sir. We also found these near the knife." Deputy Heddon placed two belt buckles and a charred pocket watch on the table.

The sheriff studied both buckles, turning them over and over again in his hands. He handed them to me. "Do you recognize these things, Milo?"

"The large curved buckle belonged to Ham," I said. "I can't say anything about the square one."

I turned my attention to the watch case and recognized it right away. With my fingernail, I scraped through some of the soot on the warped lump of metal. There they were, the inscribed words I was looking for.

Dearest Wayne
Until the End of Time.
Hedda

I looked up at Sheriff Nelson, then over to Deputy Heddon and back to the sheriff. "This was a gift from my mother to my stepfather."

He didn't smile, but there was satisfaction on Sheriff Nelson's compressed lips. Slowly, he nodded his head. "This case is closed, son. You don't need to walk around on eggshells anymore. Your stepfather is dead."

It was like the whole world glowed two shades brighter. No more nights going to bed scared. All those years of worry washed away. At that moment, Mrs. Decker walked in with three steaming cups of coffee, placing them on the sheriff's desk. She touched my shoulder and smiled.

After the meeting and the coffee, I walked by myself to the public dock jutting out into Balsam Lake right next to the boat landing. For the first time in three weeks, I had no need to watch over my shoulder. No need to reach for a rifle. No need to look for an escape route. *My God!* It felt like a set of invisible shackles had been taken off my arms and legs. I could be a normal seventeen-year-old stumblebum again.

I kicked off my boots, placed my wallet and wristwatch on the end of the dock, and faced the shore. With my toes barely gripping to the last wooden plank, I bent my knees, swung my arms, and did a back flip into the clear, cool water.

～

Ham's funeral was scheduled for eleven o'clock on Saturday morning at the Lutheran Church in Milltown. I needed some nice clothes, so Mrs. Nelson drove me to Osceola, where a man in the Federated clothing store fixed me up with proper black pants, shoes, and a white shirt with a navy-blue tie. She paid the entire thirteen dollars and forty-three cents too, because with everything Ham and I had bought recently, my wallet was tapped dry. Mom showed up right on time at 9:18 at the Milltown Depot. She was the first person off the train, and even though Sheriff and Mrs. Nelson were standing right there with me, I ran to greet her and didn't care how many people watched us cry.

After hugging her for a long time, I finally blew my nose in my hanky and turned to introduce her to the Nelsons. Mom reached out to shake hands and dazzled them with her blue-as-a-blue-jay eyes. She was dressed in black for the funeral of course, but that didn't stop her from being beautiful.

Since we had an hour and a half before the funeral, Sheriff Nelson volunteered to take us on a little sightseeing tour of the area. He started by driving through downtown Milltown, where I jabbered about my job at Gustafson Tractor and Implement. While I was at it, I pointed out Camp Milltown and told Mom how the prisoners had helped me put in the garden next to Ham's barn. As long as my mouth had shifted to fourth gear, Sheriff Nelson slowed down and let me keep on talking about the other swell places in town. Stenlund Radio, Twetten Hardware, Bimbo Grocery, and, of course, Lindoo Drug. At that very moment, Herman Schrapp stepped out on the sidewalk wearing his white paper hat and wiping his hands on a towel.

"Hey, Herman!" I yelled out the open car window.

"Hey, Milo!" he yelled back, smiling.

Mom looked at me and smiled too. "A friend?"

"My best friend," I said.

Right on cue, Rosalyn stepped out the same door.

"Hey, Milo!" she shouted and flashed an electric smile.

"Hey, Rosalyn." I waved back.

"How did you get to be so popular in just three months?" asked Mom.

I shrugged. "Guess it was an accident."

"Well . . . that girl certainly has an eye for you." Mom smiled at Rosalyn and hers grew even brighter.

With the village of Milltown behind us, Sheriff Nelson drove us along a circular path through the countryside that skirted several lakes. He took us past Balsam Lake first, then Half Moon Lake, Bone Lake, and finally Big Butternut on the edge of Luck. We took a slow drive down Luck's Main Street and I talked about my races with the train that started at the Luck Depot. We drove right past the Northern Tavern, where I got pounded bloody for stealing two packs of cigarettes and later had to apologize. For those few seconds it took to roll by, I didn't say one word.

Sheriff Nelson's next stop was Ham's farm, and the mood grew somber. Silently, Mom stepped out of the car and gazed at what was left of the barn. She lifted a hand to her mouth and blinked a bunch of times.

After a minute, I touched her elbow. "Come on, Mom, I'll show you the house."

She nodded and followed. I showed her the water pump, the kerosene lamps, the bedroom where I stayed. Nothing, not even the Monarch Malleable, drew a comment out of her. Mom paused for a long time to study the photograph of Ham and Isabella in the old-fashioned metal frame. I told her about the baby, too, and explained where they were buried. All she could do was bow her head and nod.

As we stepped out the perfectly operating screen door onto the neatly cut yard, Sheriff Nelson and his wife were waiting for us with the car doors open.

"We should get going to the funeral," he said.

As I walked alongside Mom to the car, I heard Black Cat's call from the top of the silo. *Caw!—Caw!—Caw! Caw! Caw!—Caw! Caw!*

She was making a full-blown ruckus up there, and at first I thought it was just her way of saying hello to me again. Then I looked closer. Black Cat was hollering at something across the road. I followed the direction of her beak and eyes and noticed a movement of the tall grass beyond the sumac. *Must be a skunk or a raccoon,* I told myself. *Either that or a deer. Yep, probably a deer.*

~

The biggest gut punch of the summer was the funeral.

I guess it took the sight of Ham's closed casket surrounded by dozens and dozens of black-clad mourners before reality socked me hard. While the pastor spoke and other people delivered testimonials, my thoughts whirled slowly like storm clouds, and my hanky got good and soaked along the way.

*My God! He's really gone and he's never coming back.*

My insides ached for that dear old man. I wasn't the only one to feel it either. Mom leaned closer and closer to me in the pew until her head dropped onto my shoulder.

My eyes scanned the rest of the church and found Mr. and Mrs. Hanson with Betty sitting in the second pew. Mr. and Mrs. Torkelson were right beside them. A little further back, there was Mr. Gustafson, Mr. Stenlund, Mrs. Quigley, Sheriff Nelson, and his wife. Row after row of familiar faces—Mrs. Twetten with her upside-down basket-shaped hat, and the pharmacy man from Lindoo Drug rubbing his long chin. It took me a few seconds, but I recognized the bartender from Brask's Tavern sitting next to the bartender from the Northern. Herman Schrapp was there. So was Bill Schick from the Mobil station. There were at least fifty others who I didn't recognize, and most of them wore the hard-baked lines and tanned faces that spoke of farming.

It occurred to me, all of a sudden, that neither Grayburn Jackson nor Raina had come. *Jeez!* That bugged me at first, but the conundrum solved itself as my memories backtracked to how I had seen Indians treated over the years. I remembered some of my own spoken words insulting the Indians of South Minneapolis as I roamed the streets with my foul-mouthed friends. We called them "injuns" for one thing, and decorated the slur with words like stupid, drunken, and worthless. Sure, we knew they were American citizens. Sure, we knew they were here first. Sure, we knew they were human beings—but in our eyes, just barely. Imagine that coming from a bunch of lying, thieving crumbs like me and my so-called pals.

I shook my head, and a feeling of shame washed through me.

~

After the funeral service was over, everyone filed into the basement of the church, where a group of elderly women had prepared sandwich fixings, a relish tray, and a bowl of lime Jell-O with mini-marshmallows. Folks jawboned for an hour or so, and then everybody hit the road. The only ones left were me, Mom, Sheriff Nelson, and his wife, and we all went down the street to Lindoo Drug for ice cream. After that, Sheriff Nelson drove us to the Milltown Depot so my mother could catch the train back to Minneapolis.

When it was almost time, Mom put her hand on my shoulder. "Are you sure you don't want to come back with me this afternoon? You've only got two weeks until school starts again."

"I know, Mom, but there's a lot of work to wrap up at my job. I'm rebuilding an Oliver tractor."

"Yes, but I'm sure Mr. Gustafson would understand if you wanted to go home early. Are you sure?"

"It's okay, Mom. I'll come home in time for school."

Mom looked toward the sheriff and Mrs. Nelson. "And you're sure it's okay for Milo to stay here for a couple more weeks?"

Mrs. Nelson waved her off with a smile and a little flip of the hand. "He's perfectly welcome here." She shot me a wink. "And besides, he's proven to be an excellent gardener."

Mom sat up straight and spread her smile to the whole group. "Well, I guess it's settled then. Two weeks." She tapped her index finger on the table and leaned in toward me. "And after that, we just need to get Tom back through the front door."

~

We all stood around at the Milltown Depot until the southbound train to Minneapolis chugged in and the conductor shouted, "All aboard!"

I hugged Mom, and she hugged back, with both arms squeezing me like an anaconda. When she finally got on the train, she took a seat right by the window. As it rolled away, I waved until I was certain that she could no longer see me.

# Chapter 36

On Sunday I went to church with Sheriff Nelson and his wife because I couldn't come up with any excuses. It wasn't that bad, actually. I just put on my funeral clothes, kept my head down, and followed their every move. When they stood, I stood. When they pretended to sing, I pretended to sing. When they sat down—yep, you get the picture. Afterward, I asked permission to head off on Star-Chaser for the afternoon. What could they say? It wasn't like I had a killer after me or cows to milk anymore.

From the closet in my bedroom, I lifted the blue glass jar of ashes that had been given to me by the funeral man after they were done with the make-believe casket. Ham's entire burnt-up remains weighed less than Peacock. I tucked the jar inside my shirt just like I had with the stolen cigarettes two months back. Then I headed north out of the village of Balsam Lake.

∿

Our path through the corn toward the top of the wooded knoll was the same as we had taken with Peacock. The procession was similar too. I carried the shovel and Raina hugged the root bundle of a sapling white pine. It was Grayburn Jackson who carried the blue glass jar and its contents, walking slowly with Black Cat back on his shoulder.

Over our heads, a family of three-month-old barn swallows seemed intent on traveling with us, showing off their newfound skills at swooping and ninety-degree turns. Atop a fencepost, a meadowlark aimed her open mouth at the sky and filled it with song. I glanced down toward the marsh, where the family of sandhill cranes paused for a moment from spearing frogs as all seven stilt-legged giants posed like statues. Even the pasture, now empty of cows and horses, seemed to watch us climb the knoll. A warm breeze pushed across the tops of timothy and orchard grass bending their heads to a prairie rhythm. Along their edges, the orange daylilies simply bowed.

Grayburn held up his hand and stopped us near the very top of the knoll. He closed his eyes and hummed some sounds. I looked at Raina, but she couldn't see me because her eyes were on the trees and sky. Suddenly I noticed the birch leaves fluttering all around us—a million little waving hands.

The graves of Isabella, the baby, and Peacock were strewn like thrown dice and not in any kind of a row. I touched the shovel blade to a spot roughly in the middle of all three, glanced at Grayburn, and detected a nod. The digging went quick because Ham's remains were so small and I didn't hit any large rocks.

Grayburn handed me the jar, and for the first time, I noticed that he had knotted something like a slender tree root around the rim. I knelt alongside the hole, unscrewed the lid, and spread Ham's remains in the bottom, then stood back up. Next, Raina pulled out a bundle and unrolled it. It was that nifty blanket, the one woven from narrow strips of rabbit fur. She shook it out, knelt down and tucked the blanket over the top of the ashes in the bottom of the hole. She got back to her feet, and we stood together for another minute, but no words were spoken.

After shoveling the dirt back into the hole and tamping it down, I dug another hole a few feet away for Raina's tree. She loosened up the burlap around the roots and plopped it in. Together we filled in more loose dirt and pushed it in around the edges.

I figured it was time to leave, but Raina held up her hand, a signal for the three of us to wait. A gust of wind came up, taking me a little off guard. I looked at Raina and she never changed her expression. The gust kept coming, shaking my shirt and pants—Grayburn's too. It tossed Raina's dress and hair, but still she did not react.

Then, just as quick as it started, the gust ended, which Raina seemed to take as another signal. She knelt down and placed a small object over the top of the mound of soil, then stood and backed away. Focusing my eyes, I recognized the rounded agate that Mrs. Quigley had given me and that I had given to Raina. The bright sunlight shone right through it—a vanilla ice cream and caramel swirl.

*Manitou.*

~

Back outside the house, near the wheel ruts, Grayburn stood next to Ham's old Ford truck with the crow still perched on his left shoulder. "Are you sure you don't want to keep Black Cat?" he asked me. "She's pretty good company and probably wouldn't mind moving to the city."

"I can't," I said. "Mom would kill me if I showed up with a crow. Besides, look at her. She's ready to move back with you now."

Grayburn scrunched up his bottom lip and shot me a sort of half smile, half shrug.

"Would you like to come inside the house?" I asked. "I don't have any Chippewa Tea but could fix you up some coffee."

Grayburn looked at Raina then back at me. "Maybe some water," he said.

I led the way through the unlocked door and pulled three glasses off the shelf. I grabbed the pump handle and was just getting ready to work it when I froze. There in the basin was a single glass that hadn't been there yesterday. It didn't mean anything, of course. Could have been anybody. Probably Mr. Hanson or Deputy Heddon just stopping to check on things. I shook it off and got back to pumping three clean glasses full of cold water. We drank them in silence and headed back out the door.

With Raina working the choke and throttle and me turning the crank, Ham's green Ford truck roared back to life, and the three of us, plus Black Cat, piled inside. A half hour later, we were surrounded by sand, jack pines, and the familiar sight of Grayburn's patched-together home.

Grayburn got out with Black Cat on his shoulder, and I realized that nobody in the world had a more genuine smile. "I hope you will remember us after you move back to the big city," he said.

"There's no way I could ever forget."

*Caw!*

"No, I won't forget you either, Black Cat."

Grayburn's smile glowed even brighter. "Come back and see us sometime. Minneapolis isn't that far away."

"Sure." I shrugged.

The old man nodded and walked up his front stoop. Raina silently followed him until I stopped her.

"Raina, can I talk to you for a few minutes?"

She turned to face me, and we both waited until Grayburn had disappeared through his front door.

"I need your help with something."

"What?" she asked.

"Something I want you to teach me."

"Len's the teacher," she said. "Not me."

"This isn't about fighting."

Like a timid deer, Raina Jackson took a step in my direction, then stopped. "What is it then?"

"I want to learn how to trap an animal."

～

I was headed back to Balsam Lake, but it wasn't in a straight line, since I had to swap out the truck for Star-Chaser at Ham's farm. I still felt queasy in my gut after finding the extra water glass in the basin. I could have been a scared chicken and zipped fast to Sheriff Nelson's house. Instead, I swallowed hard and walked toward the silo.

The cement sides were charred black and the wooden roof was burned off, but it otherwise appeared to be okay. I climbed a few steel-ladder rungs and looked inside. Just as I thought—empty. From the silo I strolled down to the garden and was saddened that the heat and smoke had killed most of the plants. A few cucumbers and green beans had survived on the outside edge, but they didn't amount to much and weren't worth canning. My next stop was the pasture, then the cornfield. My mind spun to questions around who owned the property now and who was going to manage the harvest.

My eyes scanned the horizon for movement as I walked to the shed. It looked the same as ever, and I rolled Star-Chaser out before sliding shut the door. The house still appeared to be untouched, but a knot swelled up in my stomach as I crept inside and wandered from room to room. Back in the kitchen, the only thing on the table was the brochure that Ham had been studying intently in the days before his death. I picked it up:

Public Lecture
AGRICULTURE AND LAND CONSERVATION
Eau Claire State Teachers College
Eau Claire, Wisconsin
Thursday, August 30, 1945, at 7:00 p.m.

My recollection returned of Ham sitting at the kitchen table studying and studying that brochure. I had watched him as he turned it over and over in his hands, reading every word more than once. Whatever that professor from Madison was planning to say, Uncle Ham sure as heck wanted to hear it. Even though Eau Claire was an hour and a half away, he had his heart set on going, and the only thing that might have stopped him was me and my rotten stepfather.

My index finger traced each line as I read through the brochure. *Land Ethic? . . . Thinking Like a Mountain? . . .* What the heck?

I pocketed the paper and almost took a step toward the screen door when I paused and focused my eyes on the basin beneath the pump spigot. There should have been four glasses.

*Jesus—Mary—Joseph!*

Now, there were five.

# Chapter 37

I flew to Balsam Lake, ditched Star-Chaser in the garage, and scrambled up the porch steps just in time to earn a scowl from Mrs. Nelson. Supper had just ended. Her lips were clamped tighter than a vice as she glanced at the clock and walked past me with her hands full of dirty dishes.

"Sorry I'm late," I said.

Sheriff Nelson winked at me and nodded at a chair for me to sit on. "You've had a full day. I'll give you a pass this time. Help yourself to the meatloaf. It's still warm."

I did as I was told and dug in. When Mrs. Nelson came back to the table, she had dialed herself back from boil to simmer and even poured me a glass of milk. "Do you want to tell us about your day?" she asked.

"I visited some friends," I said.

It sounded like a phony answer, and I guess it actually was. I didn't want to tell her the truth about the improper burial. That was a private thing. Part of me wanted to talk to the sheriff about the things I had seen at Ham's house. You know—the movement in the grass, the drinking glasses not adding up. Something kept my mouth clamped shut.

After supper that evening, I stayed inside. And no, I wasn't scared— a guy gets tuckered once in a while, you know. For three whole hours, from seven to ten, I sat in a chair and listened to comedy and radio drama programs on the Nelsons' RCA radio. I was also hoping Cedric Adams might have something to say about when our soldiers in the Pacific were coming home. He talked about the end of the war and about something called "V-J Day" coming up on September 2. All that and more, but not a word about ordinary infantrymen like my brother, Tom.

~

The next morning was a Monday, and I found myself taking a roundabout path to Gustafson Tractor and Implement. I parked Star-Chaser inside the shop and got to work on the Oliver again. For almost four hours, the challenge of fixing that burnt-up wreck kept me going. I was getting ready to head out the door just past noon when Mr. Gustafson stepped into the shop.

"Two more weeks? Is that right, Milo?"

"Yes, sir," I said. "That's when classes start up again at Washburn High."

He gave me a light punch in the shoulder. "We're going to miss you around here, son. You've done a fine job."

I smiled at the compliment.

Mr. Gustafson shifted his attention to the tractor I was working on. "Looks like it's coming along," he said. "Do you think she'll run again?"

"Absolutely!"

He smiled again and nodded. "Good work." He turned and started walking away.

Just then I remembered something. "Um . . . Mr. Gustafson? Do you have time for a question?"

He spun around. "Certainly."

"I've been wondering about that field of corn that we planted on Ham's land. What's going to happen to it? In a month or so, should we be cutting it for silage? It would be a shame to let it go to waste."

Mr. Gustafson looked sideways and toward the ceiling. "That's a good question." He walked back over to me again. "I think that's a question for the people who are managing Ham's estate."

"Who's that?"

"Don't know exactly. Give me a couple days and I'll find out what's going on with his land and other assets. I'm pretty sure the bank is involved, so I'll start there."

~

The smart and proper thing to do after my shift at Gustafson Tractor and Implement would have been to make a beeline to Balsam Lake. Mrs. Nelson probably had a delicious meal waiting for me at her kitchen table— bologna sandwich, bowl of soup, maybe a pickle.

On that particular day, I was neither smart nor proper. On top of that, I still needed to do something about my recent encounters with ghosts. Instead of pointing Star-Chaser south on Highway 46, toward Balsam Lake, I took off in exactly the opposite direction.

~

As I approached the weathered barn, red brick silo, and white house at the Zilstrom farm, I noticed corn a foot taller than the top of my head—a perfect crop. I parked Star-Chaser in the far corner of the field and simply walked between rows. Once I had reached the Bear's front yard, it was just a matter of waiting him out until I could manage a private chat with Gilbert. Two rows deep in the corn, I kicked aside a dirt clod and sat on my ass, fifty feet from the front door.

For a half hour—nothing. Then another half hour came and went. Finally, I heard a screen door slap from the opposite side of the house followed by what must have been a full two minutes of a man yelling like a maniac.

*Poor Gilbert.*

The screen door slapped again, and this time I watched as the Bear strutted toward the milk house end of the barn and disappeared inside. I made my move to the front porch and listened as dishes clanked and clattered from an unseen kitchen. I knocked three times and everything went silent. The next thing I noticed were two eyeballs peeking around a corner. They were as big and white as peeled potatoes.

"Wh-wh-what you doing here?" he asked, popping all the way into open view.

I couldn't answer, as I just stood there in stunned silence. Gilbert's face was a wreck. His purple ear was better but those two black eyes were back, and worse than ever.

"I got this too," he said. As he held up his right fist, I could see that three knuckles were scraped up pretty bad.

"Holy piss, Gilbert! You punched him back?"

"D-d-damn right!"

Now I was the one crouching to look through the window.

"Wh-wh-what you doing here?"

"I need to borrow a gun. Do you have a deer rifle? The .30-30 got burned up in the fire."

"Pa does, in his closet. Whatcha need it for?"

"Somebody's been snooping around at Ham's place. It's driving me crazy. I need to flush him out."

"But I thought your stepfather died in the fire."

"That's what the sheriff and Deputy Heddon said. Maybe I'm starting to believe in ghosts. Either way, I'm sick of hiding."

Gilbert leaned in, eager to help. "But I don't know where to find the b-b-bullets."

"That's okay, Gilbert. I just need to carry the gun. Scaring the guy is the main thing."

"Wait here." Gilbert dashed up the wooden steps and returned with a monster of a gun that must have been five feet long. I operated the bolt action and tried carrying it over my shoulder by the leather sling.

"This will be perfect," I said.

"It's an Enfield. First W-W-World War."

"Thanks," I said. "I'll bring it back tomorrow. Look for it inside your first row of corn."

He nodded.

I nodded back and scrammed.

~

I rode up one of the wheel ruts of Ham's driveway with the Enfield strapped over my shoulder like my own personal cannon and parked Star-Chaser inside the machine shed.

It was time to search the property, and the most important thing was to look tough and dangerous. Ghost or human—whatever was out there didn't need to know that I was toting an empty rifle. I worked up a sneer and held the Enfield at forty-five degrees across my chest, then marched forward to the house to get the scariest part over first.

How many water glasses would I find in the kitchen basin? That was my very first question. The last time through, there had been five. Would I find six? Seven? And what else might *somebody* have moved around?

I let the screen door close behind me with neither a twang nor a slap. Then, in one smooth and fast move, I entered the kitchen and scanned my surroundings. Everything appeared the same as yesterday. I touched the coffee pot and the Monarch Malleable—both cold. I took inventory of the cupboard doors—all closed. It was time to check the basin under the pump spigot. One—two—three—four—five glasses. Same as last time. My pulse dropped a little bit as I moved on to the living room. Nothing had changed. I explored every inch of Ham's bedroom, including the closet and under the bed. It was time for the creaky stairs and an assault on my old bedroom on the second floor. My heart hammered hard as each wooden step squealed, groaned, or squawked. I sprang through the door into what could well have been an ambush. Nothing.

Upon leaving the house, my nerves started to settle back down. The barn was gone of course, and with it a million hiding places. The bushes and tall grass had been scythed flat. Another ten-thousand hiding spots gone. In the end, I walked the perimeter of the roadside ditch and what was left of the garden before popping my head into the empty silo. From there I inspected the fence lines that bordered the cornfield and pasture. I even conducted a surprise attack on the outhouse. Nothing—not even any fresh smells.

That was it, I had conducted my own assault on my imagined enemy and prevailed. No ghost, no criminal, no hobo off the railroad tracks lurking around on Ham's homestead. If I had a rubber stamp that declared ALL CLEAR, I would have used it. As it was, I sniffed with satisfaction, shouldered the Enfield, and made my way back to Star-Chaser in the machine shed.

I was fixing to wrap two turns of the rope around the flywheel when I spotted it. A tiny object no bigger than the end of my thumb resting on Star-Chaser's leather seat. It was a rectangle. A tiny box-shape. A man-made thing with red and yellow colors mixed together with blue letters.

*Bit-o-Honey!*

# Chapter 38

I barely slept.

Mrs. Nelson glared at me over the kitchen table. Coming home at half-past eleven without any explanation hadn't sat well with her. If I had been out drinking beer or just carousing with friends, I'd have admitted it and begged for forgiveness. There was no way in hell I could explain where I had really gone after finding the Bit-o-Honey candy. It was something I had to do. Something I had to do by myself.

Mrs. Nelson cracked six eggs into a bowl like she was mad at them. She stirred them up with some milk and salt and pepper and dumped the works in a frying pan. The eggs cooked slowly and that gave her another half minute to drill me with her eyes. Looking for a distraction, I got busy setting the table and making toast. Sheriff Nelson walked into the kitchen, kissed his wife, and then joined in on the assault.

"As long as you're a guest in this house, we expect you to act like one," he said.

I nodded.

"If you're going to skip meals and stay out late, we expect a phone call next time."

"Sorry."

The sheriff sat and buttered a piece of toast. The only sound was the ticking of the wall clock and the scraping of a spatula against a cast-iron frying pan. I stared at the steam swirling off my coffee.

~

Work dragged all morning, and I was not getting much done. Every crank on a wrench, every turn of a screwdriver gave me a reason to pause and think. The storm inside my head swirled and swirled. Nine o'clock . . . ten o'clock . . . eleven o'clock . . . noon. I filled out my time card and pushed Star-Chaser out the door.

Just like yesterday, Mrs. Nelson probably had a sandwich waiting for me on the kitchen table. My stomach couldn't have taken it anyhow. With two turns of the rope around the flywheel, I brought Star-Chaser to life and took off slowly to Ham's farm, but not on the back roads. Not this time.

Up the left wheel rut and over to the front of the machine shed I rode. Leaning Star-Chaser against the shed with the engine still running, my eyes darted and I swallowed hard. The door slid open with a clatter and I stuck my head inside. Nobody home—so far so good. Ham's bamboo fishing pole and wicker creel stood in the corner and I grabbed them. The bait can would stay in the shed. I didn't need it and do you want to know why?

Because I was the bait. That's why.

After strapping the pole and creel to Star-Chaser, I lowered my goggles, motored to the center of the yard, and stopped. From whatever rathole or brush pile the creep was watching, I wanted him to get a good look. No gun. Nobody with me. Just a high school kid going fishing—all by himself. The clutch engaged, the rear wheel gained traction, and I motored down to the end of the driveway and turned north on the gravel road, driving slow.

Two more turns and I was on Highway 35, still northbound. Minutes later I was rolling through the village of Luck. Not too fast. Just slow and steady. Past the Northern, the West Hotel, and the Danish Brotherhood Star-Chaser chugged right along. A little more throttle at the edge of town and, finally, back up to almost highway speed.

I suppose you're wondering whether or not I looked back to see if he was behind me. Hell no, I didn't look back. No sense looking back. I probably couldn't have seen him anyhow. But, I could sure as hell feel him.

Onward Star-Chaser chugged with her engine at half throttle. A familiar white barn. Green fence lines still smattered with orange daylilies. I rumbled past the spot where the railroad tracks passed under the highway. My right turn on the County Road was coming up. A hand signal. A slow turn. Wouldn't want anybody behind me to miss it.

It was just five more miles through the fields and pastures with patches of woods. Then three more miles. Then one. I parked Star-Chaser right on the gravel shoulder. No sense hiding her on this particular fishing trip.

Grabbing the pole and creel, I scrambled down the embankment and got in the water without even kicking off my shoes. Just like the last time

I had visited McKenzie Creek, I would work my way upstream. It took some grit, but the plan was to walk a few steps and then wait. With an empty hook and cork bobber and my back to the road, I made casts here and there.

The stream babbled between my legs. A woodpecker hammered at a distant tree, and a chickadee sang *dee-dee-dee* as it bumped around the base of another. The next thing I heard was a blue jay screaming from somewhere. My ears practically stretched away from my head, they were trying so hard to listen.

The telltale sound finally came with the crunching of car tires on gravel. As expected, it rolled on by—real slow. He was onto me. That's all I needed to know. Sloshing against the current, my shaky legs carried me further upstream.

Around one bend, then another, and another, I kept a sliver of space between me and that murdering bastard. From a hiding place behind a clump of bushes, I waited again for him to come closer. Just like me, he was walking in the shallow water. With a glance, I caught sight of the pale skin of a face that for nine years had been stuck behind steel bars and cement walls.

As I continued to walk against the current, I casted here and there, trying to keep up the act. Maybe he could see me through the brush. Maybe he couldn't. Either way, the mud that I stirred up flowed in his direction— a perfect trail for any killer to follow. I could almost hear his snarling breath. My knees were really quivering now, and it wasn't from the cold water. The bamboo pole in my hands shook like a wind-whipped reed.

*Splash . . . splish . . . sploosh . . . splash.*

As I forged ahead, the hairs on my neck strained. I stumbled over submerged branches and ducked the overhanging ones. Suddenly, I stepped in a hole that sunk me up to my waist and at the same time got the fishing line snagged on an overhanging bush. I tried to pull myself out of the hole but my left foot was stuck in shin-deep muck. I glanced back and caught the flash of sunlight off metal.

*Son of a bitch!*

I flopped forward in the water and reached out for a clump of branches. Working every cord of muscle in my stomach, shoulders, and both legs, I yanked myself forward and into the shallows. My lungs gasped for air. My heart banged away like a machine gun.

A minute passed as I sloshed ahead some more. I glanced back and saw nothing. One more bend and there it was—the beaver dam. I clambered out of the water and into the wall of brambles and thorns. Holding the bamboo pole with one hand and shielding my face with the other, I pushed through until, at last, I reached one end of the beaver dam and took a wobbling step on top.

The tangle of mud and sticks made for herky-jerk walking as I crept along the top of the dam's curved wall. At last, I reached the center, where water spilled over the top. I had made it. The bait was in place. The trap was set. All I needed now was the rabbit.

Fishing pole in hand, I sat, Huck Finn style, atop the dam facing a lovely blue pond on the upstream side. I would not look back. I mustn't. It was just me, the wicker creel, and my bamboo pole. No gun. No escape route. No cop within miles and miles.

Just like before, I couldn't hear him wading slowly toward me. But just like on the highway, I knew he was there. I could see him through the back of my head—the eyes, the teeth, the snarl. He moved slowly, silently, all sound covered up by the gurgling of McKenzie Creek water spilling over the low point in the dam. And then there was the knife, of course—long, thin, brand new, and razor sharp.

All that remained was the waiting. If it worked, it worked. If not—oh well, nobody lives forever.

I waited . . . and waited . . . and waited . . . and waited.

And then . . .

It worked.

Had Borsthagen been paying attention to his surroundings instead of the bait, he may have seen the wires and triggers just beneath the water's surface. Had he been alert to anything besides my skinny neck, he might have noticed two young birch trees, bent over and ready to spring.

The first sounds were the *whoosh—whoosh* of those two young trees springing up and pulling hard against the snare wires. After that? A whole lot of yelling, swearing, and splashing followed. I probably would have smiled but there was still work to do. I spun around and faced him.

He thrashed wildly and flashed his teeth like a lassoed shark. The two birches on either side of the creek shook and rattled but held firm. The wires that had been sprung angled down from the tops of the trees and into the water, where the submerged slipknots remained attached to both legs. In his panic to escape the trap, Borsthagen kept falling, standing, and falling again. He reached underwater with the knife, trying to cut through the steel-core rope.

Given enough time, it was possible that my stepfather could have figured out a way to loosen the steel wire that bound his legs and kept him trapped and floundering in the water. I had expected this and had prepared for it. I grabbed Ham's fence tightener with both hands on the upstream side of the beaver dam. It only took a couple seconds to familiarize myself again with the two sets of steel jaws, ratchet bar, and lever handle. In addition to the snare trap wires attached to the saplings, I had set the trap with a third wire, which I'd fished right through the mud and sticks of the beaver dam and fastened to a submerged log. All I had to do was work the ratchet handle.

As you can imagine, this third wire attached to the others had the effect of pulling the loops in the snare trap tighter than ever to make sure that the captured animal couldn't escape no matter what. The other advantage of the third wire was that it ratcheted that creep closer and closer to the dam.

I knew the leeches had found him when Borsthagen's voice switched from yelling to high-pitched shrieks. His wild writhing just made things worse for him as the snares got tighter and tighter, and at one point he even lost his grip on the knife. The screaming eventually died down and was followed by five minutes of whimpering like a whipped dog. Gosh— for a second there I almost felt sorry for him.

Almost.

# Chapter 39

With the ride into Frederic and the telephone call and everything, it took an hour before Sheriff Nelson and his deputies could get there to take possession of Mr. Wayne Borsthagen.

The leeches hadn't killed him, but they'd tamed him plenty. Yep—my stepfather was one limp noodle, and noodle colored, too, by the time the deputies hauled him back through McKenzie Creek and into the back seat of the cop car. From there, they transported him to Frederic Hospital. Two days later and he was in the Polk County Jail, where Deputy Heddon reported that the prisoner had a new problem. Some sort of itch—poor guy.

Sheriff Nelson told me that Borsthagen would be sent off to the Wisconsin State Prison in Waupun this time. He showed me a picture of the place—gray stone walls, steel bars, a guard tower at each corner. It was perfect for him.

I went to bed that night thinking about rabbit snares, Chippewa tea, and the words of one swell Indian girl named Raina Jackson.

*Some animals are best trapped.*

~

I slept in late the next day. Hell—who wouldn't have?

Reckon it was half-past eight when Sheriff Nelson shook me awake and told me about my mom coming up on the morning train.

"Is she fixing to take me back home?" I asked.

"Don't know. Maybe. You and your mother have been asked to attend a meeting at the bank at one o'clock. I know that much."

~

Mom met me at the Milltown Depot with a hug that seemed to last about three hours. Neither one of us wanted to be the first to let go.

"Thank God you're all right—honey," said my mom, over and over.

"Thank God you're here with me," I answered back.

It was a piece of paper in Mom's hand that finally caught my attention after we unhugged. I had seen the words "Western Union" on the top center and, right away, they got me scared. Western Union telegrams were famous for bad news. It was how families from the war learned of their dead sons and brothers. Mom caught the look of fear in my eyes.

"No. It's *good* news, Milo. Tommy's coming home by the end of September."

My brain spun like a top and I'm pretty sure that my body did too. An outbreak of pure joy suddenly infected me, and I felt myself glowing like an arc welder. Mom, for her part, just stood there with a big smile on her face. It was no ordinary smile. It wasn't even a Rita Hayworth smile. It was a Hedda Egerson, thank-God-my-life's-getting-back-to-normal kind of smile, and it was brighter than the sun.

Of course, the news about Tom needed celebrating, and I knew just the place. Mom threw her purse strap over her shoulder and grabbed my elbow. Together, we walked straight down Main past the hotel, the Co-op station, Brask's Tavern, and Stenlund Radio to the ice cream counter at Lindoo Drug.

~

The meeting at the bank was in a fancy room where all the chairs had leather seats and the walls were covered with wood panels. The varnished table that filled up most of the room was so thick that it probably weighed two tons. Even the light fixture hanging from the ceiling was a fancy outfit—cut glass or some such.

A gray-haired man with a curled mustache walked into the room, all fancy looking, with creases in his gray pants so sharp they could have sliced aged cheddar. The guy had a gold watch chain dangling from his pocket and cuff links that sparkled like real diamonds.

"Hello, folks. I'm Burt Engerbritsen with the bank." He shook my hand, then Mom's. "I'm so sorry about Hjalmar's passing."

Mom nodded politely. My eyes kept flashing back to the cuff links.

When our eyes met again, Engerbritsen was looking me up and down like he was trying to square up my gangly body and the scar on my face with the story of what happened on McKenzie Creek. A look of disbelief washed over his pink face. His eyebrows popped and his lips tightened.

We heard voices in the hall, and moments later, two more men walked into the room, Mr. Gustafson and another fellow decked out in a brown, vested suit with a white shirt and dark-blue tie. Turns out, he was some kind of lawyer. Mr. Gustafson shot me a wink, then stepped across the room to offer a greeting and handshake to my mom. The brown-suit guy didn't move. He just looked me over, same as Engerbritsen had, like I was the scrawny barn cat that had just beat the hell out of a Rottweiler.

"You did a remarkable thing yesterday," said the lawyer.

I looked at the oak wall, the light fixture, and finally the floor. Mr. Gustafson gave me a solid shoulder-thump with his fist, and our eyes came together.

"He's right, you know," said Mr. Gustafson. "The world could use more young men like Milo Egerson."

"Thank you, sir," I said, and just then, Mom's hand touched my other shoulder and it stayed there.

Everyone finally sat down, with the banker and lawyer on one side of the two-ton table and me, Mom, and Mr. Gustafson holding down the other side. Engerbritsen cleared his throat and began with what everybody already knew, that Ham had been deeply in debt. Turns out that he owed money to just about every merchant in Milltown and Luck and hadn't made a mortgage payment on the farm in eight months.

The big surprise in the meeting came next. Engerbritsen gave a nod to the brown-suited lawyer, and the man pulled a single sheet of paper out of his inside vest pocket.

"What I've got here is Hjalmar Rehnquist's will," he said. "He sent it to me in the mail about three weeks ago. As you can see, it's brief and handwritten."

I zeroed in on the sheet of lined paper that looked like it was ripped right out of a Big Chief tablet like we used in school. I couldn't make out the words, but the jagged scrawling belonged to Ham.

The lawyer put on a pair of round, wire-rim glasses and gave the piece of paper a quick shake before reading out loud.

*"To whom it may concern. I hereby bequeath my farm and all of my remaining possessions to my grand-nephew, Milo Egerson. He's good with animals, knows his way around machinery, and has proven himself a pretty damn good farmer. Milo is also the only person who can see to it that the land gets taken care of good*

and proper. *And on top of all that, the boy kept me out of the Polk County Poor Farm. That's all. Hjalmar Rehnquist."*

I heard a sort of gasp from Mom and detected a forward leaning from Mr. Gustafson. As for myself—well—I quit breathing, for one thing.

After a brief pause, the banker spoke up. "Now folks, you probably already know that there's a problem with this here. The problem, of course, is Hjalmar's rather extensive debt, as we just discussed."

Engerbritsen produced his own sheet of paper and showed it around the table. It was a list of debts owed, not just to the bank but to everybody. By the time it was tallied up, the banker said it was more than everything Ham owned, including the land, house, silo, and cows. The lawyer chimed in again and said that arrangements would be made for the property and Ham's other possessions to be sold at auction. The banker was first in line to get his share of the dough. After that, it was the county, followed by the merchants. You've probably already guessed who was left at the bottom of the batting order? That's right—me and Mom.

Something like a knot of barbed wire rose up in my gut as I stared at the round belly of the banker with his soft hands neatly folded on the table. It wasn't the money part that was vexing me. It wasn't the lost inheritance part either. Do you want to know what it was?

*The Land.*

For a whole lifetime, Ham had watched over that land like it was a living thing. And make no mistake—it really was a living thing. In Ham's eyes, the land had something like a soul, way more than just property and the object of bank transactions. Part of that soul was in the gentle rise and fall of the pasture and the cornfield. Part of it was in the woods, where wild creatures roamed. Part of it was in the cattail marsh in the southwest corner, where the sandhill cranes nested year after year. Part of it, of course, was up on the knoll where Isabella, the baby, Ham, and Peacock lay buried. That high point was a special place where neither plow nor harrow was allowed to touch. A place of trees planted by a powerful Indian girl. A place with more soul, perhaps, than any human. I wasn't sure exactly, but I think that knoll in the middle of the cornfield had something to do with a word Raina had spoken to me the other day.

*Manitou.*

My eyes locked on the banker with his pinched smile.

"Are you fixing to cut up the land?" I asked.

Engerbritsen paused, sensing the hook in my glare.

I continued. "Are you fixing to drain the cattail marsh? Cut down the woods? Plant corn over the knoll?"

Engerbritsen glanced over his glasses at the lawyer, then back at me. His eyes darkened as he placed both elbows on the table and leaned forward in my direction, like he owned me.

"If the next owner desires a loan from my bank, he will do all of those things. Land has a purpose, young man, and that purpose is to generate a profit—pure and simple. Do you understand?"

My muscles tightened like coiled springs and a river of blood rushed into my face. I wasn't sure what I was going to say or do, but it was going to be something. Just then Mom's hand touched my shoulder and squeezed.

# Chapter 40

Mom wanted me to go back to Minneapolis with her right after the meeting at the bank. It was plenty tempting. I could have just skated back home and forgot about Polk County, Wisconsin, and certain pricks like Engerbritsen, Wingtip, and Melonhead for the rest of my life. I was looking forward to seeing my pals from Washburn High again, too. Heck, some of them had probably bought cars by now, and I could imagine bombing around the Twin Cities—downtown, uptown, the university, the lakes. There would be plenty of catching up to do and cigarettes to smoke in the alleys. Maybe I would get right back in the swing of things, and that probably meant kicking in a few headlights, hot-wiring a car, and shoplifting the occasional pack of cigarettes.

Three months ago, it would have been an obvious choice, but these days I was thinking different. Ain't it funny how your conscience can whipsaw you like that?

Do you know what the clincher was that kept me from going home with Mom? It was that brochure I found on Ham's kitchen table for the public lecture titled AGRICULTURE AND LAND CONSERVATION at Eau Claire Teachers College. Gosh—the old man sure had his heart set on it, and it only seemed right that somebody should go in his place.

~

Getting from Milltown to Eau Claire, Wisconsin, wasn't going to be easy. For one thing, I wasn't very good with maps. For another, Ham's truck was deemed off limits by Engerbritsen, who said it belonged to the estate. That meant I would be riding Star-Chaser, powered by the Briggs & Stratton.

Have you ever noticed how luck sometimes shows up right when you need it most? Well, you're probably not going to believe this, but I was getting Star-Chaser's gas tank filled up by Mr. Schick at the Mobil station when a gleaming black 1938 Packard Super 8 pulled up to the pumps with the flying lady hood ornament and everything. It was neat, all right—the American version of a Rolls-Royce—and who'd have guessed I'd see one out here in cow and rutabaga country. For about five seconds I pondered on who the rich guy was who could afford such a primo car. Then the door popped open and two feet in stockings and lady's shoes landed on the pavement. Mrs. Quigley.

"Good afternoon, Bill," she said.

"Afternoon, Edith. I'll be right with you as soon as I get this little motor-bike gassed up."

"No hurry. How are you, Milo?"

"Just fine, Mrs. Quigley."

"It's been quite a week for you, hasn't it?"

"Yes, ma'am. It sure has."

"And is this the motorbike that you built? I've heard folks talking about it."

"This is it." I proudly tapped the seat with my palm.

"Where are you off to? Not back to Minneapolis, I hope."

"Not yet, ma'am. I'm going to Eau Claire today, if I can find it."

Mrs. Quigley kept asking me more and more questions until I had spilled my guts about everything. I told her about the meeting at the bank with Mr. Engerbritsen and the lawyer. I told her about Ham's will. I told her about his long list of debts. And I told her about his feelings about the land and how he was excited about attending the land conservation lecture. I told her that I figured somebody needed to attend the lecture in Ham's absence and that the only logical somebody was me. In the end I popped the brochure out of my hip pocket and handed it to her. And do you know what happened next? She asked if she could come along.

Yep, in the time it took to smoke a Lucky, my prospects of getting to Eau Claire in time for the lecture bumped up about 500 percent. All of a sudden, I was a fat cat limousine rider. And I didn't even need a map, because Mrs. Quigley knew all the roads by heart.

We got to Eau Claire early enough that Mrs. Quigley decided to give me a driving tour through the city. I had Eau Claire pegged as just another cow town on the edge of the north woods. Turns out it was no Minneapolis, but it was no outpost either. For starters, they had two big rivers, one called the Eau Claire and the other called the Chippewa. For seconders, they had a bustling downtown. They didn't have anything like the Foshay Tower, of course, but they had a bunch of four-, five-, and six-story buildings, including a fancy hotel. They also had a huge rubber tire factory that went on and on along one of the rivers for what seemed like a half mile all by itself. Mrs. Quigley told me that the factory employed thousands of people and made many of the tires for US Army trucks and Air Force planes that helped us to finally win the war.

"We have time for supper," said Mrs. Quigley. "Are you hungry?"

"Yes, ma'am, I could eat." I was trying to say it politely. In truth, I was damn-near starved.

"How about that place over there," she said.

I read the sign: WIGWAM TAVERN.

"I'm willing if you are," I said.

She parked the Super 8 on the street and grabbed her knitting bag out of the trunk, and together we walked inside. The crowd was mostly men, and half of them wore U.S. RUBBER patches on their blue shirt pockets. Two guys sat at a table in the corner playing cribbage. Another four jabbered and laughed around another card game of some sort.

"They're playing euchre," said Mrs. Quigley.

"Did you say *yooker*?"

"Yes. It's a Wisconsin tavern game. It's played fast."

We both watched from a distance, and I was confused from the get-go. For starters, they only used half of the deck and dealt the cards in clumps of two and three instead of one at a time. If that wasn't strange enough, there was something funny going on with the Jacks. Sometimes they were powerful and could even overtake any Queen, King, or Ace. Other times they weren't worth their weight in dog food.

"You'd best keep away from those sharks until you've had some practice," said Mrs. Quigley.

I nodded and Mrs. Quigley guided me to a pair of open stools at the end of the bar. Two bartenders, both wearing white shirts and black pants, kept pouring beer after beer as nickels were slid across the varnished walnut. From the tap handles I noticed two beer brands that I was familiar with—Hamm's, because it was popular back in the Twin Cities and brewed in East St. Paul, and Leinenkugel's, my great-uncle's favorite. But it was the third tapper that was getting all the action, and one of the bartenders had his hand on it nonstop.

"What kind of beer is everybody drinking?" I asked Mrs. Quigley.

"Walter's," she said. "It's the hometown brew."

Mrs. Quigley signaled to a bartender and he came over wiping his hands on a towel. "What'll it be, ma'am?"

"What do you have for food?"

"Grilled sandwiches mainly," said the bartender. "Ham and Swiss, Ham and Cheddar, Ham and Colby, or just plain grilled cheese."

"Ham and Colby," said Mrs. Quigley.

"Ham and Swiss," I said.

The bartender nodded. "Anything to drink?"

"Brandy Old Fashioned for me. A mug of Walter's for the young man."

I didn't flinch, but it took an effort.

"You old enough?" asked the bartender.

"I'll vouch for him," said Mrs. Quigley just as my mouth cracked like an egg.

When the drinks came, Mrs. Quigley lifted her glass of amber elixir and clinked it against mine. "To Ham," she said, and we each took a sip.

I smiled a little and looked at the bubbles in my beer. Then she kept on talking. She told me that, with my stepfather going to the Waupun State Pen, my potential was unlimited. She said I was smart and courageous and good-hearted, and that if I could just shake the chip off my shoulder and quit looking for trouble, I might be a model citizen one day.

I started feeling all warm and gushy on the inside and was glad, for the moment at least, to be out of the alleys.

We gobbled down our grilled ham and cheese sandwiches and, even though I offered, Mrs. Quigley paid the bill. The sunlight blasted my eyes as we headed back out on the street and found our way to the Packard Super 8. Mrs. Quigley knew right where to go, of course. From the corner of Madison and Barstow, she drove us south through some old neighborhoods, including some fancy houses that looked down on the Chippewa River. The sign for Eau Claire Teachers College pointed us to a big open space by the river where we found a single red brick building.

"Is that the whole college?" I asked. "One stupid building?"

Mrs. Quigley shot me a disapproving look. "It's known as *Old Main*," she said. "And the quality of an education is not measured by the number of buildings."

I kept my mouth shut as Mrs. Quigley parked the Packard. On the sidewalk I politely offered her my elbow. She latched on and we walked inside.

～

Let me tell you something about that two-hour lecture called AGRICUL-
TURE AND LAND CONSERVATION.

It wasn't boring.

Do you remember how I was all confuzzled by some of the phrases
that were mentioned in Ham's brochure? Remember when my brain was
all twisted about certain terms like *Land Ethic* and *Thinking Like a Mountain*? I came out of there clear-eyed, excited, and wishing like hell that
Ham could have been there too.

"Shazam!" I said to Mrs. Quigley as she grabbed my elbow and we
walked out of Old Main.

"Shazam indeed," she said back.

# Chapter 41

Three days later, on Sunday, September 2, 1945, the Japanese officially signed the papers of surrender aboard the battleship USS *Missouri*. When word of the event trickled down to Milltown, a party erupted on Main Street. Sheriff Nelson caught word of the spontaneous outburst when one of his deputies called him at home following church. He asked me if I wanted to ride along and, hell—who wouldn't.

When we got there, every bar, tavern, and restaurant was packed, and people were spilling out onto the streets with their beer glasses and cocktails. I knew I'd get my chops busted if I tried to sneak a beer, so while the sheriff kept an eye on the soon-to-be drunks, I roamed over to Lindoo for my favorite treat—a chocolate-cherry malted milk shake.

As usual, Herman Schrapp was behind the counter and the smile on his face was bigger than ever. Somebody had even painted red-and-blue stripes to go with the white of his paper hat. I looked around. Heck—everybody in the joint was smiling, and that even included the druggist.

I was on my second slurp through my soda straw when I detected the form of a girl with dark-brown hair and a bright-yellow dress quietly taking a seat in the stool next to mine. I glanced over and locked on to a pair of sparkling eyes the color of which I was still trying to figure out: blue, gray, green—a mixture of all of them probably.

"Hi, Rosalyn," I said. "You look nice."

She smiled bigger than the Grain Belt sign on Nicollet Avenue. I looked around the room to see if Wingtip was in the area.

"Where's your boyfriend?"

"I don't have a boyfriend anymore."

The news almost dumped me off my stool. I mined my brain for what to say next. "Sure is a big day, isn't it? I mean with the war ending and all."

"Yes, it is."

"Can I buy you a grasshopper malt with chocolate sprinkles?"

"How did you know?" she asked.

"That's what you were having the first time I met you." Herman got busy on the concoction behind the counter while I kept talking to Rosalyn. "My mom got a telegram last week. My brother, Tom, is coming home from the Pacific in a few weeks."

"That's wonderful." She moved her hand an inch closer to mine. "Tell me about him."

With an opening like that, a fella can jabber up a cyclone. As soon as I finished the parts about Tom, I went on to Mom. And after that, Rosalyn wanted to hear all about what happened at McKenzie Creek.

It took a long while, but I spilled every detail, and when I was done Rosalyn had me up there on a pedestal with Dick Tracy and the Green Hornet. Somewhere in the telling, we ran out of ice cream and ended up going for a walk together. For some reason, we wandered in the exact opposite direction of all the commotion on Main Street and ended up in a shady place in the vicinity of the Milltown Public School athletic fields.

~

The following Monday I headed back to work at Gustafson Tractor and Implement with just one week to go before going back to Minneapolis and Washburn High. I had just started doing a carb rebuild on a 1938 John Deere B when Mr. Gustafson came up to me in the shop.

"They're loading up the army trucks at Camp Milltown."

"What for?" I asked.

"Sergeant Harrison told me that most of the men are heading south to Texas."

"What about the guys we worked with?"

"Don't know. Take a break and we'll go down there and find out."

I wiped my hands on a shop rag and walked with Mr. Gustafson along the edge of the road to the camp. Sure enough, six trucks were lined up on the shoulder. I figured thirty men to a truck and came up with almost two-thirds of Camp Milltown heading out of Wisconsin for good. Just inside the main gate, Sergeant Harrison and three guards were standing in front of six lines of men, each with a PW duffel.

"What are they waiting for?" I asked Mr. Gustafson.

"Don't know."

We walked up to Sergeant Harrison and he didn't look happy.

"Heading south?" I asked.

Sergeant Harrison grimaced. "They will be heading south if we can muster enough drivers."

"Enough drivers?" I asked. "Where are they?"

"Some of them did a little too much celebrating yesterday. That party didn't end until four in the morning."

Mr. Gustafson tried and failed to hold in a chuckle. Then he regained his composure and shook his head. "Where are they now?"

"One is laying on a cot in the infirmary. The other three are puking in the latrines. Even if they come back, they aren't fit to drive."

Mr. Gustafson shrugged and Sergeant Harrison gritted his teeth as the prisoners patiently waited in their lines. I looked down the first row and spotted the men from my garden-planting cre:. DiMaggio, Drac, Spencer Tracy, and Blondie. All four of them were fixing to ride together in the same truck.

"Hey there," I said with a wave. All four smiled big and waved back.

For another minute we watched and waited as Sergeant Harrison paced. Then a crazy idea popped into my head.

"Sergeant Harrison?"

"Yes."

"Why don't you let the prisoners drive?"

"What?"

"I know four of these men personally from when they worked on Ham's farm. They're trustworthy," I said. "And besides, the war's over."

For a long time, Sergeant Harrison didn't answer. He glanced at the men in the first row, kicked a stone, and looked at me again. At last he turned to Mr. Gustafson. "What do you think?" he asked.

"I think Milo's right. You can trust them."

Sergeant Harrison nodded to me and Mr. Gustafson. "Come with me, please." Together we walked down the first row of men. DiMaggio, Drac, Spencer Tracy, and Blondie all grinned on our approach.

"*Der Gartenbauer,*" said DiMaggio.

"*Ja,*" I said. "*Gartenbauer.*"

DiMaggio reached out with an open palm and shook my hand with an iron grip that neither one of us wanted to let go. Next, DiMaggio reached out for Mr. Gustafson's hand. After that, the other three Germans from Ham's farm shook our hands too. Gosh—it felt like a class reunion or something.

Sergeant Harrison turned to me and Mr. Gustafson. "You have confidence in these four men?"

"Absolutely," I said.

"You can trust them," said Mr. Gustafson.

Harrison nodded and turned his attention to the four Germans again. *"Wer kann einen Lastkraftswagen fahren?"*

All four men snapped to attention and raised their right hands. Sergeant Harrison tapped DiMaggio, Drac, Spencer Tracy, and Blondie on their shoulders. *"Komm mit mir,"* he said with a hand signal.

It only took fifteen minutes to get the remaining German prisoners and their gear loaded up. Sergeant Harrison ordered one of the few sober American guards to drive the lead truck and another to drive the last one. The driver's seats of the four trucks in the middle were all occupied by German prisoners. In the passenger seat of each middle truck was a green-around-the-gills United States Army soldier with a rifle and a puke bucket.

They all rolled out of Milltown shortly after nine o'clock in the morning. Other than me and Mr. Gustafson, only a few kids on bicycles watched from the side of Highway 35 to see the first large group of Camp Milltown prisoners leaving for the last time.

One at a time, the big engines roared to life and threw black smoke into the blue sky. With a signal from Sergeant Harrison, the lead truck roared and slowly came up to speed. Each of the other five trucks followed close behind. I had a notion to wave to each truck as it rolled past, but that seemed like a sort of pansy way of saying good-bye. Instead, I pumped my right arm up and down, hoping that the signal translated into German.

It worked. All six trucks, even those driven by the Americans, gave me a long, loud blast on the horn. The longest blast of all came from DiMaggio, and his grin damn-near lit up all of Polk County.

# Chapter 42

I felt like a slacker watching the new barn go up.

In just four days of work, the crew from St. Croix Falls and six of the remaining Germans from Camp Milltown had plumbed, leveled, and secured every post and beam as well as two-thirds of the rafters. I turned my attention to the cornfield, where Mr. Hanson pulled a wagon of green stalks behind his Farmall while two more Germans continued the harvest with their machetes. The machine that would chop and throw corn silage into the top of the silo was lined up and ready to go. My mind drifted to thoughts of an old man with a snow-white beard. His farm was coming back to life, and I'm pretty sure that he was smiling.

Slowly, I turned around to study every corner of the land. The bright greens of the cattail marsh had turned halfway to yellow, with their hot-dog-shaped seed heads fluffing out. As I watched, a flock of ducks sailed into the hidden pond, and a marsh hawk soared over the edges. I rotated my view clockwise and focused on Raina's grove of trees at the top of the knoll. I'd found deer beds in there just two days ago, and the few remaining prairie chickens were attracted to that spot too. Another quarter turn to the right and my eyes landed on the distant woods where hickory, basswood, and maple leaves flashed green, orange, and yellow.

I sniffed my lungs full of cool fall air, and a mixture of satisfaction and pride warmed my heart as I realized that this was how the land was going to stay—at least for my lifetime. Yep. Hjalmar Rehnquist and that professor from the University of Wisconsin weren't the only ones who were *Thinking Like a Mountain* anymore.

Mr. Hanson chugged past me with his wagonload of cut corn stalks, grinning and nodding his approval at the harvest. I shot him a wave.

You've probably heard me yakking about the need for electricity once or twice or a hundred times. Well, guess who was here to fix that minor deficiency. Three guys from Polk-Burnett Electric Cooperative, that's who.

It wouldn't be long before another truck would be driving up the wheel ruts with another delivery. Can you guess what it was? It goes in the milk house. Yep, a stainless steel, electric-cooled (and much-needed) milk storage tank.

I just stood there with hands on hips, like a king or a prince or the mayor of Minneapolis or something, as I admired everything going on all around. Then the most important person in the whole county showed up, and can you guess who I'm talking about? Nope—not Sheriff Nelson. Nope—not the banker. It was Mrs. Quigley, in her shiny, just-like-new, 1938 Packard Super 8. She was the one who made it all happen, because she's the one who fixed things at the bank so that Ham's farm didn't have to be sold after all.

You see, not too many people knew it, but Mrs. Quigley had more money than President Truman and all of his generals. She and her husband had built up a fortune by investing in a carbon-paper business, if you can believe that. Now *there* was an innovation. Can you imagine getting two or three pages from typing just one? I figured that it was an idea that would be around for a hundred years.

Anyhow, it was Mrs. Quigley who saved the day, and it went like this. From the lecture by the Madison professor at Eau Claire Teachers College, we both realized that it would be just plain wrong to allow Ham's farm to be sold off and chopped up willy-nilly. Then when she found out about Ham's will and the banker and lawyer and everything—well hell, it was just the kind of thing that she and her money had been waiting for.

I'm not sure the banker and lawyer liked it, but quick as a hummingbird, Mrs. Quigley stepped in and settled all of Ham's remaining debts. Right after that, the land was turned over to Milo Egerson (me), and what do you think of them apples?

Well that, of course, brought up the question about who was going to take care of the place with me fixing to move back to Minneapolis and get back to my life as a roustabout-in-training. The answer came following a bunch of long conversations with Mom and a couple of telegrams to my brother, Tom. As it turned out, Tom didn't know what he wanted to do with his life, and the notion of going into partnership on a farm in the middle of nowhere with a troublemaker like me and a little old rich lady named Mrs. Quigley sounded swell to all three of us.

So that's how I turned into a genuine Wisconsin farmer. And that's how I ended up enrolling at Milltown Public School and keeping my part-time job at Gustafson Tractor and Implement at the same time. Believe it or not, I almost figured out a way to get Mom to move up here too, because the lady at the Milltown Beauty Shop had a HELP WANTED sign in the window.

"Honey, I think it's best for all of us if I stay in Minneapolis." Those were her exact words. No kidding.

"But Mom, I'm not officially an adult yet," I said.

"You've grown more in one summer than in the past ten years. Ham told me you were a natural—good with animals and machinery, both—and with Tom working alongside and me just a telephone call away, it will be fine. More than fine. You've finally got something that looks like a real future."

Well, there you have it. It was going to be me and Tom and Mrs. Quigley, with Mom back in Minneapolis talking to me three times a week on the *Beauty Banter* radio show and whenever I called her on the phone. And can you guess what classes I enrolled in at Milltown Public School? Yes, the usual. Math, science, civics, composition, and—here's the kicker—boxing.

I helped Mr. Hanson stretch a big leather belt into a figure-8 shape, and we strung it between the tractor pulley and the silage chopper. Once it was ready to go, I started feeding corn stalks into the machine so the little chunks would go up the fill pipe leading to the top of the silo.

Suddenly, I remembered something and checked my Hamilton.

*Four o'clock.*

"I've got to get back to Milltown, Mr. Hanson," I said.

"Go ahead, Milo. I'll get one of the Germans to help." Mr. Hanson smiled and shot me a wink, because that's just the kind of man he was. I smiled and winked back. Then I started up Star-Chaser, jumped on, and motored for the depot.

∼

Gilbert produced a weak grin as I walked inside the Milltown Depot to wish him farewell. We shook hands like a couple of old-timers.

"I'm excited for you, Gilbert," I said.

"I'm excited for m-m-me too," he answered back.

I tapped out a Lucky Strike, lit it, and blew a cloud of white smoke at the ceiling. I offered the open pack to Gilbert. "Want one?"

"No thanks."

I nodded and put them back in my shirt pocket. "What did your father say about your going away?"

"He called me stupid."

"That figures."

I looked at Gilbert's one bag. A gunny sack with a knot tied at the top. I flicked an ash off my cigarette and smiled.

"So, you're going to be a cowboy?"

"Yep!"

"Cripes, Gilbert! As good as you are with horses, it'll be perfect for you."

"Th-th-thanks, Milo." He smiled broadly.

"Wyoming, right?"

"Yes."

"You're going to write me a letter when you get settled, right?"

"Sure thing. Then you write me back."

"Sure thing."

We both heard the screeching brakes of the Soo Line locomotive approaching the depot for the 5:18 to St. Paul and beyond. Gilbert stood. He looked calm, confident, and grown-up.

"W-w-well. This is it."

"Sure is."

On a whim, I reached into my pocket and pulled out a dollar and thirty-eight cents that I was fixing to spend on supper.

"It's a long trip. Take this."

Gilbert didn't argue and gladly accepted the money. The train hissed and threw a cloud of steam.

"Good luck, pal," I said.

"Good luck, friend," said Gilbert.

He walked through the door and across the platform and boarded the train. With a blast from the whistle and more smoke and steam, the train started rolling. Just like that, Gilbert Zilstrom was on his way.

∼

Somehow, I felt like taking a walk instead of jumping back on Star-Chaser right away. I pointed my nose toward Lindoo Drug on the other side of town and started walking toward those now-familiar buildings lining Main Street. It seemed like I was an actor in a movie. Maybe it was a western and I was the unknown cowboy walking toward a destiny unknown. Maybe I was the big-city crime fighter on my way to save the kidnapped lady from the mobsters. Maybe I was Tom Joad in *The Grapes of Wrath*, just out of prison and up against steep odds.

As the town got closer, it looked friendlier than ever before. Milltown, after all, was my town now. I was a permanent part of the community. My brother, Tom, and I were partners on our farm just south of Luck. I was enrolled at Milltown Public School. I was almost a fine, upstanding citizen, for crying out loud.

I kept walking and the buildings grew. Brask's Tavern, the Shell Station, Milltown Hotel. All of them seemed to welcome me as one of their own.

Then, all of a sudden, I was standing in the shadow of that old Co-op station, and for the first time in weeks, my thoughts trailed off in the direction of my reliable, always-waiting rival—Melonhead. I glanced through the glass. Sure enough, just like always, there he was eating a candy bar.

For a whole minute, maybe two, I just stood there thinking.

*Should I do it?*

I pondered.

*Gosh—maybe just this once, for old times' sake.*

My eyes tracked to the greasy blacktop next to the gas pumps. The bell cord was laying right there. *What the hell*, I thought. I pocketed my watch and stepped forward.

*Ding!*

# Acknowledgments

I would like to extend gratitude to the following people who helped make this book possible:

My dear Carmen, who helped me most of all with feedback, advice, and belief in the project.

Jack, Mary, Kavya, and Curtis for a ton of encouragement along the way.

Scott Breaker, Jan Dunn, Anne Hollenbach, William Johnson, Chuck Ladd, and Bev Larsen for taking a wire brush to the first draft.

Bob and Elverna Blomgren, Lester Sloper, Erling Voss, Wendle Johnson, and Harold Evans for helping me understand the history of Polk County, Wisconsin.

Dennis Lloyd, Sheila McMahon, Jennifer Conn, Casey LaVela, Jacqulyn Teoh, Adam Mehring, Kaitlin Svabek, and Scott Mueller through my association with the University of Wisconsin Press. They pulled it all together and made it real.